OCT 2019

W9-BMP-501

WHAT COMES MY WAY

Books by Tracie Peterson

BROOKSTONE BRIDES
When You Are Near
Wherever You Go
What Comes My Way

GOLDEN GATE SECRETS
In Places Hidden
In Dreams Forgotten
In Times Gone By

HEART OF THE FRONTIER
Treasured Grace
Beloved Hope
Cherished Mercy

THE HEART OF ALASKA★★
In the Shadow of Denali
Out of the Ashes
Under the Midnight Sun

SAPPHIRE BRIDES
A Treasure Concealed
A Beauty Refined
A Love Transformed

BRIDES OF SEATTLE
Steadfast Heart
Refining Fire
Love Everlasting

LONE STAR BRIDES
A Sensible Arrangement
A Moment in Time
A Matter of Heart

LAND OF SHINING WATER
The Icecutter's Daughter
The Quarryman's Bride
The Miner's Lady

LAND OF THE LONE STAR
Chasing the Sun
Touching the Sky
Taming the Wind

BRIDAL VEIL ISLAND★
To Have and To Hold
To Love and Cherish
To Honor and Trust

STRIKING A MATCH
Embers of Love
Hearts Aglow
Hope Rekindled

———◆◆◆———

*All Things Hidden***
*Beyond the Silence***
House of Secrets
*Serving Up Love****

★with Judith Miller ★★with Kimberley Woodhouse
★★★with Karen Witemeyer, Regina Jennings, and Jen Turano

For a complete list of Tracie's books, visit her website www.traciepeterson.com

WHAT COMES MY WAY

TRACIE PETERSON

WITHDRAWN

Mount Laurel Library
100 Walt Whitman Avenue
Mount Laurel, NJ 08054-9539
856-234-7319
www.mountlaurellibrary.org

BETHANYHOUSE
a division of Baker Publishing Group
Minneapolis, Minnesota

© 2019 by Peterson Ink, Inc.

Published by Bethany House Publishers
11400 Hampshire Avenue South
Bloomington, Minnesota 55438
www.bethanyhouse.com

Bethany House Publishers is a division of
Baker Publishing Group, Grand Rapids, Michigan

Printed in the United States of America

All rights reserved. No part of this publication may be reproduced, stored in a retrieval system, or transmitted in any form or by any means—for example, electronic, photocopy, recording—without the prior written permission of the publisher. The only exception is brief quotations in printed reviews.

Library of Congress Cataloging-in-Publication Data
Names: Peterson, Tracie, author.
Title: What comes my way / Tracie Peterson.
Description: Bloomington, Minnesota : Bethany House, a division of Baker
    Publishing Group, [2019] | Series: Brookstone brides ; 3
Identifiers: LCCN 2019019801| ISBN 9780764219047 (trade paper) | ISBN
    9780764233395 (cloth) | ISBN 9780764233494 (large print) | ISBN
    9781493420445 (e-book)
Subjects: | GSAFD: Christian fiction. | Love stories.
Classification: LCC PS3566.E7717 W46 2019 | DDC 813/.54—dc23
LC record available at https://lccn.loc.gov/2019019801

Scripture quotations are from the King James Version of the Bible.

This is a work of fiction. Names, characters, incidents, and dialogues are products of the author's imagination and are not to be construed as real. Any resemblance to actual events or persons, living or dead, is entirely coincidental.

Cover design by Jennifer Parker
Cover photography by Mike Habermann Photography, LLC

19 20 21 22 23 24 25   7 6 5 4 3 2 1

Come one, come all to the Brookstone Wild West Extravaganza—the only wild west show to give you all-female performers of extraordinary bravery and beauty! Women whose talent and proficiency will amaze and delight people of every age!

ONE

MARCH 1902
LOS ANGELES, CALIFORNIA

Robert! What in the world are you doing here?" Ella Fleming asked, stepping back from her hotel room door as she tightened the belt on her dressing gown.

"Looking for you," her brother replied. "I went to the train station and found the Brookstone cars, but they said you were all staying at this hotel."

Ella laughed and swept her arm toward the room. "Isn't it wonderful? It was a surprise treat from Henry Adler. He has all sorts of meetings here in Los Angeles and wanted us to stay in comfort and style. Plus, I think he wanted to be able to hold meetings in his room. Please come in."

Stepping back, Ella waited for Robert to enter, but he hesitated. Turning to his left, he motioned to someone. Ella watched as a heavily veiled woman in black bombazine entered the room ahead of Robert. The woman was petite and clad in black from head to toe. She was obviously in deep mourning. Even her gloves were black.

Ella tried to hide her shock, but as soon as Robert closed her suite door, he hurried to explain.

"I know you'll find this quite the surprise." He reached out to pull back the woman's veil.

Ella's eyes widened as her former maid's face was revealed. "Mara?"

The black woman nodded, her brown eyes wide. "It's me, Miss Ella."

Ella embraced her friend. "I can hardly believe this. I've missed you so much." She looked over Mara's shoulder at Robert. "To what do I owe this pleasure?"

"It may be pleasure to you, but it's been a grave matter for Mara. Sit down and I'll explain." Robert motioned toward the sitting area of Ella's suite.

She sat on the settee and waited for Mara to join her. "Tell me everything."

Robert pulled a cushioned wingback chair closer. "I'm not sure where to begin. Father approached me two weeks ago. He's deeply troubled about something. Personally, I've heard rumors, and I think Jefferson Spiby is forcing Father to do things he doesn't want to do. That's why Mara is here."

Ella looked at her former maid and dear friend while Robert continued.

"You see, Jefferson has been insisting that Father let Mara work for him. Mara has no desire to do so, but that hasn't stopped Jefferson from pressing for it. Father came to me and told me he feels helpless to fight Jefferson. Apparently Jefferson holds something over our father, and he's had to yield to Spiby's will more and more. Now, I know this topic isn't for the gentler sex, but you must know the truth of it. Jefferson wants Mara for his mistress."

A gasp escaped Ella's lips. "He's a monster. How can he even live with himself?"

Mara looked at the carpet as if she bore some guilt in Jefferson's shameful behavior.

"Because he's evil," Robert declared. "The things I've heard about him are . . . well, I would never repeat them. Father asked me to figure out a way to keep Mara from his grasp, and this is what came to mind. Do you suppose Mara could go on tour with you— perhaps be your personal maid?"

"Of course. I'm sure I can get the others to agree. I'll talk to Lizzy right away. She's coming to get me in an hour. We're going to tea with some people who would like to photograph us for a book."

"I thought Miss Brookstone married and gave up performing," Robert said, shaking his head. "What made her change her mind?"

"She didn't. I mean, well . . . it's a long story. Lizzy did marry. She's Mrs. Wesley DeShazer now. She's not performing, but her uncle was quite ill last year, and she's hoping to keep him in better shape. Lizzy's mother begged her to come on the tour for one more year and keep an eye on him. She and Wes both came as a favor to Rebecca Brookstone."

"I see. Do you think she'll accept Mara's being here?"

"I have no reason to think she'll refuse her. Lizzy is all too familiar with Jefferson's cruelty and my own fear of him."

Jefferson, Ella's former fiancé, had once appeared at the Brookstone ranch with her father to try to force Ella to return to their Kentucky home. And then there was the other matter. Ella had heard Jefferson confess to being responsible for the death of the Brookstone Extravaganza's former wrangler August Reichert. His sister Mary, the show's sharpshooter, was still trying to seek justice for her brother. Unfortunately, Jefferson was much too powerful, and the authorities in Kentucky refused to prosecute him.

"Then, I'll leave Mara in your care," Robert said. "Her bags are downstairs. I'll have a bellboy bring them up. It worked out well to bring Mara here, as I was planning to come anyway to deliver some horses. I'll be in San Francisco in two days, and I understand the show will be there as well."

"Yes. We have three performances there. Saturday and Sunday evening and a matinee on Sunday."

Robert nodded. "Good. I'll catch up with you there and make sure it was acceptable for Mara to stay on. For now, however, I have to hurry, or I'll be late to my meeting."

He got up, and Ella and Mara rose as well.

"Thank you, Mr. Robert, for savin' me," Mara said in a hushed voice.

"It was my pleasure, Mara." He turned to Ella and hugged her close. "I don't know what all is going on, but as you mentioned, there is a terrible secret at Fleming Farm. A secret big enough to implicate the entire county and its officials. I intend to get to the bottom of it, and I believe Father holds many of the answers. Given his current state of mind and obvious distress, I think perhaps he'll be more inclined to confide in me."

Ella pulled back. "I hope so, but I hope too that you won't put yourself in any danger. Your family needs you, and so do I."

Robert smiled. "Never fear. I'll be on the lookout for trouble."

And then he was gone as quickly as he'd come.

Ella turned to Mara and shook her head. "I never expected to see you—not in a million years."

"I's mighty glad to be here."

Ella smiled and gave the black woman another hug. "I've missed you so much. You've always been my dearest friend and confidante, and now I have you back. This life on the road is sometimes wearying, but I think you'll enjoy seeing so many things and places. It's amazing when you think of all the miles we cover."

"I's just thankful to be safe. There wasn't gonna be no safety for me back at the farm."

Ella frowned. "Why do you say that? Father surely would never have let Jefferson take you."

"Your father couldn't stop that man. He had his way with me more times than I care to remember."

"What?" Ella knew her expression bore her disgust. "Jefferson . . . he forced himself on you?"

Mara looked away and nodded. "I's ashamed to say so, but it's true."

"Did you tell my father?"

"No. A black woman speakin' out against a white man?" She shook her head. "Nobody in that county would be listenin' to anything I had to say. 'Specially with Mr. Spiby involved."

"Oh, Mara, I'm so sorry."

Again, Ella hugged her friend. They had been in each other's company since Mara's mother had wet-nursed Ella as a baby. They'd grown up together, and even though Mara was older, she and Ella had been the best of friends. How it hurt to imagine her friend suffering at the hands of that evil man.

Ella started at a knock on the suite door. She pushed Mara toward the bedroom. "Go. Hide."

Once Mara was out of sight, Ella went to the door. "Who is it?"

"Bellman. I've brought the lady's bags."

"Just a moment."

Ella went to get a dime from her purse and drew out her small pistol as well. She hid the gun in the folds of her skirt and went to open the door. A uniformed bellman stood on the other side with two small bags.

"Set them just inside," Ella instructed.

He left the bags and quickly went to the

exit. He turned at the door. "If you need any-thing else . . ."

Ella extended the coin. "Thank you."

"No, that's quite all right, ma'am. The gentleman already paid me." He tipped his cap and disappeared down the hall.

Ella closed and locked the door behind her. She let out a long breath and replaced her gun in her purse. "It's all right. You can come out now."

Mara had completely shed the mourning hat and veil as well as the black gloves she'd worn. With everything she'd had on, no one could have known her skin was dark.

"There's plenty of room in this suite, al-though just one bed." Ella chuckled. "It won't be the first time we've shared a bed. I remem-ber all those times when we were afraid of a storm, or a cold snap made us seek each other for warmth."

"Mama said she always knew where I'd be if I wasn't in my cot," Mara said, grinning.

Ella had grown up with all the extrav-agance a wealthy Southern horse breeder could offer his daughter. As a child, Mara had been her constant companion, and she had continued working for the Flemings as an adult. Ella had no idea what she'd been paid, but hopefully she could make as much or more working for the Brookstones.

"We need a plan," Ella said, tapping her finger against her chin. "I'm going to ask Lizzy to give you a job. How much was Father paying you?"

Mara looked confused. "Paying me?"

"Money. How much money did you make working for my father?"

"Room and board was my pay. Some clothes too."

Ella frowned. "You weren't paid a wage?"

The black woman shook her head. "We had regular duties and hours, and the pay was our keep."

"Well, that hardly seems fair, but I suppose if you had to pay rent and buy food, clothes, and other supplies, it would have all figured out the same." She went to the dressing table and began to run a brush through her long blond hair. "I need to finish getting ready. When Lizzy shows up, I'll explain everything to her and see about getting you a paying job."

Mara came to where Ella sat and took the brush from her hands. "Sure good to see you again, Miss Ella."

"Just Ella. Friends don't call each other by titles." Ella looked up and smiled. "I have missed you."

"Missed you too."

Mara dressed Ella's hair as she had so often done over the years. When she finished pinning curls into place, Mara gave Ella the hand mirror. Ella cocked her head first one way and then another and nodded.

"It's perfect. Much better than I could have done for myself." She got up and undid the buttons of the dressing gown. "I'll just finish getting ready. Why don't you relax in the sitting room? There's some fresh fruit in a bowl if you're hungry."

"Mr. Robert done fed me. Had them bring breakfast to my room so nobody could see me." Mara's voice took on a sort of awe. "I had me a right fine room too. Not near as beautiful as this here one, but pert near. Never seen nothin' like it. White folks surely know how to live."

Ella nodded and stepped behind the dressing screen. "I'm glad Robert treated you well. I don't understand what is going on at the farm, but I'm glad Robert is on our side."

"Me too. Folks ain't doin' so well, and there's trouble brewin'," Mara countered.

Ella frowned and pulled on her powder blue skirt. She smoothed it down over her undergarments, then reached for her blouse. "We've known that something bad was going on there for a long time now. That's why I left. I wasn't about to be married off to Jefferson in some prearranged barter, sold off to the man who could do the family the most good. It's ridiculous in the 1900s that a girl should even have to concern herself with such things."

She stepped out from behind the screen, still buttoning her blouse. "I could never bear the idea of slavery in any form. I remember your mama talking about the horrible days when slaves were whipped merely for daring to speak back to their masters."

Mara bit her lip. She looked for all the world as if she'd like to reply to Ella's comment but couldn't.

Ella shook her head. "You know you can say whatever you like. I've never wanted there to be any secrets between us."

"There's some things what's not good to speak of. I think we be better off to just drop the matter." Mara helped Ella tuck in her blouse and secure her skirt.

"You don't have to wait on me, Mara."

"I like helpin' you. You've always been good to me."

"We're friends, first and foremost. Do you understand?" Ella reached out to still Mara's hands. "I don't ever want you to think otherwise."

"I know that. But I got to earn my keep, and maybe Mr. Brookstone will be wantin' me to be your maid." Mara gave her a smile. "A job with you beats out a whole lot of other things I can think of."

"Well, I can understand that. I've had a few jobs these last months that I'd rather not have done."

She thought of the days when Jason Adler was helping run the show. As the son of Henry Adler, he felt it important to give his father as big of a profit as possible. Henry Adler's investment was what had kept the show going, as Ella understood it. Still, when she was required to clean up after her own horse, Ella thought Jason had gone too far. Of course, he was gone now. Disappeared into thin air after trying to force Lizzy to run off with him.

Ella sighed. "We can discuss all of this later. I just want you to remember that we're friends. I'll keep your secrets, just as you've kept mine. Feel free to talk about whatever is troubling you, whenever you like." She went to where she'd hung her matching peplum jacket. The powder blue coat was trimmed in darker blue cording and silver buttons. It was one of her favorite outfits.

"Well, as your friend, I want to help. What can I do?" Mara asked, looking around the room.

"Very well. There's a dark blue hat with light blue feathers in a hat box in the bathroom. Would you get it for me while I find my gloves? I thought I left them on the dressing table, but now they're not there."

She searched for the gloves and finally located them on the pillow of her unmade bed. "Oh, I remember now. I had to mend one of them," she said, holding them up.

"You want me to help you with the hat?" Mara asked, holding up the large creation.

Ella giggled. "It's almost big enough for the both of us, isn't it?"

Mara smiled and nodded. "Yes'm, sure is. I ain't never seen a bonnet this big."

"That's part of the reason I bought it. I think it's magnificent. And it matches perfectly with this suit." Ella sat down at the dressing table. "We'll tilt it just to the right and let the brim ride up on the left. I like it best that way, and it really brings color to my eyes."

"Your eyes already blue enough," Mara said, helping place the hat as Ella suggested.

"That's perfect," Ella declared, reaching for two long hat pins. "Now I'll fix it in place and be off. I know Lizzy will be wondering why I'm making her wait. I think, however, she's going to be so excited to know you've joined us."

"Will I have to keep hiding behind that veil?" Mara asked.

Ella grew thoughtful. "I don't know. Let me talk to Lizzy and Mary. They always have the best counsel. Maybe once Lizzy knows, we can talk to her uncle Oliver. He runs the show along with an Englishman named Henry Adler. Oliver is a very nice man, and there are always dozens of jobs to do on the show. I'm sure someone as talented as you will be useful."

"I sure hope so." Mara frowned and shook her head. "I can't be goin' back to Fleming Farm."

Ella nodded. "I'm afraid that's true for us both."

"And then they removed the veil, and lo and behold, it was Mara," Ella told Lizzy and Mary over tea at the hotel after their meeting with the photographers.

Lizzy shook her head. "Mara from the farm? Your maid?"

"Yes, exactly." Ella sipped from a china cup.

"What in the world was your brother doing with her?" Mary asked.

Ella continued her story while Lizzy glanced across the room to where Wes and Chris were deep in conversation with Uncle Oliver. Los Angeles didn't sit well with Wes, especially after the photographers had revealed their true desires to hire some of the stunt riders away from the show. They even wanted Lizzy to perform for them, reminding her and the others that she was the top trick rider in the country. Wes had immediately pointed out that she was retired. He didn't want Lizzy performing at all—not for any reason—and the fact that Uncle Oliver had suggested that perhaps they could revisit the issue after the show's current season only put Wes in a fouler mood.

Lizzy actually felt sorry for him rather than angry. He had only agreed to come on tour for another year because Lizzy's mother had begged him. Even Lizzy wasn't that excited to go. Her heart was on the ranch in Montana—the ranch her grandfather, father, and uncle had built together. She hadn't realized just how important that place was to her until her father had died while on tour with the show. After that, the wild west show had lost its appeal for Lizzy. Not only that, but she'd also suffered a lot the year before and had hoped to put it all behind her.

Yet here she was again, facing the grueling schedule and constant work. Well, it wasn't quite the same—she wasn't performing this time around. Wes had put his foot down about that. Now that they were married, he didn't want her risking her life trick riding. A part of her wanted to protest, but she was getting older, and the performances took a lot out of her. Besides, she and Wes hoped to have a family soon, and she didn't want to risk any unborn child just to get a few cheers from an arena full of strangers.

Still . . . she missed the unity she felt with her horses. She missed the challenge. And she really did miss the applause.

"Lizzy, I don't think you're even listening to me," Ella protested.

A sigh escaped Lizzy. "I'm so sorry. I'm afraid my mind has been on so many things. We've barely started this tour and already there are problems to deal with. And of course the people we met today mostly lied about their intent."

"Mostly?" Mary, the show's star sharpshooter, said with a raised brow. "They completely lied about what they wanted. They wanted to create an entertainment in the city that features trick riding every night. Given the outrageous amounts of money they're offering, I'm afraid one or two of the girls will be enticed to stay behind."

"You don't really think they'd leave Brookstone's, do you?" Ella asked. "I know I never would. This has become my family."

"As I recall, it was Lizzy they wanted most," Mary said with a shrug. "I thought Wes would pop a vein."

Lizzy thought of her husband's dismay. "I did too. But I told them no and so did Uncle Oliver. But they offered a lot more than the show can pay. Not to mention the other benefits like a place to live and a personal assistant. Goodness, there are times I wish I had a personal assistant."

"The girls who would consider leaving must not understand the delicate balance of the show," Ella said, shaking her head. "We have a very specific act planned out. Maybe we should talk to them and explain."

"That was my thought exactly," Mary said, reaching for a small sandwich. "I think we should remind them of the contract they signed and how important it is that they keep their word. Like your daddy always said, 'The show must go on.'"

Lizzy was glad they felt just as she did on the matter. "In the meantime, we will of course hire Mara on to help. I have enough authority to see to that. She can work in the laundry and sewing room. I'm sure our new head seamstress can use an extra hand. She seems a bit . . . overwhelmed."

"You don't like Amanda much, do you?" Mary asked.

Lizzy hadn't meant to be so obvious. Frankly the seamstress was much too familiar with Uncle Oliver. Not only that, but she always seemed to find ways to get out of her work. "I don't know her well enough to like or dislike her. She's definitely no Agnes."

At the reference to their former seam-stress, who had retired after last year's tour, the other two nodded.

"Nobody is as good as Agnes," Mary declared. "I was more than sorry to hear of Brigette's illness. Especially after all that time Agnes put into training her. It's a shame she wasn't able to join the tour this year."

"Well, she'll always have a place with the show if she wants one. Meanwhile, I'm waiting to see if Miss Moore proves herself," Lizzy said in a curt manner to stress that the topic wasn't open for discussion.

Wes was making his way over to the table.

"I see the boys are finished with their conversation. Why don't we adjourn to your room, Ella?" Lizzy suggested. "Then I can talk to Mara about the days to come. I'm sure we can keep her busy and safe."

⋅⟫⊰ TWO ⊱⟪⋅

I wish you weren't so upset." Lizzy could see by the wary look in Wesley's eyes that he was worried about her encounter earlier in the day. She hadn't even had a chance to tell him about Mara.

"I wish folks would stop trying to buy you. You aren't a commodity."

Lizzy touched his arm and smiled. "No, I'm not. But, more importantly, no one could ever separate me from you. No matter how much money they were offering. Just remember, I've wanted to be your wife for a very long time."

He shook his head and strode over to the large hotel window. "It just rubs me the wrong way that they would even ask. Especially after we made it clear the first time."

"I suppose they're used to getting what

they want. They cajole and offer more and more until a person agrees."

"We should have never come on the tour. We would have been better off staying at the ranch. Phillip would have been better off by far. He's drinking a lot. I try to keep tabs on him, but he always manages to slip away."

"He's a grown man. You can't be his conscience. You're a good brother, but you can't make him a good man."

Wes frowned and turned to look out the window. "I've got a bad feeling that this was a mistake."

Lizzy knew there was nothing she could say to change his mind, so she chose instead to change the subject. "There's something I want to talk to you about. It has to do with Ella."

He didn't even turn around. "What about her?"

"Her brother showed up and brought her a surprise."

"Not that fiancé of hers, I hope."

Lizzy shook her head, then realized he couldn't see her. "Wes, would you just come sit with me for a few minutes?"

She saw his shoulders drop as he sighed. Nevertheless, he turned back to face her and then followed her to the sofa. Once he was seated beside her, Lizzy put her hand on his thigh.

"Robert brought Ella's maid, Mara, to stay with her. Apparently there was a problem with Jefferson Spiby. He wanted Mara to be his mistress."

Wes said nothing, but his scowl deepened.

"Anyway, it seems that Spiby is exerting more and more control over Ella's father, and he was worried he wouldn't be able to refuse Spiby's demands. He told Robert about it, and Robert snuck Mara out of town and brought her here."

"Why here?"

"It was the only place he could think of. Ella was delighted. She and Mara have always been dear friends, and Ella has asked that Mara be allowed to join the show."

Wesley's expression left no doubt of his surprise. "As a performer?"

Lizzy shook her head and smiled. "Of course not. Mara is a very talented seamstress. Ella also said she can clean if needed. I'll talk to Uncle Oliver and Mr. Adler at our meeting in San Francisco, but I'm confident they'll say yes. I plan to put her to work helping Amanda Moore in costumes."

"Doesn't that put everyone in danger? I mean, Spiby came after Ella when she ran away. What's to stop him from showing up again to get Mara?"

Lizzy shrugged. "I suppose nothing, but

I can't imagine he'd go chasing after a mistress as he did a future wife. At least, I hope he won't."

"People are strange. They do things you'd never expect them to do. Like you being willing to work for a man whose son tried to kidnap you and force you into marriage."

She could see an almost accusing look in his expression. "Wesley DeShazer! You know as well as I do that we're here because Mother begged us to come. I didn't want to be here any more than you did. I'm only here for Uncle Oliver. I'm not even performing, just as you commanded."

He raised a brow. "I didn't command you."

She felt an air of smugness wash over her. "You want to rethink that comment?"

He looked away. "We both agreed that you were getting too old and that we wanted a family."

"And I agreed with that logic, but you told me you wouldn't agree to come—even to see to Oliver's care—unless I stopped performing. That's a command in my book. Or if you don't like the word *command*, we could use *ultimatum*. Honestly, Wes, I didn't want to fight about this. We're here now, and we committed to being here for the duration unless our health or well-being dictates otherwise."

He shook his head. "You make me out to

be such a bad guy. Yet the real villain, Jason Adler, walks free somewhere. No one has even bothered to look for him, as far as I know."

The very mention of Jason Adler had darkened his mood. Lizzy couldn't blame him. Thinking back on Jason caused her more discomfort than she cared to admit. "Well, that's where you're wrong. Mr. Adler told me he hired an entire army of investigators to search for his son."

"Looking for him and finding him are two different things."

Lizzy felt the tension between them increase. Coming with the show was not the best decision they'd ever made together, but it was one that made her mother happy, and for Lizzy that was the most important.

She sighed. "I don't want to fight with you, Wes. I know you're unhappy, and because of that, I'm unhappy. I love you and I wish we were back home, but we made a promise and we need to see it through. It's just until autumn, and we both agreed we weren't going to Europe with the troupe. The months will pass quickly, and then we'll be back on the ranch. Phillip and Uncle Oliver too, since they aren't doing the Europe shows."

"Your uncle will be lucky to make it through the American shows. As for Phillip . . ." He shook his head. "I have no idea how long he'll make it. Adler always has liquor around, and it's like taunting a child with candy."

"True, but the world is full of temptations, and we each have to make a decision whether to yield to them or not. You can't force Phillip to give up drinking, and you can't make him better by making me out to be the enemy."

Wes sighed and gave a nod. He looked at her long and hard, and she could see the love in his eyes. She never doubted it was there, but his anger was doing an excellent job of burying it.

"I'm sorry, Lizzy. I know you aren't my enemy, and I don't want to fight with you. It's just that I see Phillip doing so much worse lately. I'd send him back to the ranch, but he'd just continue to drink, and I wouldn't be there to keep him in check."

"Phillip has to want to stop drinking. Something is obviously driving him to it. Have you tried to talk to him about it?"

"Of course I have!" His raised voice made Lizzy cringe, which in turn made him launch into another apology. "I'm sorry. I can't seem to do or say anything right. When I try to talk to Phillip, he accuses me of being holier-than-thou. When I try to talk to you, I make a mess of it all by losing my temper. I'm really sorry, Lizzy. It's something about this place. I just don't like it."

She could see the sadness in his brown eyes. She reached out and took his hand. "We'll get through this together better than apart, and there is one thing we haven't yet tried."

"What's that?"

"To pray together. Since leaving the ranch, we haven't done much of it at all—at least not together. There's strength in numbers, you know."

"You're right." He pushed back her long brown hair before leaning forward to kiss her. "Please forgive me. You deserve better."

She moved closer, cherishing the feel of him as Wes put his arms around her. "We're going to get through this, Wes. With God to help us, we'll make it."

The first order of business when the show arrived in San Francisco was a meeting Henry Adler had planned well in advance. He was big on meetings and generally held at least one major meeting each week with smaller gatherings each day.

"I hope you've found the hotel suits your needs," he began. "I know it might be strange that we're in hotels instead of the train cars, but we've managed to include the rooms in some of our negotiations for performances, and I believe you will be better rested in these lush accommodations. Especially for days when we do more than one performance."

Ella suppressed a yawn. She was more concerned about whether or not Lizzy had spoken with Adler or Oliver Brookstone about Mara. Worry over her friend had given her more than one sleepless night.

"As you know, we will have our first show tomorrow evening. It's already sold out, as are the Sunday matinee and evening performance. Your reputation precedes you. Well done."

Ella smiled, as did most everyone else. The only people who seemed less than enthusiastic were Phillip and Wesley. Ella's gaze lingered on Phillip DeShazer. She'd lost her heart to him despite her attempts to resist. He was such a sweet-natured man, but he bore so much pain and regret. There was a haunting darkness to him that she couldn't understand. She knew he blamed himself for his father's death—he'd told her that one night when he was drunk. He would never say more than that, and ever since, Ella had wondered what had happened. Whatever the truth, he was hurting, and she wished she could give him peace of mind.

He caught her gaze and smiled. Even that, however, was a sad attempt. She would have to double her prayers on his behalf.

"Several people here in the West are experimenting with moving pictures. Apparently by coming here, they hope to avoid complications due to Mr. Edison's patent." Mr. Adler paused a moment and looked at his notes. "One man has asked to come to our practice session prior to the show. He'd like to attempt to film something of each act. I've given my permission for him to do so. He asks only that you ignore his presence."

"What about him being in the way? How can we perform our tricks while making sure he doesn't get hurt?" Alice Hopkins asked. Several other performers nodded as she continued. "I'll be racing around the arena, shooting arrows from horseback. I can't be bothered with worrying about whether this man is in the wrong place."

"I've explained that to him. He will position himself out of the way. He assured me of that. Once we're at the arena, you can let your concerns be known should you find his positioning less than acceptable. I promise, I will support your concerns."

That seemed to put the matter to rest, and Adler continued speaking about a variety of things related to the show. Ella glanced at the clock on the wall and wondered how much longer they'd have to be here. She pulled a shawl tight around her to ward off the damp chill of the room and sighed.

It seemed Lizzy had said nothing to her uncle or Mr. Adler regarding Mara. Or at least if she had, Henry Adler wasn't interested in bringing the matter to everyone's attention. Maybe that meant he'd said no—that he didn't want Mara on the tour.

Ella frowned. She could hardly send Mara home, although she might be able to talk Lizzy into letting her go to the Brookstone ranch in Montana.

"If there are no further questions," Mr. Adler concluded, "we'll adjourn early so you can enjoy the city. There are a great many attractions here, and I'm told they have some of the finest restaurants in the West."

This met with most everyone's approval, and the performers and crew began filing from the room.

Ella caught Lizzy's attention and made her way to where she stood with Wes and Phillip. "Lizzy, I was wondering if you'd had time to speak to your uncle regarding my matter."

"Oh, I'm so sorry. Of course I did. Uncle Oliver said it was perfectly fine to hire Mara on to help with the sewing and laundry. She'll be paid room and board and fifteen dollars a month."

Ella breathed a sigh of relief. "I'm sure she'll be thrilled. Father only paid her room and board. Look, she can stay with me when she's not busy elsewhere. We spent a good portion of our lives living close."

"That's exactly what I thought too. I told Uncle Oliver and Mr. Adler that Mara would stay in your room."

"Thank you." Ella smiled. "So, are you going sight-seeing?"

"We were just discussing that. Would you care to join us?"

"Yes, do come with us. I'll see to it that you have a great time," Phillip declared.

"I can't." Ella glanced over her shoulder to make sure no one was listening to their conversation. "Robert is supposed to come today. He's in town on business and planned to speak to me about Mara and anything else he's learned. It's important that I see him. But maybe after practice in the morning I'll have a little time."

Phillip grinned. "I'm going to hold you to that."

"Well, I should get back upstairs and let Mara know the news. She's been worried."

"Tell her that we're happy to have her on board," Lizzy said. "Then later, after you're finished with your brother, bring her around to meet Amanda and the rest of the work crew."

"She'll be the only person of color," Ella said, then bit her lower lip.

"I know," Lizzy replied. "I thought of that, but I don't think it should be a problem. Our workers are decent folks—most are Christian, and the color of a person's skin shouldn't matter to them."

"It shouldn't, but that doesn't mean it won't. I don't want Mara to be given a difficult time. I've heard of horrible things done to people of color. I don't want her hurt."

"Nor do we. We'll do our best to make it clear to everyone that they will either accept her and work without complaint, or they'll be dismissed."

Ella worried her lip a bit more, then nodded. "I'll let Mara know."

❖═ THREE ═❖

When she reached her hotel room, Ella was surprised to find her brother had already arrived. She embraced him and gave him a smile. "I had no idea I'd see you so soon."

"I completed my business early," he told her, then nodded toward Mara. "Mara was gracious enough to let me wait here for you."

"I was afraid when the knock came on the door," Mara admitted, shaking her head, "but Mr. Robert called out to let me know it was him."

Ella could well imagine. She smiled at her friend. "Let's sit. I have news." The sitting area wasn't quite as large as she'd had in the other hotel, but they made do. "I just came from speaking with Lizzy. She said her uncle is happy to hire Mara on to help with the sewing and laundry—if that meets with your approval." She looked to Mara with a smile.

"It does. I'd be happy to help sew and wash clothes."

"I'm glad to hear it's all working out." Robert unbuttoned his coat and took a seat on a wooden chair. "And will they pay Mara a fair wage?"

Ella frowned. "Definitely fairer than what Father offered. Did you know she worked for room and board only?"

"Is that true, Mara?" Robert had a strange look on his face.

"When I turned twenty-one, Mr. Fleming had me sign a special paper that said I'd agree to work for that, as well as my clothes and anything like medicine or such. He said he had spent lots of money raising me, and my work would pay that back. All of his workers signed the paper, so I signed it too."

Robert's expression betrayed his concern. "What about spending money? What if you wanted to go to town?"

"Or save up to move away?" Ella asked.

"We never went to town, 'cept for church. We weren't allowed."

Ella shook her head. "Weren't allowed? You're a free woman. How could you not be allowed to go to town whenever you wanted, so long as your work was done? Didn't Father give you time off?"

Mara shook her head. "Not exactly. We could go to church. We traded Sundays with other house staff so that there was always someone to see to the white folks. But our papers say we had to work every day unless Mr. Fleming say otherwise."

Robert looked at Ella, shaking his head. "I knew Father wasn't allowing you to go to town or parties. I suppose as far as the staff was concerned, he figured that if he provided everything needed, there was no reason for excursions to town, but I don't understand the attitude of paying no wage. I'll ask him about that when I get back."

Ella nodded and turned to Mara. "Well, for now you'll make fifteen dollars a month and have room and board. You're going to have a much better life. I can hardly wait to show you around the cities where we've performed in the past. We're going to have a lot of fun."

———

Lizzy heard laughter coming from her uncle's hotel room. High-pitched, female laughter. No doubt Amanda Moore was visiting. It was highly inappropriate for a single woman to be entertained in a bachelor's hotel room, even if he was twenty years her senior.

When she knocked in an authoritative manner, Lizzy wasn't surprised that the laughter stopped abruptly.

"Well, if it isn't my darlin' niece," Oliver said, swinging the door open.

"Hello, Uncle." Lizzy stepped inside and kissed him on the cheek. "I gather from the raucous laughter that you aren't alone."

"You gather correctly. Amanda came to see me and bring me the shirts she mended for me. And to measure me for a new coat."

"I thought we had a new coat made at the ranch. Is there something wrong with it?" Lizzy glanced around the room, but there was no sign of Amanda. "Where is she?"

Oliver looked a little embarrassed. "She's gone to hang up the shirts. What can I do for you, Lizzy?"

She could tell he was anxious to be rid of her. "I want to discuss the third act. I was talking to Ella a few days ago and then again earlier today, and we both agreed that some changes need to be made. It will affect your announcements."

"We can talk about it in the morning. I'm going to have a light supper and call it an evening. I'm much too tired to make sensible decisions at this hour."

"It's only six."

"And I was up at four this morning. I need my rest. I'm completely done in."

Amanda chose that moment to return. She wore a sage green skirt and an embroidered cream-colored Mexican blouse that dipped entirely too low in the front. She stopped when she saw Lizzy and her expression soured, but she quickly put on a simpering look. "Why, Lizzy, what in the world are you doing here?"

"I might ask the same question, but Uncle Oliver explained that you are delivering his mended shirts."

Amanda touched a hand to her blond hair. "And so I did. Just doing my job."

"I'm glad to see it. I was just about to tell Uncle Oliver that there seems to be too much work for you."

Amanda gave a sad nod. "I'm glad someone has finally noticed."

Lizzy gritted her teeth. This wasn't going the way she'd expected. "I've decided to hire on another woman to work with you."

"Well, that's a relief." Amanda lifted her chin. "She'd better be able to sew. Oh, and wash and iron. We have more laundry than one person can keep up with."

"Then it's a good thing you already have two laundry assistants to keep things on track." Both girls had complained to Lizzy about Amanda's lack of willingness to work alongside them. She thought she might as well address the matter here in front of her uncle. "Although, when I stopped by to see how things were going this morning, you were nowhere to be found. The girls were working alone. Do you want to explain?"

"I don't answer to you. Oliver knows my abilities and where I am at all times. You act like it's my fault that there's too much work to do. I'm only one woman." She looked at Oliver. "Maybe you should explain that this is your affair, Oliver—that we've already discussed my duties, and it's no longer Lizzy's business to worry over."

"Brookstone's show is my business," Lizzy said. "My family *owns* this business, in case you've forgotten."

Amanda had the decency to remain silent.

Lizzy continued. "I expect you to be working alongside those girls, especially when the workload is as arduous as you portray it."

Oliver patted Lizzy's shoulder. "Now, now, Lizzy. I'm sure Amanda knows what she's doing. No sense in dressing her down when she's done nothing wrong."

Lizzy raised her brow. "I suppose that would depend on who you talk to."

"All I see *you* do is tell other people what to do. You don't know how hard I work." Amanda turned to Oliver with tears in her eyes. She reminded Lizzy of a pouty child.

"We simply need things to run in an orderly manner. I'm trying to ensure the performers have what they need." Lizzy was angry enough to tell Amanda what she really thought of her and her lack of modesty and work ethic. Instead she turned back to her uncle. "Uncle Oliver, I want to talk to you first thing in the morning. Can you meet me for breakfast?" She paused a moment for effect, then added, "Alone?"

"Certainly, child. Never fear. I'll be there."

Lizzy stood seething. She wanted to force Amanda from the room but knew she had no right to do so. She'd just bide her time and pray. Hopefully her uncle would see the truth for what it was.

Ella enjoyed supper with her brother at a seaside restaurant. The food tantalized from the first aroma to the last bite, and the setting was beyond perfect. From their table they could watch the sun set over the Pacific Ocean. It was like watching gold melt into the water as orange and yellow hues spread out across the horizon.

"I must say, the view is spectacular," Robert said, sounding as if he admired it as much as Ella did. "Puts me in mind of a painting our grandfather had. Do you recall it? The large one that hung over the fireplace in the dining room. It always gave me a sense of well-being."

"I've never known you to be sentimental." Ella sipped her tea and then marveled again at the setting. "But you're right. It is a very grand view. Wouldn't it be amazing to live on this cliff?"

"Indeed." Robert dabbed his mouth with his napkin. "I suppose, however, I must put aside pleasantries and tell you what I've been able to confirm in the last couple of days."

Ella was intrigued. "Regarding the farm and Father?"

"Yes. I still don't know what's going on, but I didn't want to speak in front of Mara the other day. You see, Father recently confided in me that he had some bookkeeping problems. The former bookkeeper, Mr. Buford, left some time back. I knew he was in San Francisco and decided to look him up."

"And did you?"

"I did, but he was of little help. He told me Father dismissed him without any reason. He gave him a very good letter of reference, however, so Buford took it and the generous financial settlement Father gave him and came west. I told him how Father has been suffering headaches and that the bookwork has been miserable for him, so

I offered to help. However, when I started looking at some of the sale ledgers, I was confused."

"By what?"

"That's exactly what Mr. Buford asked," Robert said with a smile. "There were accountings for the sales of horses that I was unfamiliar with. When I questioned Father, he said it was part of a herd that he kept on Jefferson's estate. A special new breed they were working with. He told me it was no concern of mine and that Jefferson would be highly offended if he found out that I had any knowledge of their special horses."

"How strange. Especially if he was already selling stock from this group. Obviously they must be advertising the stock."

"Exactly." Robert shook his head. "Mr. Buford said that Father had more than one separate business arrangement and wouldn't allow Buford to manage the books for those accounts. Father has me completely baffled. He's not himself, and frankly I think Jefferson has some hold over him. I think whatever it is, it was the same reason you were promised to him in marriage."

Ella cringed. "I've often wondered why Father was forcing the issue. I thank God daily that Mother was able to convince him I was too young to get married. Otherwise I might have been forced to marry Jefferson at sixteen, as he wanted."

"Well, there's enough oddity about the entire situation that I intend to keep searching. I'm wondering if this new breed of horse is what August Reichert saw."

Ella thought back to the night August Reichert had been killed. She had already decided she would never marry Jefferson Spiby and would run away with the Brookstone show. She had arranged with Mara to escape when August took the Brookstone horses back to the train cars that evening. But instead, word came that he had been trampled to death.

Later, Ella overheard Jefferson admit to killing August—that he'd seen too much. She didn't know what he'd seen, but she'd run away from home, terrified of being the next one Jefferson might put an end to.

"If August did somehow get in the middle of this business and offend Spiby, then it wouldn't surprise me if Jefferson killed him to keep him quiet," Robert said.

"That would make sense." Ella nodded and picked up her teacup. "August knew horses better than anyone else in the troupe. If he'd seen the breed and questioned Jefferson about it . . ."

"Still, that's a lame excuse for killing a man."

"Perhaps they hadn't started selling them yet and Father and Jefferson wanted to keep it a complete secret. It doesn't excuse murder by any means, but if a lot of money is tied up in the matter, I could see that driving Jefferson to kill. Money is all he cares about. Well, that and having his own way."

"I suppose you may have something there," Robert said. "My plan is to ferret out the truth. Father seems genuinely troubled by whatever is going on. Enough so that he can't figure out his own books and is suffering terrible headaches."

"And," Ella added, returning her gaze to the ocean, "he apparently can't seek Jefferson Spiby's help."

Robert escorted Ella through the hotel lobby. Light shimmered down from the crystal chandeliers overhead and sparkled off the jewels of the wealthiest patrons. Furnishings with rich upholstery and highly polished wood graced the marble floors. The room was crowded with well-dressed men and fashionably gowned women, all in a hurry to be somewhere.

"Well, hello, you two," Mary Reichert

said, coming alongside Ella. "Chris thought that was you. Did you have supper out this evening?"

Ella smiled despite her inability to think of anything but what August might have seen that cost him his life. Mary always reminded Ella of what had happened on Fleming Farm. Even if Robert hadn't brought up the matter with his information about the new horse breed, Ella would have thought of the brother Mary loved so dearly and missed so much.

"We went to Cliff House," Ella announced. "Have you been there?"

"No, but I have heard others recommend it," Mary replied.

Chris joined them. "Sorry for the delay." He took off his hat and gave Ella a nod. "My, Ella, you look beautiful. That color suits you."

"Doesn't it, though?" Mary agreed. "Dusty rose brings out the color in your cheeks."

Ella's face warmed. "They're sure to darken even more with all your praise. Might I offer you a compliment in return, Mary? You've always looked good in red, but the cut of that velvet gown is lovely."

"I told her the same thing," Chris declared. "And I think every man who sees her thinks the same. I'm not sure I like this dress at all. It makes her too beautiful."

Robert chuckled, and Mary rolled her eyes. "Who would ever expect a man to complain that his fiancée looks too beautiful?"

Ella smiled. "Did you two enjoy an evening on the town, despite the troublemaking gown?"

"We did," Mary replied. She smiled at Chris with such adoration that it was easy to see they were in love. "We had a light supper and then went to a ballet. It was beautiful, and the dancers were so graceful. I wanted to dance right along with them, and if not for my two left feet, I might have tried."

Chris chuckled. "I really think she might have. I kept hold of her for most of the evening, just in case."

Ella grinned. "Well, even if you can't dance as well as they can, Mary, I'm willing to bet none of them can shoot anywhere near as well as you."

"She makes a good point, my dear," Chris said, raising Mary's gloved hand to his lips. "You have your talents, and they have theirs."

"Speaking of talents, how is your book coming along, Chris?" Ella asked.

He gave a little shrug. "It's faring quite well, if I do say so. I was searching for an angle, something to really hook the reader, and it came to me that I might combine history with the wild west shows."

Robert piped up at this. "What do you mean?"

"I'm sorry. Where are my manners?" Ella glanced up at Robert. "I know you've met Mary, but this is her fiancé, Christopher Williams. Chris, this is my brother, Robert."

"A pleasure to meet you," Chris said, extending his hand. They shook briefly, then Chris continued to speak. "I'm writing a book about wild west shows. I know the idea of them is somewhat exotic and attractive to many people, but I also wanted to find another angle to draw in readers who might otherwise not care about the entertainment value. I decided to couple that with the history behind not only the shows themselves but also the acts. For instance, Mary is a sharpshooter. I thought it would be interesting to bring in stories about the history of firearms and the various sharpshooters who've made a name for themselves. The same with trick riding. There's a lot of history surrounding people doing stunts while on horseback, from the Russian Cossacks to the Indians of the American frontier."

"I think that will definitely make the book more interesting." Ella fought to suppress a yawn. "I'm sorry, but I'm exhausted. If you don't mind, I'd like to return to my room and go to bed. I have an early morning practice."

"Of course. I was just about to bid good night to Mary." Chris smiled at the dark-haired beauty. "Until tomorrow." He kissed her hand in a formal manner, then released her. He bowed to Ella. "Sweet dreams to you both."

"I'll see you tomorrow," Mary said, leaning over to give Ella a hug.

"I'll say good night as well," Robert declared as Mary headed for the elevator.

"Are you going to the farm now?" Ella asked.

He smiled and nodded. "In the morning. I'll catch an early train. One way or another, Ella, I promise I will figure out what's going on."

A sense of foreboding washed over her, and Ella hugged Robert close. She didn't care that she was making a spectacle of herself. "Please be careful. I don't want anything to happen to you. Father's threats should never be taken lightly."

"I promise I'll be careful." He held her tight, then bent to kiss her cheek. "Don't worry, Ella," he whispered in her ear. "Trust in God. He is our source of strength."

She stepped back, nodding. "He is. He is indeed."

⟶⟞ FOUR ⟝⟵

Phillip DeShazer frowned as he saw a tall, beefy man embrace Ella Fleming. He didn't know who the man was, and he didn't care, especially since the man was leaning down to kiss Ella.

Phillip took a step forward and stumbled. A sudden sea of people momentarily stunned him. Of course, the excessive amount of whiskey he'd consumed that night certainly didn't help keep him steady. He grabbed one of the lobby chairs, irritating the older gentleman occupying it.

"So . . . sorry."

Phillip straightened, but when he looked again, the man was gone and Ella was standing alone. Phillip frowned. Had the man kissed her? Were they in love? Maybe he'd only imagined her companion.

He started out again, and this time his footing was surer. Ella had turned to go by the time he'd worked his way across the busy lobby. He thought about calling out to her but changed his mind. Wesley and Lizzy might be close at hand, returning from their evening out. He had refused to accompany them, telling them he planned to stay in the hotel all evening. And that *had* been the plan, but things changed when he learned of a great place for entertainment and libation just a couple of blocks away.

He reached Ella just as the elevator doors opened. "I wanna talk." He took hold of her arm.

Ella pulled away. She turned and fixed him with a look of disdain, and then recognition and surprise filled her face. "Phillip. You startled me."

"Going up?" the elevator operator asked.

"Yes. Sixth floor, please," Ella replied and climbed into what to Phillip resembled a gilded cage. He followed her inside. She frowned. "You've been drinking. I can smell it."

He grinned. "You have the cutest nose. I've always . . . liked it." He staggered and leaned hard against the polished wood. As the wood-paneled doors closed, the cage disappeared, and in its place was a tiny, intimate wooden room. It might have been romantic except for the slender uniformed man operating the controls.

"Where's your room, Phillip?" Ella put her arm around his waist as he started to slide toward the floor.

Her touch prompted him to straighten. "Six—six-oh-two." He grinned. "Where are you?"

"I'm in six-ten. So I'm just down the hall."

"I don't like seein' you kiss other men." He looked at her, but her face was blurred.

"That was my brother, silly."

"Your brother?" His tongue suddenly felt too big for his mouth. He rolled it around, trying to lessen the discomfort. "I got a brother." He started to sink again.

"Yes, I know." Ella drew his arm over her shoulder. "You'd better lean against me. I'll help you get to your room."

"Sixth floor," the attendant called out.

Phillip forced his legs to move and let Ella half pull, half push him from the elevator. When they were clear of the contraption, the operator closed the door, and they were alone. The long hall was void of any other person.

"Your room is just over here," Ella said, steering him toward a door with 602 clearly marked in gold lettering.

"Don't go. Not now," he whispered. "I wanna talk to you. I need to . . . talk to you. I care about you." Ella looked up, and Phillip lost himself in her eyes. He thought her the most beautiful woman he'd ever known. "You're so pretty." He reached out to touch a blond wisp of hair. "No." He shook his head hard. The motion sent his vision swirling. "You're not pretty . . . you're beautiful."

"Well, thank you for the compliment, but it's time to go inside and get some sleep. Do you have your key?"

He tried to force the words to make sense. Key? Did he have a key? Phillip rubbed his eyes and fought to stay upright and awake. A key for what?

"I care about you, Ella."

"I think all you care about is alcohol," she said firmly. "Now, find your key, or I shall be forced to find it for you."

Again, the words didn't completely make sense, but he felt his coat pockets, then patted the outside of his trousers. Something hard and metallic refused to yield. He reached inside and pulled out a key. With a happy laugh and a grin, he held it up.

Ella took the key from him and slipped it into his door. Once it was open, she gave him a nudge toward the room. "Go on now. We can talk more tomorrow."

Phillip stepped over the threshold and promptly fell to the ground.

"Oh, Phillip, why must you do this?"

She sounded so sad, and Phillip struggled into a sitting position. He looked up at her standing just outside the door. He shook his head. What was he going to say? Hadn't she just asked him a question? No . . . it was something else.

"Come on," she said, coming into the room. She put her purse on a nearby chair and went to Phillip. "I can't lift you, but if we work together, I should be able to help get you back to your feet."

Phillip nodded and got on his knees. Ella took his arm and steadied him as he stood. Without another word, she led him to the bed. He sank to the mattress and sat looking at her.

"You're always . . . good to me."

Ella didn't seem to hear him. She was pulling off his boots instead. Why was she doing that?

"What . . . are you doin'?"

"Taking off your boots so you can go to bed."

"I care about you," he muttered, feeling his body grow heavy.

"The only thing you care about is the bottle. Honestly, I don't know why you drink."

"My ma . . . said the same thing. My folks didn't drink."

"Then why do you?" Ella picked up his boots and straightened.

Phillip shrugged. "Helps . . . me forget."

"I've heard you say that before. But what is so awful that you have to forget it this way?" She put the boots at the end of the bed, then came back to where he sat.

"I did a lot of bad things," he murmured.

She helped him out of his coat. "We all do bad things—things we regret."

"I knew these . . . these people, and they were bad." He tried to keep the room from tilting by blinking hard, but it was no use. "My folks didn't like them, so I ran off." Ella went to the other side of the bed, and Phillip frowned. "Where'd you go?"

"I'm just turning down the bed. I can't undress you any further, so once I go, you'll have to tend to yourself."

"Don't go."

She came back to him and prompted him to stand. "I can't stay, Phillip. It's inappropriate enough that I'm here with you now. It won't be good for my reputation if I'm seen here."

"If anyone says any . . . anything bad . . . I'll punch him."

Ella nudged him to sit back down. "There.

Your bed is ready for you, and now I need to go."

"No. I didn't tell you."

She frowned. "Tell me what?"

"About the . . . the bad things."

"You can tell me later. You're drunk and sleepy now."

"I ran away," Phillip said, paying her words no mind. "My friends were bad. They made me . . . bad. We weren't nice to folks. We got into fights and we gambled and drank." His slurring only worsened as he rambled. "Pa—he came to get me."

Phillip had been confident no one would even care if he left. With all the trouble he'd caused, he was certain his folks would simply say "good riddance" and be glad he was gone. Instead his father had hunted him down.

"He said he loved me." Sadness and loss washed over him.

"Of course he loved you. Really, Phillip, I must go." Ella turned, but Phillip grabbed her hand.

He glanced up at her and shook his head. "How could he?"

She gave him an odd look. "Fathers usually love their children. Just because you did bad things didn't change the fact that he loved you. It's just like with God. We sometimes do bad things that He doesn't like, but it doesn't change the fact that He loves us."

The words struggled through the clouded images in his head. "I ran off, and he came after me."

Phillip let the memory come, even though he'd fought it off a thousand times before. His friends were all worthless rowdies who cared only for themselves. They embraced Phillip as someone to mold in their own image, and mold him they did. Whenever someone dared to cross them, they would beat that person senseless, then rob him blind. They weren't afraid of anyone, not even the law, and people feared them. As time went on, their antics only got worse and deepened his regret and shame.

"Phillip, you must go to sleep. You can't think clearly in this drunken stupor."

If only she knew. The memories were clear enough. "Pa came after me. They . . . they beat him."

She frowned. "Your father? Your friends beat him up?"

Phillip nodded, feeling more than a little nauseated. "I tried to help him, to make them stop." He closed his eyes. "They beat Pa . . . put him on the ground. I tried to stop them, but John Bryer hit me and knocked me down. Pa got up . . . got up bleedin'. He came to help me because he . . . he thought John Bryer was gonna hit me again."

Phillip could see it clearly despite his drunken stupor. John Bryer was six feet five and had at least fifty pounds on his father. No one interfered with what John wanted.

"Pa tried to help me up. John hit him with the butt of his gun." He closed his eyes, as if he could block the image from his mind. "He killed him." Tears seeped out. "I killed him."

When Ella sat down beside him, Phillip opened his eyes. Her expression was full of gentle kindness. "You didn't kill him, Phillip."

"He shouldn't have come after me."

"He came after you because he loved you. Did they get the man who really killed him, this John Bryer?"

Phillip nodded. "They hanged John Bryer. There were witnesses." He sat in silence for several seconds, then jumped up. "You can't tell anyone—especially Wesley. He doesn't know what happened. He doesn't know it's all my fault—that Pa was saving me."

"He'd understand. He wouldn't blame you."

"Yes, he would. Everyone would. You got to promise me you won't say anything."

She stood. "I won't, but don't you see? This secret is killing you."

"Wesley doesn't know Pa got killed coming after me. He'd never understand. He'd never forgive me, and he's all I got left."

"So you drink to forget that it ever happened," she murmured. "Phillip, you have to stop."

Her expression was so sympathetic, so sad. Phillip reached out to touch her cheek before he could stop himself. The effects of the alcohol were fading.

"I can't stop. When I'm sober, I can still hear him."

To his surprise, she didn't move away. The softness of her skin was unlike anything he'd ever known. She was so beautiful.

"Hear who?"

Her question broke the spell. He pulled back his hand as if her skin had suddenly grown hot. "My father."

Ella nodded. "What did he say?"

Phillip could still see his father's bloodied face looking up at him—his life's blood pouring from the head wound. He was barely conscious. "He said, 'I'll always love you, son.'" He looked at Ella and shook his head. "He loved me, and I killed him."

"No. He did what he did because he loved you."

"Then love killed him."

Ella shook her head again. "No. Hate killed him. Hate killed him just as it nailed Jesus to the cross. Jesus died for us because He loved us. He even loved the people who killed Him. Your father came after you because he loved you. He had to know that what he was doing was dangerous, but the love he bore you was far stronger than fear. His final words were of love, Phillip. Don't turn that into something ugly because of your fears or anger."

He tried to understand her words. Tried to focus on the sweet lilt of her voice and the touch of her hand on his arm.

"Phillip, your father spoke those last words because he didn't want you to focus on John Bryer or on the hatred. He didn't want you to think that you'd disappointed him. He wanted you to know that none of that mattered. Only the love remained."

A sob broke from Phillip's throat as he bowed his head. Ella pulled him into her arms and held him while he cried. He wrapped his arms around her and forgot for a while how alone he truly was. Why couldn't it be like this forever? Just Ella and him—together?

Because you aren't worthy of her love.

The voice echoed from somewhere deep in his brain.

You're worthless. You make everyone around you unhappy. You're the reason your father is dead.

The accusations went on and on, and despite Ella's closeness, Phillip couldn't silence the voice.

⟶⟩═ FIVE ═⟨⟵

Ella finished a grueling practice and rubbed her burning thighs. She'd started out with a new trick that Lizzy had helped her with. It was a series of spins, layovers, and drags that even had her looping around under the horse's neck to pop up on the other side.

After that, she had worked with the other Roman riders to perfect their act. The Roman riding tricks used to be simple. The riders would mount in a variety of ways and then stand on the backs of the horses. Usually they handled just two horses at a time, which was more than enough. There were a couple of riders who were very good and could handle as many as four, but the more horses they added, the greater the danger.

Then Henry Adler got the idea that their tricks should become more acrobatic. He'd seen a circus act and was convinced it would add a certain dazzle to the show, so now the girls were performing more and more tricks. One of the girls would always act as anchor and handle the team, but then they'd add as many as three or four other performers who climbed all over the horses, executing dangerous stunts as they went. The audiences loved it, just as Henry had thought.

Ella didn't mind doing both trick and Roman riding. She found herself craving the rush of excitement and the approving cheers of the crowd. All her life she had sought approval, it seemed. She could easily remember longing for her parents' approval when she was young. It seemed only Lucille, her black nurse, had plenty of that to offer. Lucille always told Ella that no matter what she did in life, God would always love her, and so would she. Ella could count on one hand the number of times her father had told her that he loved her. Even her mother's love was sparsely given. Or perhaps that wasn't fair to say. Her mother's presence was sparsely given, and Ella equated that to her love.

"You performed well, Ella," Lizzy Brookstone said, coming to join her. "I was watching from the stands. You always amaze me with your natural talent."

Ella straightened. "I love working with

your horses. I wanted so much to train my own horse, Pepper, to do the show, but you were right. His back is just too long, and it makes it difficult to do some of the tricks."

Lizzy nodded. "Well, since I'm no longer performing, I hated to deny Thoreau the opportunity. Longfellow seems happy to do less, but even he wants to get out there and hear the applause."

"They're both incredible. You trained them so well."

"Thoreau has really blossomed under your handling," Lizzy said, her voice full of admiration. "I'm glad you two spend so much time together."

"It's like you said, the horse and rider need to become one and know each other's moves." Ella wiped her perspiring face with a towel.

Laughter sounded from across the arena. Ella caught the frown on Lizzy's face.

"What is it?"

She turned and saw Lizzy's uncle walking arm in arm with Amanda Moore. The seamstress was dressed in a beautiful new ensemble and seemed delighted to show it off.

"I assume that's a new outfit," Ella said.

"Yes. No doubt Uncle Oliver paid for it," Lizzy muttered. "I wish we'd never hired her."

Ella had to agree with her friend. "It's not

like she's doing much work anyway. If she spent less time escorting your uncle around, I might not have to give my mending to Mara. Perhaps you could dismiss her."

"Uncle Oliver would never allow it."

"Yes, but maybe Henry Adler would." Ella raised a brow.

Lizzy shook her head. "It's getting ridiculous. Annie and Melba both had costume trouble when they performed their Roman riding last night. I told them to get with Amanda and see what could be done. She couldn't have had time to fix their costumes already."

As Oliver and Amanda approached, Lizzy planted her hands on her hips. Ella could see she was preparing for battle.

"Uncle Oliver, I wonder if I might have a word with Amanda." Lizzy's words were curt.

"But of course, my dear."

Amanda smirked. "Do you like my new outfit? We purchased it yesterday, and it's the very latest fashion from Paris." She let go of Oliver's arm and gave a whirl. The emerald fabric flared out around her. "I think it's just divine."

Lizzy fixed Amanda with a stern look. "I see you have time to shop and stroll about with my uncle. I'm wondering if you've taken care of Annie and Melba's costumes?"

Amanda returned Lizzy's stare with indifference. "There was nothing wrong with their costumes. I looked them over."

"The problem isn't in a tear or other flaw, it's in what needs to be done to allow them more give during their performances."

"If they drop a few pounds, they'll have room enough." Amanda elbowed Oliver. "Isn't that right, dearest?"

Lizzy scowled. "You aren't paid to make those kind of judgments, but to accommodate the performers when they have needs. I told the girls you would adjust the costumes, and you will."

Instead of protesting, as Ella had presumed Amanda might do, the older woman turned to Oliver and pouted. "Do you hear how she talks to me, darling? I try to be civil, but she's always yelling at me."

"I haven't raised my voice at all," Lizzy countered.

"Well, she's ruining our celebration." Amanda slipped her arm from Oliver's. "I'm going to have a bottle of champagne sent up to our room while you straighten her out. She's much too mean to me, and I simply cannot bear it."

She stalked off with a dramatic flair.

Lizzy looked at Ella and then back to her uncle. "What is she talking about? Celebrations and champagne? You know you can't drink, Uncle Oliver. The doctor said it would kill you."

He waved his arms as if trying to stuff something into a box. "Now, Lizzy, you mustn't be so cross. I only had trouble with alcohol because I was lonely. I'm not lonely anymore. Amanda has come into my life and changed all of that."

"What are you saying?"

He smiled. "I've asked her to marry me, and she's said yes."

Ella was just as surprised as Lizzy. She couldn't imagine anyone wanting to deal with Amanda's ill temper on such an intimate level.

"You scarcely know her," Lizzy protested. "She's not even doing her job."

"And that's my fault."

"No, it's not. It's her own fault. If she had any pride in herself, she'd see to her work first and then worry about chasing after you."

Oliver laughed. "I've never had anyone chase after me. It feels good, and I don't intend to let this misunderstanding ruin it for us. You hired that new woman, Mara, to help with sewing. Amanda isn't going to want to work once we're wed, so we'll make Mara head of costumes and sewing."

Lizzy's mouth dropped open. "And when do you plan to marry?"

He shrugged. "Not exactly sure. Amanda needs time to plan it. We might even do it as part of one of the performances. That's been so popular since we featured your own engagement."

"But you're planning to have Mary and Chris's wedding. You don't need to have one of your own. You need to think this through."

He smiled and patted Lizzy's hand. "Stop fretting. I've given it a lot of thought."

"She's only been with the show a few weeks. It couldn't have been that much thought."

He shrugged. "Sometimes a fella doesn't need a lot of time to know what's right. Now, you stop worrying about everything. God will get us through this."

He walked away, and Lizzy appeared too stunned to say or do anything to stop him.

"I'm sorry, Lizzy," Ella said, touching her arm.

"That woman doesn't care a fig about my uncle. She's just using him. She wants his money. I've seen women like her before on other tours. She thinks she can woo and sweet-talk him and get whatever she wants."

"Well, it appears she's managed to get a wedding proposal, so you seem to be right about that much."

Lizzy shook her head. "This is madness."

Ella was relieved to see Wesley approaching. Perhaps he'd have some words of wisdom to calm Lizzy's fretful heart.

From the frown on his face, Wesley already realized there was a problem. He approached Ella and Lizzy, looking from one to the other. "What's wrong?"

"Uncle Oliver has proposed to Amanda. He plans to marry her, Wes!"

Wes shrugged. "What's wrong with that?"

Lizzy gave an exasperated sigh. "Everything. In fact, there's nothing right about it. I can't believe you asked that question."

"If he's happy—"

"But he's not!" Lizzy interrupted. "At least, not in the right way."

This made Wes smile. "Now, who are you to say what the right way is for someone else to be happy? If Oliver loves Amanda, then you need to accept that and welcome her into the family."

"No! She doesn't care about him. She's after his money. I know that's all it is. She doesn't even care that he's not supposed to drink. She was arranging for champagne. She knows Uncle Oliver can't have it, because I've told her. I told her quite clearly, in fact, that alcohol will kill him."

Wes shook his head. "I'm sorry, Lizzy. I don't know what to say."

"You need to have a talk with him."

"No. I won't interfere with another man's romance."

"Then I will."

She started to leave, but Wes caught her and spun her around.

"You need to stay out of it. This isn't one of those times when interfering will help. If a man has his heart set on a woman, he isn't going to listen to his niece or her husband tell him he's wrong. Why don't you pray about it instead? Ask God to show him the truth."

Lizzy seemed to calm at this. She considered his words for a moment and nodded. "I suppose you're right. I just saw red. I can't believe that after a few short weeks, my uncle would lose all his common sense."

Wes chuckled. "Love has a way of doing that to a fella. Now, if this crisis is resolved, I need to get back to work." He leaned down and kissed his wife's forehead. "Love you, Lizzy."

She gave a hint of a smile. "I know you do, and I love you."

Ella envied their love. It was so apparent that they belonged together. She thought of Phillip and how deeply she cared for him. If her love for him could make his past disappear and his longing for alcohol abate, he'd never have to worry about anything ever again.

"Are you finished here?" Lizzy asked.

Ella nodded. "I'm heading back to the hotel for some lunch and a bath." She smiled. "You're welcome to join me. Well, for lunch, anyway." She chuckled. "I have something to tell you. Something my brother discussed with me."

Lizzy glanced around and then nodded. "I suppose there's nothing else for me to do here. I need to figure out how to help Annie and Melba."

"Mara will know how to adjust the costumes." Ella looped her arm through Lizzy's. "Come on."

───◆◆◆───

"And then Robert said Father declared that he and Jefferson have a new breed of horse. A secret herd he's keeping at Jefferson's estate."

"A secret breed of horses?" Lizzy shook her head. "Surely if he was selling them, they wouldn't be secret for long. Besides, it's hard to hide an entire herd."

Ella had already considered all of this. She picked up the second half of her sandwich. "I wish I knew what was going on. Robert says that things aren't good. My father is so upset that he can't keep his own affairs in order. That isn't like him."

"I'm betting Spiby is behind it," Lizzy said.

"Me too," Mara agreed. She had joined the girls for lunch. "That man always be up to sumptin'."

"I don't know what Jefferson has on him, but it's apparent Father is completely obligated to him. Maybe it has to do with this new bunch of horses, but whatever it is . . . it isn't right."

Ella took a bite of her chicken salad sandwich and considered all that had happened over the last couple of years. Her family had always had its share of secrets mingled in with business. Her father was very protective of new horses and breeding stock. He was also very selective about who he allowed to come to the show room. He never advertised. He didn't have to. His reputation preceded him, and people came from all over the country to purchase Fleming Morgans.

Still, even if there was a new breed of horse, how could that equate to so much trouble? Why would business as usual suddenly weigh so heavily on her father that he needed Robert's help? He'd never let Robert do much when it came to the breeding and sales. He always kept Robert busy elsewhere, sending him off to deliver horses or to handle other parts of the farm's business.

"And I was sure you could help," Lizzy said.

Ella realized she hadn't been paying attention, but Mara was nodding.

"I's sure I can, Miz Lizzy. You can count on me."

"I'm not sure how soon we'll change things officially to put you in charge, but the sooner I can arrange it, the better."

Mara grinned. "I ain't never been in charge of anything before."

Lizzy smiled. "Well, you're very talented, and Ella assures me you can handle the job. We'll get someone in to be your assistant. There's also the laundry to consider. We have two girls who help with that, but if it's too much, let me know, and we'll bring in another girl."

"It seems so funny to go from Jason's streamlined troupe to Henry's very generous one." Ella took a sip of her iced tea.

"I agree," Lizzy declared. "However, it does my heart good. It's more the way my father wanted to see it. He always wanted a huge show like Buffalo Bill's, where there were hundreds of people and animals. Buffalo Bill hired Indians as well as whites and reenacted wars and attacks. My father thought it some of the most marvelous showmanship to be found. I thought so too." She smiled at the memory. "It was quite the life, and now I see this show taking on some of those elements. Henry was even talking about having an act with diving horses."

"Diving?" Ella asked.

"Yes. There are people who take their mounts up onto a high platform and then jump them into a huge tank of water. I've never seen it, but it sounds intriguing."

"And dangerous. I can't imagine a horse wanting to jump off a platform into a tank of water. How high up do they go?"

Lizzy shrugged. "Henry mentioned something in the neighborhood of forty to fifty feet being normal."

"On horseback?" Mara asked, her eyes widening. "I wouldn't be jumpin' off somethin' that high even without the horse."

"Me either," Ella admitted. "You won't catch me being talked into that."

"Well, I'm sure if Henry wants to have it as part of the show, then that's what will happen." Lizzy shook her head. "I think it would be amazing to see, but I wouldn't want to perform the stunt. Still, it might be a great thing for the show. Sometimes I wish I could go on being a part of it, and other times I'm glad those days are nearly done."

"So you will miss it?" Ella asked.

"Of course I'll miss it. It's been a part of

my life since I was a child. But I enjoy life back on the ranch too. I know once I'm there and Wes and I start having a family, I'll be more than content. I love the ranch—it's home."

Ella frowned. "I wish home meant to me what it means to you. I don't even feel like I really have one anymore."

"You and Mara will both have a home with us so long as you need one," Lizzy countered. "No matter what, you can count on that."

"I 'preciate that, Miz Lizzy. Ain't never felt quite so misplaced as I do now. I grew up on Fleming Farm. That's all I ever knew." Mara wiped a tear from her eye. "Still, it wasn't the same without my mama."

"No, it wasn't. Lucille kept us both on the straight and narrow." Ella smiled. "I miss her so much. She was more of a mother to me than my own. I suppose that's why I don't understand all this nonsense about people of different colors. Did you ever wish you could be white, Mara?"

Mara shook her head. "Ain't like bein' black is something to fix. It's not the skin, but the heart and head what need to be fixed. Folks need to see that all folks belong to God no matter how they appear."

"Very wise words," Lizzy declared. "I couldn't agree more."

"Sadly, I don't think some people will ever see it that way." Ella shook her head. "I knew people my age who thought my friendship with Mara was completely uncalled for. They called me all sorts of terrible names. I couldn't believe anyone could be so heartless. I remember we even had a lynching nearby when I was a child. A young black man who was walking home from town. Some white boys decided to beat him up, and then they hanged him."

"I 'member that too," Mara said, and again there were tears. "My mama told me to stay close to her even when we went to church. We knew better than to be out alone. It was terrifying, and I 'spect it's gonna get worse. Some folks are just full of hate. Scared me plenty when I was little and don't make me feel much better now that I'm grown."

Ella shook her head. "Why didn't you ever tell me how you felt? We used to tell each other everything."

Mara shrugged. "I guess there were just some things a black girl couldn't tell a white one. Especially one she was workin' for."

The thought made Ella sad. Here she had believed she and Mara could tell each other anything. They would seek each other out when they were afraid. Well . . . at least Ella sought out Mara. She thought back on their youth and realized that Mara never came to her. She always went to Mara. Ella could still remember dragging the poor girl from her cot in the middle of the night to come to her bed because she had been afraid. Mara never complained, and by morning Lucille had always seen them back in their proper places.

"Do you ever think we'll see a day when people just see people instead of their skin color?" Lizzy questioned.

Ella met Mara's gaze. She could feel a sense of sadness between them. "I hope so," she said, praying that it might be. "I hope so."

⤙ SIX ⤚

L adies and gentlemen! Boys and girls!"
Oliver Brookstone announced. "I'm sure
you've been quite amazed by our bow
shooter, Alice Hopkins. Let's give her another
round of applause."

The audience went wild with enthusiastic
clapping. Brookstone smiled as he waved his
black top hat back and forth to encourage
their cheers. After a time, he lowered the hat
to his head, and the crowd calmed.

"Now I will give you one of the most im-
pressive shows you will ever see. Our Mary
Reichert has been shooting since she was a
little girl and is rivaled only by Annie Oak-
ley. Help me in giving Mary a warm Denver
welcome."

Mary stepped out from behind a stack of
boxes, dressed in her dark buckskin skirt and

red calico blouse. She wore her custom-made red Stetson atop her head, and dark brown knee boots rounded out her costume. At her hip, a leather holster held her favorite five-shot Smith & Wesson .38.

She gave a wave to the audience as she made her way to the area where the crew had set up her targets. Oliver began speaking again, and the crowd went silent. He explained the first of many tricks.

"Our Mary will show her precision by shooting dimes out of the air. Our crewman will toss these high, and Mary will shoot them through the center."

Phillip came out with a small bag of coins and held it up for the viewers to see. Next he opened the bag and let some of the dimes spill into his hand. After this he glanced to Mary, who gave him a nod, and then he began tossing them into the air.

Mary shot five in a row with her pistol, then reloaded while Phillip collected the dimes and tossed them to members of the audience. She didn't have to look to know she'd hit all five.

After that, she went to the table where her Stevens Crack Shot rifle waited. She picked it up and turned to the audience. They seemed to sense that she was about to do something important and quieted. She strolled over to

Oliver Brookstone as she had done in every show.

"Well, this is it," Oliver whispered. "I don't think anyone is expecting a thing."

"Maybe not expecting, but definitely anticipating." She smiled at him. "At least if Henry has done his advertising correctly."

Oliver turned back to the audience. "Miss Mary needs a volunteer. The man in question will have to be brave and of a strong heart. The tricks performed here are both highly dangerous and unpredictable."

The hands of hundreds of men went up all over the arena, but Mary zeroed in on Christopher Williams, sitting just three rows up from the floor. She walked toward him, looking all around at the ocean of people. When she finally let her gaze settle on him, she couldn't help but smile. How handsome he was in his brown tweed suit. His sandy-colored hair had just been trimmed the day before, and his blue eyes were intense as they returned her gaze. When he winked, Mary thought her heart would burst with joy. He loved her, and it made her so happy.

She went to Chris and took his hand, much to the disappointment of the crowd. There were audible moans from those who'd not been chosen.

"Take me instead," the man beside Chris begged.

Mary ignored his plea and pulled Chris back to the performing area, then set him up with a lit stub of a candle in his mouth. The candle wasn't but two inches long, and though Mary had performed this trick many a time, she couldn't help being just a bit hesitant. After all, this was the man she loved, and she would never be able to forgive herself if anything happened to him.

The audience quieted once again as she took aim at the wick of the candle. She steadied her grip, took a deep breath, and then let it out and squeezed the trigger. The sound of the rifle wasn't all that loud, but the bullet did its job and extinguished the flame without harming Chris in the least.

The crowd again broke into wild cheers and clapping. After this, Mary did a series of tricks with Chris holding various things. She ended the display by having him stand sideways and hold a very small feather between his teeth.

"I hope you know what you're doing. Just remember, if you nick my lips, it will be a long while before I can kiss you," he whispered with a grin before raising the feather to his mouth.

"I always know what I'm doing. Besides,

I wouldn't risk missing out on your kisses." She left him with a grin and walked to the table where her rifle waited.

She took aim, then shook her head and turned to place her back to the target. She picked up a mirror and carefully leveled her rifle on her shoulder. Gasps were heard throughout the arena, and one woman even shrieked in fear.

"Ladies and gentlemen, boys and girls, I must ask for absolute silence!" Oliver proclaimed. "The life of this poor man is dependent upon it!"

A hush fell over the audience.

Mary smiled. It was always the same.

She glanced at the mirror, adjusted her aim, and then took the shot and ended her performance. She was so confident of her shot that she didn't even look at Chris as the feather blew apart and floated to the ground. The audience rose to their feet, stomping and clapping and yelling their approval.

Mary gave a bow and then put down her rifle and went to where Chris stood. She raised his hand in hers, and together they took another bow. Chris wrapped his fingers around hers, and instead of letting go once they straightened from their bow, he dropped to one knee and held up a ring box. Mary hadn't thought it possible that the crowd could cheer any louder, but they did. The sight of Chris proposing to their favorite sharpshooter appealed to one and all.

Mary nodded, and Chris stood and slipped the ring on her finger. Then, to everyone's approval, he swept her into his arms and dipped her backward.

"Always the showman," she said, gazing up into his amused expression.

"Hey, we have to give them their money's worth."

She laughed, and he kissed her passionately.

"Well, have you ever seen the likes?" Oliver Brookstone announced through his megaphone. "I do believe we have just witnessed an engagement. Miss Mary, come introduce us to your young man."

Chris finally ended the kiss and straightened. Mary looked at him in wonder. "Your lips seem to be working just fine," she whispered. He gave her a lopsided grin that sent her heart racing.

She put her hand to her chest and drew a deep breath. Many in the audience roared in laughter at the thought that this amazing sharpshooter should be unnerved by a kiss.

Mary reached for Christopher's hand and

pulled him with her. "Troublemaker." She grinned back at him as he obediently followed her.

Oliver helped her make the introductions, then announced that the couple would be wed at one of the upcoming shows. "We can't say where or when, but it will definitely be in the next few weeks during one of our American shows. I'll see to that!" He put one arm around Mary while still holding the megaphone to his lips. "We have flyers available listing all of our upcoming events, so let all your family and friends know."

A small orchestra struck up a musical intermission while the arena floor was cleared for the third and final act. Mary gathered her rifle and made her way from the arena with Chris right behind her.

"You two were amazing," Lizzy declared. "I'm impressed, and I think you left the audience completely enthralled. I wouldn't be surprised if there aren't quite a few proposals made this evening by folks in the crowd. You no doubt inspired them."

"Aw shucks, weren't nothin'," Chris said with a forced drawl.

Mary elbowed him. "Nothing? Proposing to me is nothing?"

He chuckled. "You know better. Do you want me to prove it to you?"

A grin broke across her face. "Maybe later."

Lizzy laughed. "You two are going to be so happy together."

Chris put his arm around Mary. "I know we will be. After all, she's armed. I have to cooperate."

"Like it would ever be difficult for you to love her," Lizzy replied. "You two belong together. Unlike two others I know." Her gaze went to something behind Mary.

Mary turned and saw Amanda and Oliver together. "I agree that she's most likely after his money, Lizzy, but you have to be careful how you manage yourself, or you'll just throw them together all the more."

"I know." Lizzy's voice bore her displeasure. "I just wish I could convince Uncle Oliver of her true motives."

"Pray about it. I'm sure in time God will let the truth be told."

"Yes, but what will the truth do to Uncle Oliver? I want him to be happy, and I'm afraid when he realizes what she's really up to, it will kill him."

———◆———

At the crew meeting the morning after the engagement, everyone was still highly energized. Ella was particularly excited for Mary and Chris, even though they'd been promised to each other since before the show's start in March.

"I'm sure you know that the engagement was very well received," Henry Adler said. "We sold a record number of programs, and I think we're going to have to start having autograph signings after the shows. People have been asking for that, and I believe Americans in particular are keen on that kind of thing." His English accent thickened as he hurried his words. "We owe it to our audience to see that they're happy—after all, they're spending their hard-earned money to attend our performances, and we need to honor them."

Ella didn't mind the idea of signing autographs. She'd done so several times, mostly for love-sick young men who'd cornered her after performances. Of course, there were an equally large number of young girls who wanted to trick ride like she did and asked Ella how they could learn.

"As for the wedding, we've chosen Chicago, as most of you know. Oliver and I have decided to throw quite the grand affair. We're going to have a white buckskin outfit made for Mary. Miss Moore assures me she can arrange that. There will also be attendants' outfits. We still need to discuss the style and determine the decorative arrangements. The Chicago show will take place in four weeks, so there should be time enough to prepare the outfits, right, Miss Moore?"

Everyone looked to Amanda, who was seated beside Oliver and nodding. "Of course. I'm sure I can have everything ready."

This surprised Ella. She had been confident Amanda's days of sewing were over. Ella felt certain Mara would be the one who ended up making the costumes in the end.

After several additional announcements, the meeting finally concluded, and a late supper was announced in the adjoining room. Ella was starved, but she wondered where Phillip was and if he was all right. He'd made himself scarce since she'd put him to bed that night in San Francisco. No doubt he was embarrassed by what he'd said and done.

She made her way to where Wes and Lizzy stood talking in hushed tones. Lizzy smiled at her, but it was clear she was upset.

"Did you hear Amanda?" Lizzy asked. "I swear she'd lie right to God Himself."

"I did wonder about that. I'll let Mara know that the responsibility will probably fall on her shoulders."

"We certainly can't count on Amanda to honor her word."

"What was that you said about my word?" Amanda asked, coming up behind Ella and Lizzy.

"I said I don't believe we can count on it," Lizzy replied. "I dare you to prove me wrong."

Amanda gave a harsh laugh and didn't even try to pretend to be the docile darling she was around Oliver Brookstone. "I'm not interested in your dares. You're just out of sorts because I intend to marry your uncle."

"Well, I plan to do whatever I can to see that it never happens," Lizzy said, moving toward Amanda. Wes held her back.

Amanda was undaunted, however. She pointed her finger in Lizzy's face. "You need to mind your own business. Your uncle is happy with me. Stay out of it, or you'll suffer the consequences."

"Meaning what?" Lizzy asked, straining against Wesley's hold.

"Meaning," Amanda began, her voice thick with contempt, "that you might lose him forever if you interfere much more. He loves me and intends to marry me. We could just up and disappear after that, and you'd never see him again."

Lizzy shook her head. "You'll never separate us. We're family, and you're nothing."

"Sometimes family can be such a bother. I haven't seen mine in years." With that, Amanda sashayed off toward the supper room.

"Oooh, I hate her!" Lizzy pulled away from her husband. "I can't stand her at all."

"I couldn't tell," he said sarcastically.

Lizzy turned to look at him in frustration.

Ella felt sorry for her and reached out to touch her friend's shoulder. "Don't let her make you so angry, Lizzy."

"You heard what she said. She wants to separate my family."

Ella nodded. "I know. I wonder if Oliver realizes her intent. Maybe you should talk to him about it."

"Maybe I will." Lizzy seemed to calm a bit. "Maybe Uncle Oliver doesn't realize her plans."

"Maybe he doesn't care," Wes said, turning Lizzy to face him. "You know, same as I do, that when a man marries, he's supposed to cleave to his wife. Lizzy, if Oliver really and truly loves her and they marry—you can't interfere in what God has joined."

"They aren't joined yet," Lizzy countered. "I won't be sinning if I try to get Uncle Oliver to see the truth before they marry." She jerked away and stormed off past the supper room.

Ella frowned and looked at Wes. "She's really upset. I know she's afraid that Amanda is just taking him for his money."

"I know that too," Wes admitted, "but unless Oliver sees the truth of it and cares enough to do something about it . . . there's not a whole lot we can do."

She knew he was right, but it didn't help. It was the same with Phillip. Until he cared enough to do something about his drinking, there wasn't a whole lot she could do to stop him.

"I know you're worried about her," Wes said.

Ella looked up and smiled. "I actually wasn't thinking about Lizzy just then. I'm worried about Phillip."

Wes nodded. "So am I." His voice took on a level of concern that only deepened Ella's own apprehension.

"I tried to encourage him to talk to you." She didn't want to say too much. She'd never betray Phillip's confidence, but it was important to let Wes know that she was trying to do the right thing.

"God knows I've tried to get him to talk. He's all bottled up inside. He's always been that way. Always kept things close to the vest, didn't want folks to know too much or get too close."

"I . . . I care about him, Wes."

He smiled down at her. "I know. And I know he's smitten with you. If anyone can help him make a new start, I think it's you. But I have to warn you that you can't love him into changing. He has to want it for himself, and he's most likely going to have a rough go of it. He's been drinking since he was a young man."

"Yes, he told me. I've prayed for him and tried to share the Bible with him, but he has a lot of . . . memories that still hurt him. I think he feels that God deserted him."

"Most folks feel like that at one point or another, but Phillip has gotten stuck in that place. He feels alone and unloved, yet here we all are, just waiting for him to see how much we do love him. Sometimes I feel that I've failed as a big brother."

Ella shrugged. "I suppose everyone fails everyone in some way. I don't think we can be responsible for the expectations others put on us. After all, they're the one assigning them, and if we fail to live up to them, how is that our fault?"

"You make a good point, but probably not in the way you intended. Makes me realize that my expectations of Phillip are just that. Mine. It's not fair for me to hold a grudge or grievance if my brother fails to live up to my standards and expectations."

"It's true. I guess we just need to find ways to make him realize his value so that he'll want to strive for a better way. Not for our sake, but his."

Wesley nodded and offered Ella his arm. "I think you're a very wise young woman, Miss Ella Fleming. I don't know about you, however, but I'm famished."

She grinned. "I don't know that I'm wise, but I am hungry. Let's go get something to eat."

·✦⇒ SEVEN ⇐✦·

When Ella woke the following morning, Phillip was the first thing on her mind. She heard Mara humming a tune across the room and sat up to find her friend ironing.

"Where in the world did you find an iron?" Ella asked. "I had to send things to our laundry girls to get them pressed before."

"I borrowed the iron and the board from one of the hotel maids. They said they has a laundry here in the hotel. I didn't figure it made sense to pay someone else to do it, and I didn't feel like makin' my way with a basket of fresh wash all the way to the train station."

Stretching, Ella smiled. "There's times when I prefer living on the train. Everything is only a few steps away. It might be in another car, but it's all connected, and we're just one big happy family."

"Oh, I nearly forgot. This message came for you this morning." Mara fished an envelope from her pocket.

Ella took it and looked at the writing. It was Phillip's. She quickly tore open the envelope and read the missive.

Need your help. I'm in the city jail.

"When did this come?" Ella glanced around for a clock. "What time is it?"

"Jes' about seven thirty."

"That it came, or is that the time?" Ella tossed back the covers and jumped out of bed. Without any concern about propriety, she began throwing off her nightclothes.

"That's when it come," Mara declared. "What are you doin'?"

"I have to help Phillip, but you can't say anything about it. He's in jail and, well, it's not the first time I've had to rescue him." She started tearing through the wardrobe. "I'll just wear my practice clothes—if I can find them. Where did I put them?"

"I washed them and been ironing the blouse. The skirt be hangin' up in the washroom. I 'spect it's near to dry. I washed it last night."

Ella made a dash for the bathing room. Her well-worn brown skirt was hanging from a hook on the back of the door. She grabbed it and pulled it on. She managed to locate her stockings, which Mara had also washed, and donned those as well.

"What time is it?"

"Eight fifteen. Ain't been that long, Ella. 'Sides, if that boy got himself thrown in jail, it won't hurt him a bit to sit and think about what he done."

"He drank too much. And unfortunately, he spends a lot of time thinking about that."

Ella finished dressing and headed for the door. "If anyone is looking for me, just tell them I had to go out and I'll be back shortly."

Mara nodded. "Are you sure you don't want me comin' with you?" She handed Ella her purse. "You might be needin' this. Sometimes there's a price to pay."

Ella nodded. "There always is. As for you coming with me, I think it's best you stay here. If Father or Jefferson sent someone to find you, we'd be hard-pressed to fight them off by ourselves."

"I 'spect you're right on that account." Mara shook her head.

Downstairs, a hotel doorman hailed a cab, then assisted Ella into it. He offered to instruct the driver, but Ella dismissed him.

She didn't want anyone to be able to ask the doorman for her destination.

The driver turned and looked down at her with a curious gaze. "Where to, miss?"

She gave him the address that had been on the stationery, then sat back to observe Denver. The entire time, however, her mind was on Phillip. What could she do to help him? How could she make him see that liquor would never take away his pain and sadness? She had prayed so much that he might see the truth, so why wasn't it happening? Was God not moved by her prayers? Didn't He care about Phillip's loss and the pain he'd endured? Didn't He see that Phillip was remorseful?

The cab stopped in front of a large brick building. "Here we are, miss."

Ella waited for the driver to assist her from the carriage. She handed him a dollar. "Please wait for me."

He tipped his hat. "Of course."

She glanced again at the building and then nodded to no one in particular. The city's jail was large and busy. She was used to helping Phillip in smaller venues, so this experience was rather intimidating.

"I've come," she told the clerk, "to retrieve Phillip DeShazer. I believe he was most likely brought in drunk and disorderly."

The officer looked her over and nodded. He called to another uniformed man, "Mrs. DeShazer is here to get her husband."

"He's with the others waiting for the judge to pass sentence," the second officer declared. He looked at Ella. "If you want to wait over here, Mrs. DeShazer, we should know the outcome shortly."

Ella didn't bother to correct him. She feared if she told him she wasn't Phillip's wife, he might not allow her to take him from the jail.

An eternity seemed to pass before Phillip was finally brought to the desk. He gave her a sheepish nod, then waited as she paid his fine. Apparently he and another man had been brawling in the street. Phillip had been caught, while the other man escaped. No damage was done to any public structures, so the charges were minimal.

They made their way outside, and the bright sunshine caused Phillip to wince. He raised the coat he carried to block the light.

Ella took his arm. "If you need to close your eyes, just do so."

"I'm fine. Sorry about this."

Ella was glad she'd asked the driver to wait. He was still there and actually climbed down to help them get into the carriage.

"Back to the hotel?" he asked.

"Yes. Perhaps just drop us off down the block, and we'll walk the rest of the way." She looked at Phillip as they settled into the carriage. "Better put your coat on and button it up so no one can see your torn shirt."

He glanced down. "Yeah. I guess you're right." He struggled into his coat and did as she suggested.

Ella didn't know what to think or say. Phillip was a good man deep inside. She knew he was. He was just so troubled and fearful of life. He felt cut off from the people who loved him because he was convinced they couldn't possibly continue feeling that way if they knew the truth about him.

"But I know." She hadn't meant to murmur the words out loud.

"What?" he asked.

Ella smiled and patted his arm. "It's nothing."

For a few moments they rode in silence, but Phillip finally turned to her. "Ella, I'm sorry for this. Sorry for all the other times too."

"I know, and I forgive you."

He gaped at her. "Why? Why do you forgive me so easily?"

"How can I not? I want to be forgiven my trespasses too. The Bible says that if we forgive others, our Father in heaven will forgive us. However, if we don't forgive, we won't be forgiven. That's in Matthew, chapter six."

He shook his head. "I don't deserve it."

"None of us do. And, I'll admit, I think that rather than simply beg forgiveness, we should strive to be done with sin as well."

"What do you mean?"

The driver hit a particularly large hole and sent Ella crashing against Phillip. He caught her to keep her from falling forward. Their faces were just inches apart, and Ella wished the circumstances could be different.

She sighed and pulled back. "I mean that if we just keep sinning without any intention of stopping—what good is it to be forgiven? It means nothing to us unless we work to stop doing wrong."

"You think your forgiveness means nothing to me?"

"I believe forgiveness means the world to you, but I don't think it's mine you are seeking. I think you want Wesley's. And even more than that, I think you want God's."

He stiffened. "Wes would never forgive me if he knew the truth. I doubt God would either."

"Oh goodness. How very self-centered you are."

His eyes widened. "What?"

"Phillip DeShazer is the only man in the

world God cannot forgive. His sins are far worse than anyone else's—worse than murderers, thieves, and liars. Phillip DeShazer has done more evil than anyone in the history of human beings."

"That's not what I said," he argued. "I just, well, it was a bad situation, and . . ."

"And Jesus died on the cross for everyone but you? Is that what you're saying?" She crossed her arms in frustration. "Jesus couldn't fit you in with the others? He died on the cross for the entire world except you?"

"Of course not." Phillip shook his head. "That's not what I meant. But folks are hard-pressed to forgive sins that are close to their hearts."

"Maybe it will be hard for Wesley. I don't know. What I do know is that seeing you drink your life away is killing him."

Phillip frowned. "No, it's not. He doesn't know how bad it is unless you've told him."

Ella rolled her eyes and sat back against the leather seat with a huff. "I don't have to tell him. He knows, and he cares so much about you. You aren't fooling anyone, Phillip. Everyone in the troupe knows you drink. When you don't show up at night, they figure you're in jail or lying in a gutter somewhere. Wes is no fool. He's worried about you because he loves you."

For several long moments neither of them said anything more. Ella hoped and prayed that Phillip would understand the truth of his situation. He longed for forgiveness, that much was clear. It was also clear that he had convinced himself that forgiveness wasn't possible.

"Do you think God will really forgive me?" he asked.

"Yes." She didn't offer anything more, as nothing more was needed.

"Do you think Wes could forgive me?"

She thought for a moment. "I don't know. I really don't know Wesley that well. But it doesn't matter what I think, because it is still up to him." She sighed and took his arm. "Phillip, it might take time, but you've been running from the truth for over twelve years. Don't you think it would be worth at least trying to set aside the past and letting the truth be known? You need to do this for your own sake. Only God can heal you and make this better."

Phillip leaned closer. "You make it better, Ella." He put his arm around her and tried to kiss her, but Ella jerked back.

"Don't!"

"But why not? I know you care about me." His brown eyes looked sadder than she'd ever seen them.

"I do care about you. Maybe too much, but my love can't save you. Only God can do that."

"But I love you, and I know you love me."

His words struck deep, and Ella felt herself wanting to give in to his desires. "Even if I do love you, Phillip, we can't be together. We can't have a future until you resolve the past. It's that simple. It will never work otherwise."

"But if I tell Wes the truth, he'll hate me. He'll never speak to me again."

"That's a risk you'll have to take. If not, you'll bear this guilt and drink yourself to death." She held his hand. "I won't stand by and watch you die. If you truly care about me, then you won't ask that of me."

The carriage came to a stop, and before Phillip or the driver could offer their assistance, Ella jumped down and started walking in the direction of the hotel.

Phillip watched Ella hurry away and felt the emptiness threaten to swallow him whole. He had used her again to save him from his circumstances. Circumstances he'd brought on himself. She was completely innocent and good, and he was treating her poorly.

He stuffed his hands in his pockets and contemplated what he should do. He felt ill, as he often did the morning after drinking. His stomach was green, and his head throbbed. He vaguely remembered fighting with some man, but for what reason, he couldn't say. He supposed it didn't much matter. Part of him was always looking for a fight. As if that could somehow set the past to rights.

Ella's words came back to him. *"Phillip, it might take time, but you've been running from the truth for over twelve years. Don't you think it would be worth at least trying to set aside the past and letting the truth be known? You need to do this for your own sake. Only God can heal you and make this better."*

"But running is what I'm good at, and maybe it's time to move along," he muttered to himself.

A man passing by glanced over with a frown but said nothing. Phillip looked down at his clothes. They were dirty and torn in a couple of places. He would no doubt raise eyebrows when he returned to the hotel. Maybe it would be best to go in through the back entrance.

He cut down the alley and made his way around back, hoping no one would think him a beggar and turn him away. He pulled out his hotel room key in case he needed to offer proof, but thankfully no one was around. Without bothering with the elevator, Phillip made his way up the stairs and breathed a sigh of relief once he was safely behind his locked room door. He knew he was late for work, but he needed to change his clothes and pack. They were leaving after the evening performance.

Ella's words continued to echo in his thoughts. *"Only God can heal you and make this better."*

"Maybe He is the only one, but will He do it for someone like me?" Phillip glanced toward the ceiling. "I've made a real mess of my life, Lord. What if I've made too big of one?"

Wes looked around the stalls and pens for Phillip. He was nowhere to be found. He questioned some of the assistant wranglers, but no one had seen him. Then, just when he was ready to give up, Phillip came waltzing into the place like he hadn't a care in the world. There was bruising over his left eye, however, and a slight swelling along his jawline. He'd been fighting.

"Where have you been?" Wes asked.

Phillip grinned. "Good morning to you too."

"Morning? It's nearly noon. You should have been here at six."

"I wasn't feeling too good," Phillip said with a shrug. "I'm better now, and I apologize."

"Seems you're always apologizing." Wesley decided not to bring up the subject of Phillip's fighting. He cared so much about his brother, but it was obvious Phillip didn't care about anyone but himself.

"We're heading to El Paso tonight, right?" Phillip asked.

"That's right. Why do you ask?"

The younger man shrugged. "I worked there once."

Wes narrowed his eyes. "I thought you mostly stayed around Wyoming. Or was that a lie?"

If his tone offended, Phillip didn't show it. "No lie. I was in Wyoming more than anyplace else, but I got around. I told you I worked clear down to Texas and back up. El Paso was just one of those places." He pushed back his hat and sobered. "It's a rowdy town, and we might have trouble. It'd be good to keep a close eye on the ladies . . . and the livestock."

Wes nodded. "I'll keep that in mind, but what about you? Will I need to keep a close eye on you, or will you have my back?"

Phillip picked up a rope, then met Wesley's gaze. "You'll have my help. I promise."

Wes wanted to believe him, but past experiences had soured his trust. "I hope so. I really want to believe you."

Phillip's expression was regretful. "I know. I want to do better."

"Well, at least that's a start." Wes decided to leave it at that. "Come on. There's work to be done."

Later that night, wrapped in Lizzy's arms, Wes tried to fall asleep to the rhythmic rocking of the train. Unfortunately, sleep eluded him, and his thoughts were all about Phillip. He wondered if he could count on his brother to keep his word. Wes wanted to believe in him—wanted to trust him—but it was obvious alcohol held a tight grip on Phillip.

"Are you going to stop worrying anytime soon?" Lizzy murmured.

"Sorry, did I wake you?" He pulled her even closer.

"I haven't been able to sleep with you so restless." She rose up on one elbow. "Want to talk about it?"

"I'm just afraid of losing Phillip again. Afraid I've already lost him to liquor. I want to believe he can stop drinking—that he can overcome this—but I don't know that he can."

"With God, all things are possible."

"Yeah, but a fella's got to want God's help. I think Phillip is content to face his demons alone."

Lizzy touched his unshaven cheek. "He'll come to the place where he realizes he can't do it on his own. We all do. When he does— just make sure you're there for him."

Wes couldn't see her very well in the darkness, but occasionally light from the open window flashed enough of a glow that he could just catch a glimpse of her sweet face. He was blessed to know she loved him. Blessed that he had her encouragement and support. Unfortunately, he didn't think she really understood his position. If Phillip wasn't willing to stop drinking and putting the people he loved at risk, Wes would have to fire him. Yet how could he do that? How could he walk away from his brother?

"Do you think God ever calls us to give up on folks?" he asked.

She yawned, and he felt guilty for keeping her awake.

"Never mind, just go to sleep, sweetheart."

Settling down in his arms again, Lizzy sighed. "I don't think God ever gives up on us. He does let us go our own way and reap the consequences, and I suppose if a person completely rejects Him, then God lets him go like Jesus did when He was talking to the rich young ruler who didn't want to sell everything and follow Him." She yawned again.

Wes hugged her close and settled his face against her hair. She smelled sweet, like the lilac and rose scent of her soap.

"I love you, Wes." Her voice was fading. "Just give it to God. With Him to guide you . . . you'll make the right choice."

⊷⹀ EIGHT ⹀⊷

Ella accompanied Lizzy and Mary to the costume car in search of Amanda—and Mary's wedding costume. Lizzy was confident that Amanda hadn't even begun the creation and wanted to gather the supplies so that Mara could get to work immediately.

"Try not to worry, Lizzy. Mara will be able to make the outfit without any trouble. I'm sure of that." Ella tried to sound convincing even though she wasn't sure Mara had ever sewn with leather.

Due to the increased number of performers, Henry Adler had devoted one car to nothing but costumes, laundry, and sewing. Most of the clothes used for performances hung against the wall, running the entire length of the car. The girls overseeing the laundry had their equipment at the far end. There was a washroom set up with tubs and hot water, as well as lines where the clothes could be placed to dry. At the other end was the sewing machine and a cabinet full of supplies for just about any sewing need. Henry Adler had thought of everything. The only thing missing was Amanda.

"She's so seldom at her job," Lizzy declared. "I don't know why I bothered to look for her here. I should have gone straight to Uncle Oliver's office."

The two laundry girls came from the far end of the car. One of the girls, named Sue-Ellen, offered a smile. "If you're looking for Miss Moore, she isn't here. She told us she had to go work on her wedding plans."

Lizzy frowned. "Do you know if she's worked at all on Mary's wedding costume?"

Sue-Ellen looked at the other young lady. Ella couldn't remember her name, but she couldn't have been much more than sixteen. The girl shook her head, and Sue-Ellen shrugged.

"I don't think she's worked on much of anything, truth be told."

"That's what I feared." Lizzy began to look through the cupboards. "Do you know where that white doeskin is? Uncle Oliver had it specially delivered in Denver."

Sue-Ellen pointed. "I think she put it in the big trunk over there."

Lizzy went to the trunk and knelt. She raised the lid. "Yes, here it is. Let's gather up whatever you think Mara will need. I know Uncle Oliver got a special sewing kit for leather. In fact, here it is under the hides." She began to pull the items from the trunk. "Ella, why don't you rummage through the cupboards for material to use for linings and other supplies."

"There's some white tulle here. It would make a lovely veil if you were of a mind to have one." Ella held it up.

"Bring it," Lizzy commanded. "If not for that, then perhaps we'll need it for the under-garments."

"What about something for you and Ella?" Mary asked.

"What in the world's going on here?" Amanda all but yelled, stomping into the costume car. She threw a glare at Lizzy. "You have no right to be going through my things."

"These aren't your things, they're the costuming supplies. And, just as I suspected, you haven't even begun to work on Mary's wedding costume."

Amanda shrugged and plopped down at the sewing table. "Didn't much feel like worrying over someone else's wedding when I have my own to be concerned with." She smiled, and Ella could see that Lizzy wanted nothing more than to slap the grin from the seamstress's face.

"You're impossible. I'm so glad God provided us with Mara," Lizzy said, looking back into the trunk. She gathered up several more things along with the hides and stood. "We won't be entrusting you with this project. But there are a great many other projects you should direct your attention to. There are a lot of repairs to be made, and I suggest you get them done."

"Or what?" Amanda asked, her voice dripping with sarcasm. "Will you fire me?" She laughed. "I don't think Oliver will allow that. He'll never believe you over me."

Ella took what she could of the white material and went to stand by Lizzy. "We should just go, Lizzy. There's a lot of work to do."

Lizzy stared hard at Amanda for another heartbeat, then stormed out the door. Ella could see that Amanda was enjoying herself. She didn't care at all about her offenses. Mary followed Lizzy out of the car, and Ella knew she shouldn't delay any longer lest she say something she'd regret. Where Amanda Moore was concerned, that would be quite easy.

Phillip finished cleaning the horse stalls and rolled the wheelbarrow to the open side door. Hot, dry air rushed in against his sweat-soaked body and refreshed him. They were moving through open wasteland. He had no idea where they were, but the desolation of the landscape matched his soul. He dumped the manure and soiled straw out the door and momentarily found himself wishing he could jump off with the debris. His life was worthless. He had done nothing but cause pain and grief to those he cared about.

For the last few days, he'd continually thought about Ella's words and Wesley's concern. He knew they loved him, and he hadn't had a single drink since Denver. But he wanted one. He wanted one more than he'd wanted anything else, and at the moment, that desire was enough to make him want to abandon his chores and go to the lounge to see what might be available. Why couldn't he just forget about alcohol? Why was it the first thing on his mind each morning? Why was his desire for it so overwhelming?

He glanced around to see if anyone was watching him, wondering what he was up to, standing here in the open door of the train car. Thankfully the rest of the crew was elsewhere—busy currying animals or tending to the gear. Phillip was alone with his thoughts and regrets. It was times like these that all his mistakes and poor choices came barreling at him like boulders loosed down a mountainside. He didn't like to be alone. He despised his own company. The only time he found it tolerable was with a bottle in his hand. How was he ever supposed to stop drinking?

One of the horses at the far end whinnied as the door to the next car slid open and Wes walked in. He paused to console the gelding. For reasons he didn't understand, Phillip felt the urge to talk to his older brother—to tell him everything. Ella had said it would change things. She was convinced he would never truly be able to live until he confessed his part in their father's death. But the risk was so great. What if Wes wanted nothing more to do with him? What if he sent Phillip away? Brookstone's show was all he had. It had become a family to him. And it was where Ella was.

But I have to tell him.

It was eating him alive to be with Wes day in and day out, knowing the truth of what he'd done. It was like a burning ember deep within that roared into a huge flame every time they were together. The time had come. All the turmoil and discomfort that had guided his life needed to come to an end.

But he'll hate you.

It was that accusing voice again. Every time Phillip got the gumption to do the right thing, that voice spoke up to remind him of all that he feared.

"How's it going?" Wes glanced through the stall rails. "Looks like I'm too late to help you muck out."

"Yeah, I already took care of it."

Wes shrugged. "I'm sure there's something else I can lend a hand with."

"There is." Phillip pushed the empty wheelbarrow aside. "Can you spare me a few minutes for a talk—or maybe I should say, a listen?"

Wes seemed to sense the importance. "Of course. I always have time for you." He plopped down on a bale of straw and said nothing more.

Phillip drew a deep breath and then let it out. "I, well, I don't know where to start, but I guess I should just go back to when everything began."

"All right." Wes untied his kerchief and wiped his forehead. "That seems reasonable." He replaced the kerchief and waited.

Phillip paced the small area, swaying with the train's rough movements. Like a sailor at sea, he had learned the tricks to balancing his steps on the rails. "It was hard when you left the family to go to work for the Brookstone ranch. I felt like . . . well, it was like losin' a part of myself."

Wes smiled. "It wasn't easy for me to go. I knew it was important that I leave, but it was never easy."

"I convinced myself you didn't care about us anymore." Phillip shrugged. "So I decided I wouldn't care either. It seemed almost appealing at the time, but I knew it was wrong. I got in with a bad bunch. There wasn't a one of them who was worth a plugged nickel. Still, when I was with them, I didn't miss you quite as much." He paused to offer Wes a hesitant smile before going back to his pacing. "There was this one fella—his name was John Bryer. He was a big guy and always spouting orders and directions. He reminded me of you."

"I don't know if I deserve that or not," Wes replied.

Phillip held up his hands. "I didn't mean it in a bad way. It's just that when you were around, I always felt . . . well, I don't know. I guess I always felt like I knew what I was supposed to be doing. You kept me going to school long after I wanted to quit. Church too. I mean, Mama and Papa wanted me to go to both, but it was your opinion that really mattered to me."

Wes frowned. "I didn't know."

"No, because I wasn't going to tell you. It didn't seem like the kind of thing to do. But I felt that way, and when John Bryer took me under his wing, I felt that same sense of purpose again. It was like I didn't have to worry about making up my own mind."

"Or doing your own thinking."

Phillip nodded. "I'm sorry to say that's true." He stopped and looked down at Wes. "I'm ashamed to say I did things that were wrong—things that hurt other people. I never knew for sure just how much our folks knew or how much they told you."

"Enough. They were pretty worried about you."

The thought saddened him more than he could say. Phillip pressed on, knowing that if he didn't continue his confession, he would never bring up the subject again.

"John Bryer said a man was judged by how he managed his liquor, his women, and the men who tried to best him. He said it was important to prove myself—to make it clear to every man around me that I wouldn't be controlled by anyone."

"Except John Bryer?"

Phillip hadn't seen it that way then, but

of course now he did. "Yeah. John figured he was in charge of all of us who kept company with him. I never saw anyone defy him—except one time."

He'd come to the place where he had to confess what had happened to their father. He had to admit his role—his fault in their father's death. If not now, he might never have the courage to do it.

"I ran away. I wanted to run with John and the boys full-time. I could get all the liquor I wanted when I was with John because folks were too afraid to say no. Drinking helped me forget the wrong I was doing and the good life and reputation I'd lost. Pa found me in town and convinced me to come home. I did, but I knew I couldn't stay. I wasn't comfortable there. If they'd known what I'd done . . . well, I couldn't live with the thought of it. My guilt ate me alive." He paused, shaking his head. "I never stopped to realize they already knew quite a bit. I was just so ashamed, and I left. Ran off in the night. I figured I'd never see either one of them again, but Pa . . . Pa . . ." Phillip fell silent.

"He came after you." It was more a statement than a question.

Phillip nodded. "Yeah. He did. He told me he wasn't going to give up on me. He told me it didn't matter what I'd done—that I was forgiven and that he wanted me to come home. I . . . I actually broke down and cried like a baby. I couldn't believe that I could be forgiven of robbing and beating up on folks. I had tried to tell myself that because I wasn't all that involved with the actual deeds that I wasn't as guilty as the others, 'cause I mostly just kept watch. But I knew the truth."

For a moment Phillip said nothing. It was painful to remember, but even worse to speak the words aloud. And now, as he remembered their father's death . . . it was almost too much to bear. Maybe this had been a mistake.

"Go on," Wes encouraged.

Phillip took a breath. "John Bryer got word about Pa and came to where we were. He wasn't going to let Pa force me to go home. He threatened Pa, and when that didn't work, he threw a punch. Pa dodged it, but that only made John mad. He started hitting Pa, and I tried to stop him, but I wasn't much against that brute. He knocked Pa to the ground. I thought maybe he'd killed him, because Pa didn't get up. Something inside me made me attack John for what he'd done. That was a mistake, because then he started in on me. Pa came to and must have felt the need to rescue me." Phillip's voice cracked, and tears came to his eyes.

"Pa pushed John out of the way, then bent

over to help me up." Phillip could no longer hold back the tears. "John wasn't about to be bested by an old man. He came at Pa. I saw him raise his hand to hit him, but I didn't see in time that he had hold of his gun. He hit Pa in the head with the butt of his revolver." He bowed his head and sobbed. "I saw Pa's eyes go all blank. He fell to the ground. There was blood everywhere, and it was all my fault. It's my fault that he died. I killed him same as if I'd done the hitting."

He was too afraid to look up and see Wesley's reaction. His brother would no doubt hate him. Didn't Phillip hate himself? Wasn't that the reason he'd never admitted his guilt? He cried all the harder. All the tears he'd tried to bury deep inside and drink away came pouring out.

Warm arms closed around him as Wes hugged him close. Phillip sobbed uncontrollably. How could Wes even bear to be near him, much less hold him? He didn't deserve this kindness. He certainly didn't deserve this comfort.

Phillip shook his head. "I killed him. I killed him." He couldn't stop the confession that had been stuffed deep inside.

"No, you didn't," Wes whispered against his ear. "John Bryer killed our father."

"But . . . I'm . . . to blame. I didn't want

. . . to tell you. Didn't . . . want you to hate me . . . when you learned the truth." It was as if he were still that young boy. As if he'd remained that boy for the past twelve years—unable to grow up because of all that had happened.

Wes pulled back and Phillip looked up, certain he would see contempt. Instead he saw tears in his brother's eyes and compassion in his expression.

"I've always known, Phillip. I've always known what happened that day."

"How? How could you? I only confessed it to Ma, and she promised she'd never tell a soul."

"She didn't have to," Wes said, holding Phillip's shoulders. "I talked to the sheriff myself. I just didn't know that you blamed yourself. Not like this."

"He died because of me, Wes. Because he loved me. He told me that with his dying breath—that he'd always love me."

Wes smiled. "What a blessing. He told me that when I left for the Brookstone ranch. I've always carried that as a comfort. You should too."

"But he wouldn't be dead if he hadn't come after me."

"He came after you because he loved you. He couldn't stop himself. His life didn't mean much if he couldn't live it for his family. That was the way Pa was. His love for us was what made him the man he was."

"I just wanted to be like you—like him—but I'm not. I'm not worth anything. I made a mess of my life, Wes. I know that. I'd give anything to undo the wrong, to start over."

"So let God help you. He can create a new man out of you, if you accept Him into your life. He'll forgive the sin and wash you clean."

Phillip found the words calming. "But what about . . . do you . . . can *you* forgive me?"

Wes's smile broadened. "You will always have my forgiveness, Phillip. You're my brother, and nothing you ever do will keep me from loving and forgiving you."

Phillip wanted to cry anew, but there was one more thing he had to ask. He had to know the truth. Had to hear it from his big brother. "Can God . . . really forgive me?"

"Well, I can't speak for Him, but the Bible does, and it says all we have to do is ask. First John, chapter one, verse nine says, 'If we confess our sins, he is faithful and just to forgive us our sins, and to cleanse us from all unrighteousness.'" Wes shrugged and smiled. "So I guess in a sense, we can speak for God. At least we can share His words and promises."

In the midst of such great relief, Phillip also felt more broken than he'd ever been before. He felt helpless and without the strength even to stand, and he sank to his knees. Wes did likewise.

"I need help," Phillip whispered to Wes. "I can't go on like this."

Wes nodded. "I know."

"I mean all of it, Wes. The drinking and the lying."

Again, his brother nodded. "I'm here to help you. I've always been here, and I'll always be here."

"What should I do? What can I do?" Phillip held out his empty hands as if hoping Wes might lay the answer in them.

Wes took his brother's hands and gripped them tight. "We're gonna pray first, and then I'm taking you home."

Lizzy went to Henry Adler's office with the full intention of telling him her concerns about Amanda. Instead, Henry motioned her inside like a long-lost daughter and told her to take a seat.

"I was just coming to find you. I've had a letter from my wife." He held it up as if in proof. "Jason has been found and has agreed to go to a sanatorium."

Lizzy couldn't conceal her surprise. "Where was he?"

"Hiding with some of his American relatives, family of my wife's. Apparently he sought their help when he made his plan to take you away." Henry smoothed out the letter on his desk.

"I see." Lizzy frowned, remembering that night the previous year when Jason had tried to kidnap her and force her to marry him. Henry had been mortified that his son had tried something so desperate, but had confessed at a later date that Jason had always suffered from a weak mind.

"He has agreed that a rest would do him good. We found a skilled doctor who believes he can help Jason."

"I'm glad," Lizzy replied, uncertain what else she could say. She had already agreed not to press legal charges against Jason, much to Wesley's dismay.

"I believe in time, with the proper treatment, Jason might be returned to us whole."

"I pray it's so." And she did. She didn't want ill will between the families. Not when Uncle Oliver was so dependent upon Henry Adler for help.

"I hope you know how much it means to us that you didn't want to see him arrested."

"It would hardly have helped."

Henry nodded and tapped the letter. "At least you no longer have to worry about whether or not Jason will suddenly appear and repeat his offenses. I know it's a relief to me and your uncle."

"I doubt Uncle Oliver will even notice. He's rather preoccupied with Amanda Moore." Lizzy got to her feet. "I think you should know that Mara will be making the wedding costume for Mary instead of Amanda. We found out that Amanda hadn't even started it, and since you want to have the wedding in Chicago in a matter of weeks, it was important that someone should get the job done."

But Henry was looking at the letter, and Lizzy wasn't sure he'd even heard her. It was easy to understand how difficult all of this must have been for the Adlers. Lizzy had never wanted them to suffer for the actions of their son. Their social standing in England and America was at risk because of Jason's foolishness. There's no doubt that news of Jason's appearance was a huge relief.

"Well, if you don't need me for anything else, I'd better get back to work," she said.

"Of course. Of course. Thank you for your understanding and forgiveness."

Lizzy smiled and moved to the door. "Of course. God charges all of His children to be in the business of forgiving."

She closed the door behind her and burst into tears. She hadn't expected the rush of emotions. Lately she seemed so out of sorts. She knew it was because of Wesley's distress and her uncle's foolishness, but tears weren't going to help one bit.

Wiping her eyes on the edge of her sleeve, Lizzy did her best to force her thoughts back into their proper places. A part of her longed for home, where she could go for a long ride to sort things out. Mostly, she missed her mother's counsel. If Mama were here, she'd be able to talk sense into Uncle Oliver. Lizzy felt ill-equipped to reason with him. After all, she'd only ever loved Wes, and it hardly gave her much experience to draw from when trying to warn her uncle of Amanda's deceptions. Then again, what if Amanda truly loved Oliver and just hated Lizzy?

She sniffed back her tears and fought to regain control of herself. She couldn't allow Amanda's ugly spirit to distract her from what needed to be done. Lizzy knew that Wes was right. She couldn't convince Oliver not to love someone. Especially when all she had to base it on were assumptions and feelings of ill will.

The train hit a junction, and the car gave a violent jerk to the right. Lizzy caught hold of the doorjamb and barely kept herself from falling headlong to the floor. With a new determination to put it all in God's hands, she straightened and squared her shoulders. She had given that advice to Wes and now needed to take it herself. She couldn't help but smile, however.

"It's a lot easier to suggest someone else leave it with God than to follow that advice yourself," she said, shaking her head. "A whole lot easier."

NINE

Wes sat down across from Henry and Oliver. "Thanks for agreeing to see me." They had arrived in Dallas, Texas, and even now, most of the crew and performers were busy figuring out the arrangements for the show. Lizzy was in charge of overseeing the performers, but Wes had asked Carson Hopkins to take his place helping the wranglers today.

"You said it was urgent," Oliver replied.

"It is." Wes leaned back in his wooden chair. "I'm afraid I have to leave the show. Phillip too."

"What?" Henry Adler looked at Oliver and then shook his head. "You can't. You're our head wrangler, and Phillip is your assistant. You signed a contract."

"I know what my job is, as well as his." Wesley's tone was harsher than he'd intended. "Sorry. The thing is, this isn't easy for me.

I'm not a man to shirk my commitments, but this is life and death. Oliver, I know you'll understand."

Oliver looked puzzled, prompting Wes to continue.

"Phillip has come to a place where he can't go on with his drinking. He's ready to quit, but he can't do it here. I want to take him back to the ranch in Montana."

"But can't it wait until we leave for Europe?" Adler asked. "I'll have some of my own men in New York accompany us to England. From there, I can utilize my own staff. I can hardly just hire someone here and now."

"You're sitting in Dallas," Wes countered. "Some of the best horsemen in the world are right here. I don't think you'll have any trouble hiring wranglers. Besides, Carson is more than capable of taking charge. He took the job when August Reichert was killed and did just fine."

"But the show is much bigger now," Adler argued. "Look, if it's a matter of money, I can help. What if we send Phillip to the ranch and you remain? I could even hire someone to escort him, if you're worried he won't go on his own."

"No. I made a promise to him, and I intend to keep it. He needs me to see him through this."

"What about Lizzy?" Oliver asked. "Will you force her to leave as well? We need her here."

Wes frowned. He had hoped they could all leave as a family, but he'd already considered it might be too great of a blow if he announced she was leaving as well. "I don't intend to force her to leave or to do anything else, for that matter. It'll be up to her. She planned to come home before the troupe went to Europe anyway, so I figure I can bear her absence until then. So long as you can guarantee her safety."

"I see," Adler replied, seeming to calm a bit. "Well, I'm sure she probably told you that my son has been found and has agreed to go to a sanatorium in England."

Wes shook his head. "No. She didn't tell me." His frown deepened. Why hadn't she told him? She knew how much he worried about Jason Adler sneaking back into the show to steal her away.

"Well, I only just shared it with her. I'm sure she means to tell you. But the point is, she'll be perfectly safe. Jason poses no threat to her well-being."

"I'm glad to hear it." Wes leaned toward Oliver but kept his gaze on Adler. "Look, I'll help you find a couple of men if that's important. I know Oliver can pick them without me, however. The important thing right now is Phillip. He's in a bad way, and I intend to see him through this." He turned to Lizzy's uncle. "If anyone understands, it should be you, Oliver. You know it isn't easy."

"I do," Oliver admitted. "Alcohol truly is a demon that takes hold of you and refuses to let go." He looked at Adler. "I think we'll have to find a way to manage without them, Henry."

The Englishman's forehead furrowed as he considered all that had been said. Wes knew it was a lot to spring on them, but he couldn't help it. He knew this was life and death for his brother.

"Very well," Henry said. His expression revealed he was already trying to think of solutions to the situation.

Wes got to his feet. "Now I need to break the news to Lizzy."

"You didn't discuss this with her first?" Oliver asked.

"No. I suppose I should have, but it was important to catch you both first thing so we can get someone hired on. Phillip and I will leave as soon as we can pack and get a train north."

He left the office and made his way through the train to the car where Lizzy kept her office. She wasn't there, but he hadn't expected her to be. She was no doubt already at the fairgrounds where they were slated to perform. The wagons had been moving equipment since their arrival, and Wes knew Lizzy wouldn't want to leave things unattended.

He spotted Ella and gave a whistle. "Have you seen Lizzy?"

"She's getting ready to head over to the fairgrounds."

"I figured she'd already be there."

Ella adjusted her straw cowgirl hat. "She would have been, but someone misplaced some of the belts for the trick-riding saddles. She was frantic until she found them."

"I can imagine. Where is she now?"

"Tack car."

"Thanks." Wes wasted no time making his way to the train car in question. He found Lizzy giving instructions like a general to her soldiers.

"Make sure this doesn't happen again. Everything has a place, and everything needs to be in its place when it's not being used. If you put it back the same place every time without fail, you will always have it at the ready. Understand?"

Wes suppressed a smile as the young men gave a murmured affirmation. "You men have a lot of equipment to finish getting over to the fairgrounds," he said. "If Lizzy's done with you, I need you to get on it."

The men looked over their shoulders in unison at the sound of Wesley's voice. They looked back to Lizzy.

"I'm finished. Go on." She waited until the men had exited the car to address her husband. "I figured you'd be busy with the horses. What brings you here?" She stretched up to kiss his cheek, and Wes bent to accommodate her.

"I need to talk to you about something. It's important."

She frowned. "Is something wrong?"

"You know what I told you about Phillip?" She nodded, and he continued. "I have to get him away from here. He's never going to stop drinking as long as he's with the show. It's just too hard—too available."

"I understand, but we made a commitment to Uncle Oliver and Henry."

"I've already spoken with them. They understand the situation, and I assured them Carson would be able to step up and take charge of the wranglers. They can hire a couple of extra men here in Dallas."

Lizzy's face bore a look he knew very well. She wasn't happy with him. "You didn't think to speak to me first?"

"I needed to catch them when I could. I

knew I could talk to you most anytime. After all, we do sleep in the same bed." He grinned, but it only made her more upset.

"Wesley DeShazer, I can't believe you'd go and decide something so important without my thoughts on the matter. Doesn't my opinion count in this?"

He stiffened. "No. Not exactly. I do want your support, but I'll leave without it if need be. My brother needs me more than you do right now."

She looked stunned. "How would you even know what I need? You never bothered to ask."

Wes tried to take hold of her, but she backed away. "Lizzy, would you just listen to reason."

Tears welled up in her eyes. It wasn't like her to turn emotional on him. He wondered if he'd made a mistake. Maybe the best thing he could do would be to start over.

"Look, I'm sorry. I'm doing this poorly. Please just sit with me for a minute. I know the timing is bad and my decision is probably not completely thought through, but this is important to me." He took her hand, and this time she didn't pull away.

"Hey, boss, are we going to use that newer team of blacks tonight?" one of the wranglers asked from the doorway.

Wes glanced over Lizzy's shoulder. "Talk to Carson. I'm busy."

The wrangler's eyes widened, but he said nothing. Instead he gave a nod and left as quickly as he'd come.

"Let's go to our car and discuss this," Wes said to his wife.

He anticipated Lizzy giving him a fight, but instead she wiped her eyes and let him lead her through the various train cars until they reached the one that contained their bedroom. The car was set up with four bedrooms and a large sitting area in the middle. Wes led Lizzy to one of the chairs and then took the seat beside her.

"I'm sorry I didn't discuss this with you first. That was wrong of me, but my mind has been on Phillip. He's a broken man, and he needs me."

"I understand," she whispered. "It's just that I need you too."

"Then come home with us."

She looked appalled at the suggestion. "And leave Uncle Oliver? Mother would never forgive me."

"You know that isn't true."

"Well, if he started drinking again, I wouldn't forgive myself. Amanda Moore has her claws in him, and she's always encouraging him to drink. I can't leave him here to fend for himself."

"And I can't send Phillip off to fend for himself."

"You wouldn't be," Lizzy protested. "You could send him back to Mother. She would take care of him."

"First of all, I'm not sure Phillip would make it back on his own. Second, he's not your mother's responsibility. He's my brother, and I gave him my word."

Lizzy started to get up, but Wes held her hand.

"You gave me your word too," Lizzy countered. "We're married. We are no longer two, but one, and you should have talked to me about this before making a decision."

Wes gritted his teeth. She was right, but he wasn't going to let that change his decision. "I told you I was sorry, and I am. I should have discussed it with you first, but now that it's done, I'm asking you to understand. I'm not making you come with me. Stay, if that's what you think is right, or come back with us if you feel inclined. I'm not trying to impose my will on you."

She seemed to calm a bit. "I agree that Phillip should go back to the ranch, but I don't understand why you have to go as well. Mother helped Uncle Oliver with his drinking problem, and she cares a great deal about Phillip. I know she would be happy to help see him through this."

"I know that too, but as I said, I gave Phillip my word. When we talked, he made it clear that he isn't strong enough to do this without me. Surely you aren't so selfish that you would begrudge him this."

"So now you think I'm selfish?"

Wes rolled his gaze heavenward. "I didn't say that. I said that surely you *weren't*."

"The implication is there," Lizzy said, crossing her arms. "I can't believe you would accuse me of being selfish. I care about your brother. He's my brother now too. The issue of drinking and the trouble it causes is something near to my heart because of Oliver. But it's exactly because of Oliver that I don't feel I can quit the show and go back to the ranch."

"Then stay. I'm not asking you to go." His frustration mounted as he did his best to choose his words carefully. It seemed that no matter what he said, however, it irritated his wife.

"You're impossible." Lizzy burst into tears.

Wes didn't know any way to make this right. "Look, Lizzy, I prayed about this, and I have to do what I feel is right. This has nothing to do with a lack of love for you. It has to do with my love for my brother. Try to understand."

"I'm not . . . without understanding," she said, sniffing.

"I know that. That's why I came to discuss this with you. I knew that once you heard what I had to say, you would understand." He hoped that would soothe her hurt feelings, but either way, he needed to get on with his plans. "I suppose you'll stay with the show, then, until they leave for Europe."

She looked away and fixed her gaze on some spot behind him. "I suppose so. Uncle Oliver needs me, and apparently you don't."

"That's not fair."

She surprised him by jumping to her feet. "Life doesn't seem overly fair to me right now. You've made your choice, Wes. Now I'm making mine. I'm staying here to honor my commitment and see to Uncle Oliver like I promised my mother. I wouldn't even be here except for that promise, because I was willing to quit the show—for *you*."

He got to his feet as well. "Be fair, Lizzy. You planned to quit the show anyway. It's already June. You'll be home by August."

"Unless Uncle Oliver decides he's going to Europe."

Wes decided to ignore her comment. "I need to get our tickets and settle things with Carson. I'll come see you before I leave."

Lizzy shook her head. "Don't bother."

With that, she went into their bedroom and slammed the door behind her.

Wes stared after her. He knew she was struggling with his decision. Knew too that she hadn't slept well last night after he'd told her about Phillip. Maybe he just needed to give her some time to think it over.

He glanced at his pocket watch. He'd get tickets to Montana and then come back to get his clothes and say good-bye. Maybe by then she'd have calmed down.

When Lizzy emerged a few minutes later, Wes was gone. She knew she'd acted unreasonably, but a part of her was truly hurt that he hadn't consulted with her before making his decision. Weren't married couples supposed to talk things through and make decisions together? Still, she felt terrible and wanted only to find him and make things right. She didn't want him leaving with Phillip without smoothing things over.

She exited the train and glanced up and down the length of the bright red Brookstone cars. She saw Mary and Ella and gave them a wave but didn't attempt to join them. She needed to find Wes and apologize.

"I was hoping to find you," Henry Adler said, coming up behind her.

Lizzy turned. "I'm looking for Wes."

"I imagine he's with Phillip. I know they

were collecting his things. I'm sorry to be losing them. They are by far my best workers. It won't be the same without them."

She nodded, feeling herself close to tears again. "I wish they weren't going."

"Does that mean you're staying?"

"Of course. I can't possibly leave Uncle Oliver. I don't trust Amanda Moore. She's after him for his money and no doubt to get some control of the show."

"How would she do that?" Henry asked, seeming genuinely puzzled.

"I'm sure she thinks that once she marries Uncle Oliver, she'll have a say in the show, since he owns half of it."

Henry frowned and shook his head. "Oliver doesn't own the show anymore. He sold his shares to me in England last year when he thought he was going to die."

"What?" Lizzy took a step back at the shocking news. "Why wouldn't he tell me? Mother owns the other half of the show. He should have sold it to her."

The older man's frown deepened. "I'm sorry to be the bearer of bad news, Lizzy, but your mother has no ownership of the show whatsoever. Your uncle was the sole owner at the time he sold it to me."

"That can't be." She shook her head. "My

father and uncle owned it jointly. When Father died, it would surely have gone to her."

"I don't know what happened, Lizzy. I know that your uncle asked me to make him an offer for everything, with the provision that you and he would always have a job should you want one. I agreed to that, and my lawyer drew up papers. I assure you, Brookstone's Wild West Extravaganza now belongs to me."

·-= TEN =-·

Phillip found Ella just as she was getting ready to leave for the fairgrounds. She was dressed in clothes that suggested she'd get right to work once there, but as always, she was beautiful. He loved the delicacy of her face—full cherry lips, pale pink cheeks, dainty nose, and arched brows. The fact was, there was nothing about her that he didn't love.

"I see you're ready to start practice," he said as he approached.

"Yes." Ella smiled. "And you? Are you heading over now?"

"No. I'm not going to the fairgrounds. In fact, I'm leaving the show. That's why I wanted to come find you."

Her brows knit together. "You're leaving?"

He nodded and pushed up his hat. "I have

to, Ella. I'm not the man I need to be. I've been drinking way too much, as you know. I can't seem to stop for long, and yet I know I must."

"It's good that you want to. That's better than before. Did you take my advice and talk to Wesley?"

"I did." He looked down at the dirt. "I told him everything, just like you suggested." He fell momentarily silent.

"And what happened? Is he making you leave?" Her tone was almost accusatory.

Phillip's head snapped up. "No! Wes wouldn't do that. He's a good man, and he was . . . well, he was completely understanding. He already knew the truth."

Ella's mouth dropped open.

Phillip nodded at her surprise. "It's true. He said he got in touch with the sheriff and learned the entire truth about what had happened to our father and me that day. I had no idea he'd done that."

"All this time, he knew." She barely whispered the words.

"Yes. I suppose that should be proof to me, if nothing else, that he truly does forgive me. But not only that, he's willing to help me stop drinking."

"So you're both leaving?" She glanced down past the train cars. "Does Lizzy know?"

Phillip nodded. "Yeah. Wes said she didn't take the news real well. She's supportive of me but wasn't happy about him going. I was hoping I'd get a chance to talk to her before we head out." He hesitated. "There's something else, Ella. Something I need to ask you."

"What is it?" She looked perplexed.

He smiled. "I'm hoping maybe . . . that is, I was wondering. . . ." He couldn't seem to find the right words. What if he shared his heart with her and she rejected him? "Ella, I care a great deal about you, and I know you care about me. I believe that you love me, but right now I'm not worthy of anyone's love." She started to speak, but Phillip put his finger to her lips. "Please, just hear me out."

She nodded, and he pulled back his hand. "Thank you. See, I want to become a man worthier of you. I want to let God help me change my life, but I know it's not going to be easy. I'm hoping you'll pray for me."

"Of course I will. You must know that I've been praying for you all along."

"I do. I probably wouldn't be alive if not for your prayers and intercession. But besides praying for me, I'm hoping you will wait . . . for me."

Ella said nothing for a moment. "Are you proposing to me?"

Phillip shook his head. "Not exactly. I'm

asking you to give me a chance to prove myself. I'm asking you not to let any other fella sweep you off your feet and steal you away while I'm gone."

A smile broke across her face. "I can definitely promise that."

"You will? You'll wait for me?"

She nodded, her eyes seeming to glow.

"I don't know how long it will take, but if it starts taking too long, I'll release you from your promise. I won't take unfair advantage."

"I know you won't." She looked at him as if he was someone she admired. Her gaze warmed Phillip's heart and made him feel a sense of well-being for the first time in a long time.

"Thank you, Ella." He reached out and took her gloved hand. Raising it to his lips, he kissed it.

"You ready to head out, Phillip?" Wes asked as he and Lizzy approached.

Phillip could see Lizzy had been crying. He hated that he was hurting her. She'd always been so kind to him. "I'm ready." He looked back at Ella. "I'll come back as soon as I'm able."

She nodded. "I'll be here."

Wes kissed Lizzy, and the two exchanged some murmured last words. Phillip wished he had the right to kiss Ella, but he knew that day would come. Just considering a future with her would help him keep his determination to stop drinking—forever.

He smiled at Ella and touched her cheek. "I know you will be."

———◆◆◆———

Later that afternoon, Ella couldn't stop reflecting on her conversation that morning with Phillip. She was both excited and fearful about his plans and the fact that he'd asked her to wait for him. It was funny. They had never talked about their feelings for each other with regard to the future. They both knew there was something between them that went deeper than friendship, and yet they hadn't found a way to discuss that intimacy.

"Miss Ella?" one of the young wranglers called out.

Ella looked up from where she'd been adjusting buckles on the saddle. "Yes?"

The young man looked sheepish. "There's a fella here says he's your brother."

She gazed behind him toward the open door of the stables. "Robert!" She thanked the wrangler and immediately went to where her brother waited. She hugged him. "I didn't expect to see you."

He looked grave. "I know, but there's news, and we need to talk."

The seriousness of his tone sent a shiver through her petite frame. "Very well. Let me tell the others where I'm going, and I'll join you."

Mary was the first person Ella spotted. She joined her friend as she set up to practice her act. "I need to leave for a short time," Ella told her. "My brother has come, and there's something he wants to discuss."

The look on Mary's face reminded Ella of how intricately they were connected. "Do you suppose it has to do with August?"

"I don't know. Perhaps. If it does, you know I'll tell you as soon as I get back."

Mary hugged her arms to her body. "It's just been so long, and I fear we'll never get justice for him."

Ella gave her a brief hug. "Try not to fret. Robert has been faithful in working toward answers. I know he won't forsake the matter."

The sharpshooter nodded. "I'll look forward to hearing what you learn, and if anyone asks after you, I'll tell them you had something to tend to."

Ella rejoined her brother, and his serious expression had not changed. She was almost afraid to know the truth he bore. What if it was more than she could stand? What if something had happened to their mother or even to Father? It was true he'd hurt her deeply by trying to force the marriage between her and Jefferson, but she still loved him. Fear coursed through her, causing her to tremble.

"You're not alone," a voice seemed to whisper deep within.

She glanced heavenward. *Help me, Lord. Help me bear whatever Robert has to say.*

"Where can we talk privately?" Robert asked.

"The train car would be best for complete privacy."

They made their way to the train cars, which had been left on a siding at the fairgrounds. Ella mounted the steps to her car and checked the berths to make sure no one else was inside. "Everyone is busy since we just arrived. We should have all the privacy we need."

She motioned for him to take a seat at the table where she and the other girls often talked or played games. She sat across from him and folded her hands, drawing in a deep breath to steady her nerves.

"Tell me everything," she said.

Robert shook his head. "It's so preposterous, I can scarcely believe it."

"You have found the truth?"

"I have. But Father doesn't realize it, and once he does, my own life may not be worth much to the folks back home."

She frowned, her anxiety rising. "What in the world is going on?"

He swallowed. "Father and Jefferson Spiby are in the business of selling humans—not a new breed of horses."

"What?" His words made no sense.

"Remember how Mara said Father demanded she sign papers?"

Ella nodded. "A contract for her room and board."

"No. A contract for her life is more to the point. To explain, I'll have to go all the way back to the War Between the States." It was stuffy in the train car, so Robert unbuttoned his coat and put it on the chair beside him. "It seems that after the war, our grandfather, Father, and Jefferson Spiby and his father formed a pact. There were a great many slaves held between the two families, and losing them would ruin the horse farm and the Spibys' plantation. The slaves were obviously determined to leave, so the men of our family and the Spibys decided they had to do something to keep them. They called the former slaves together and told them they were indeed free, but that everything they wore or used in their small homes belonged to the Flemings and Spibys. They could purchase these things if they wanted, or work for them."

"How awful. Of course they couldn't leave

without clothes to wear and food to sustain them on the road."

"Exactly. The people were trapped, forced to sign papers that bound them to work for the various things they needed. Of course, they had to have housing and food while they worked, and that was an additional charge. Our grandfather was shrewd. He knew exactly how much to charge to keep his workers from ever being able to pay off their debts."

"But how did that involve anyone else? How is it still happening today? Grief, Robert, it's 1902."

"And have you ever studied the conditions and plight of former slaves? They were set free into complete poverty. A few aid societies offered help, but most were in the North, and it was nearly impossible for southern slaves to get to them. Few jobs were available to them, because while the Emancipation had been signed, little regard was given to how to help the freed slaves afterward. Most couldn't read or write, and few had any sort of education. Such things were illegal in most of the South."

"I remember. I used to sneak lessons to Mara. Father never knew, but I always supposed he'd punish me if he found out."

"I'm certain he would have. Knowledge is power, and he didn't want any of his slaves having that. Anyway, a great many people talked big about wanting freedom for all mankind—but there were suddenly hundreds of thousands of people who needed work and no one to offer them jobs. With the exception of our farm and the Spibys'. Word got around that they were sympathetic and would hire on. Of course, those working at the farms were forbidden to tell the truth—that this was just slavery by a different name. Over the years, a great many former slaves made their way to the Spibys' plantation or to our farm, where our father agreed to sign them on. They started there, but soon enough it would be announced that their contracts were being sold to other farmers elsewhere. When protests arose, Grandfather or Father would point out that each person was free to buy out their contract and go on their way if they didn't like it."

"But no one could possibly pay." Ella could see the trap quite clearly.

"Exactly. They were never given money. They were forced to work nearly every day with very little time to themselves. They had very few options to earn money on the side, mostly because they weren't allowed to go into town except for church, and even that was done in such a fashion that it cost them. If they didn't walk, the cost of wagon rides was added to their lists of expenditures."

"But how did people know they could come and buy the contracts?" Ella was sickened by the entire matter, but she wanted to know it all.

"Grandfather used the horse farm to generate business. There were always men coming to buy stock, and word got around. Local authorities who figured out what was going on turned a blind eye for extra money in their pockets, but few people know exactly what's happening. Our grandfather and Father had excellent reputations in the community, as did the Spibys. No one was going to question what they were doing, and those who did faced either wrath or bribery."

"But I don't understand how it worked. Did buyers just agree to purchase these workers sight unseen? They could hardly have a slave auction."

"But they did. They advertised them as private stock sales. Men would come supposedly to see horses, and instead workers were paraded around the showroom."

"How could that be legal?"

"It's not. And that's why I'm here today. I can't let this go on, Ella. I can't stand back and allow a slave trade. Even if Father and Spiby could somehow find their way around the legalities, it's morally and ethically wrong.

As you said, it's 1902, and slavery is a thing of the past—or should be."

It felt like Jefferson's hands were once again around her throat. Ella could scarcely draw breath. "This is what got August Reichert killed." Her voice was barely audible.

"Yes. I believe so. I imagine he happened into the showroom as Father and Jefferson were parading workers and accepting bids."

"Oh, how terrible." She buried her face in her hands.

"Ella, listen to me. You must understand the full implications here."

She raised her head. "I think it's clear. Father has broken the law, and if it's found out—he'll go to jail."

"It's possible no one will say or do anything, but there are people out there who actively support the cause of bettering the plight of the Negro. There might well be a lawyer or minister who holds great sway with the public—someone who has the newspapers' ears. And depending on who wants to take on this matter, Father might well suffer a great deal." Robert reached out and took her hand. "I don't know what will happen, to tell you the truth, but I do know that I can't stand by and do nothing. I have good friends in Washington, D.C., and feel if I get their help in the matter, it will definitely put an end to what's been happening all these years. But it will forever destroy our family."

She hadn't thought of that. She could well imagine their mother and father wanting nothing more to do with Robert. She already felt the weight of their disapproval and rejection. What in the world would that do to Robert, the only son and heir?

"I'm so sorry, Robert. I hadn't even considered how this would affect you and your family."

He shook his head, all the while holding her gaze. "I'm not even sure I'd have a family left to me."

"You should secrete some money away before you go to the authorities. Perhaps speak with our sister as well."

"I've already considered that." He stiffened at the sound of voices outside the train car. Whoever it was passed by, however. "I believe I'll be fine financially. My assets and affairs have been separate from Father's for years. I just don't know what this will do to Virginia and the boys. My wife is a Southerner through and through. There may be a great deal of hatred and trouble to bear, and I'm not sure she's up to the ordeal. We just learned she's expecting again. She struggled last time, and something like this might cause her to miscarry."

Ella smiled. "Congratulations. Despite the troubled times, that's very good news."

"It would be better if I knew what to expect once the authorities learn the truth. It could go either way. Someone might want to make an example of Father and Jefferson. If they can get the newspapers to stir up a frenzy about it, then the entire country will know soon enough."

"And shouldn't they?" She bit her lower lip. She didn't know which was more troubling—the thought of the country hating her father and family, or losing their home and possibly causing Virginia to lose her baby. Or that no one would care enough to punish her father and Jefferson for the lives they had stolen.

"One thing I know, Robert." She squeezed his hand. "We must pray. We must pray a great deal."

❖≒ ELEVEN ≒❖

Ella carefully explained everything to Mara later that night as the two women sat huddled together in Ella's room. Neither seemed able to speak for several long minutes after Ella finished relating what Robert had told her. It was almost impossible to imagine all that her grandfather and father had done. The very thought of their cruelty sickened Ella. She thought of all the workers she had known on the farm. Most said very little. They worked hard and kept to themselves, and now Ella understood why.

"I'm just so sorry, Mara. So sorry for what happened—for what it meant for your mother and the others before you. I can't believe anyone could be so heartless. I always thought Father was a fair man, a good Christian. Now I realize what a monster he truly is. I hate him!"

"Don't be hatin', Miss Ella. Ain't nothing good ever come out of hate."

"How can I not hate him? How can you not? What he and Jefferson did was evil."

"Yes'm, I believe that too, but hate will just cripple you up inside, and it won't change what's happened. It won't make wrong things right."

Ella pulled a shawl around her nightgown. The evening had cooled considerably after a thunderstorm rumbled through around dinnertime. But she didn't think it was the weather that chilled her. Fear and confusion left her feeling ill.

"I can't bear thinking of Daddy cheating people that way." She wiped away tears. "It's just too horrible."

"He was wrongly taught," Mara countered. "Folks get trained up to think somethin' is right when it's wrong and other things be wrong when in truth they're right. It don't mean they can't learn the truth. Maybe your papa will finally be learnin' a better way."

"How could he not already know it? He knew it was wrong, or he wouldn't have been so secretive about it." Ella pulled her knees close and hugged them to her chest. "I'll try not to hate him, but this is more horrible than anything I could have imagined. My entire life there was based on lies and deceit. It hurts more than I can say. How can you even bear to be with me?"

Mara surprised her by chuckling. "You ain't done nothin' but love me since we were children. You ain't like most white women. You don't see the color of my skin. You look on deeper to my heart. And I know *your* heart. That's why I can bear bein' with you. You got a good heart and nobody can convince me otherwise."

"But my father—"

"You ain't your father, Ella." Mara fixed her with a stern gaze. "Your father will account for his own sins same as every man. If'n he turns to Jesus, he'll be forgiven, and if not, then he'll suffer for it. Only God has the right to judge him."

Ella scooted closer so she could hug Mara. "You always did know what to say to make me feel better. Thank you for being such a godly woman. You are dearer to me than my own sister."

"What happened?" Oliver asked in the midst of the chaotic crowd.

"Carson is hurt. Bad," one of the young wranglers announced. "He was on the ladder to help hoist the banner and fell. He's bleeding from his head something fierce, and a minute ago he said his back felt broken."

Moans and groans filled the air along with Alice Hopkins' inconsolable sobs. Ella tried to comfort Alice, but she was far too upset. One of the wranglers had taken off his kerchief and was trying to put pressure on the wound at the back of Carson's head. Carson was barely conscious.

"Has anyone sent for the doctor?" Oliver asked.

"Yes, sir. We did that first thing."

"My back," Carson moaned. "Help me."

Oliver pushed through to get a better look at him. "Carson, try not to move. You won't do yourself any good if you thrash about."

Lizzy joined them. She assessed the situation, then went to where Alice knelt beside her husband. She looked at Ella. "What happened?"

Ella shook her head. "It was terrible. He was high up on the ladder and just seemed to lose his grip. He fell from the top."

"That's nearly twenty feet," Lizzy gasped, then put her hand over her mouth as if she'd said too much.

Most of the troupe had gathered in the arena, including Mara, who stood beside Ella. It seemed to take forever, but finally the doctor arrived with an ambulance.

"I'm Dr. Obermeyer. Let me through. Give me room to work," the older man said, pushing aside members of the troupe. "What happened here?"

"He fell from atop the ladder," Oliver told him.

The doctor did a quick evaluation, then stood. He motioned for two men to bring a stretcher forward. "Everyone out of the way. We need to get this man to the hospital immediately. His vital signs are not good." He looked around. "Does this man have a wife or family here?"

"This is his wife," Lizzy said, putting her arm around Alice's shoulders.

The doctor looked at Alice as if assessing her ability to hear the truth. "You'd best follow us. Your husband's condition is failing."

Alice began to wail, and Lizzy took her in hand. "Come on, Alice. We'll get you to the hospital. I'll stay with you."

"Oh, Lizzy. Don't let him die."

"Of course not." Lizzy threw a glance Ella's way. "Can you help Uncle Oliver keep everyone on track for the show?"

"Yes, I'll do whatever I can." Ella knew what was expected of the trick and Roman riders but was clueless when it came to the others. "What about the sharpshooters? Should I tell Mary what's happened?"

"Yes, she needs to know that Alice won't be able to perform. She can plan accordingly."

"I'll find her and let her know."

As the ambulance left and the crowd began to disperse, Ella looked down at the large puddle of blood and shivered. Someone needed to clean that up. She saw one of the young men who helped with the horses and motioned him over.

"Yes, Miss Ella?" he asked.

He couldn't have been much more than eighteen. He looked so young and innocent. Would cleaning up another man's blood bother him? She felt unable to give the order.

Henry Adler entered the arena from the other side with two black men following him. One man was tall with a powerful build. His broad shoulders and arms suggested he worked hard for a living. The other man was younger and half the bigger man's size.

"What's going on here?" Adler asked. "Why is everyone standing around?" Then he noticed the blood on the ground. "What's happened? Somebody clean this up." He looked at the young wrangler. "You, what's your name?"

"Ben, sir."

"Ben, get some straw to soak up this blood and clean it away."

The boy nodded and hurried off to get straw.

"Carson Hopkins fell from the ladder. It's serious, and the doctor just now took him to the hospital. Lizzy and Alice went with them," Oliver reported.

"Will he live?" Adler glanced at the group around him.

"We don't know. I plan to get everyone squared to their jobs and then go to the hospital myself," Oliver declared. "Unfortunately, we're now down another head wrangler."

"Good thing I was able to arrange for these two men," Adler said, looking over his shoulder. "Gentlemen, I'd like you to meet Oliver Brookstone, the man who helped start this wild west show. Oliver, this is Abraham Green. He has over twenty years of experience working with horses. And this fella is Josiah Washington, but he informs me that he prefers to be called Half-Pack."

Oliver nodded with a smile. "I'm mighty glad to have you two join us. We've been rather unlucky where wranglers are concerned this year." He shook hands with Abraham and then the smaller man. "Why do they call you Half-Pack?"

"'Cause that was all I could carry when I was a boy. I was sick most of the time and no bigger than a string bean."

Abraham rubbed the top of the young man's head. "He's hardly bigger than that now."

Oliver chuckled. "Well, you're both very welcome. I presume you've had experience with horses as well, Half-Pack?"

"Yes, sir. I've been helping Abe for the better part of seven years. I've learned a lot."

"Well, I'm sure we can find enough work to keep both of you busy. Why don't you come with me, and I'll introduce you to the other men?"

Ella turned to Mara, only to find her watching Abraham with open-mouthed wonder. "Are you all right, Mara?"

Her friend didn't reply, just watched as the men went off with Oliver.

Ella found it very amusing that Mara, who was usually quite staid in her manners, was struck speechless. She leaned close. "Are you already planning the wedding?"

That did the trick. Mara put her hand over her mouth and looked at Ella as if she'd just revealed her darkest secret.

Ella laughed. "I'm sorry. I couldn't resist teasing you. I've never seen you so besotted. I suppose the big fella is the one you're taken with. The other hardly looks old enough."

Mara nodded, then looked at the ground as if to compose herself. "Sorry, Ella."

"There's nothing to apologize for," Ella whispered. "Come on. We've got a lot of work to do before the show. But I'm certain we can find some excuse for me to send you to Mr. Green. I might need to talk to him about the horses."

Mara couldn't keep from grinning as she raised her head. "I 'spect you might need to talk to him. Maybe more than once."

Ella laughed and put her arm around Mara as they headed for the tents where they would be dressing. She found Mary in the performers' tent. She was busy cleaning her rifle and seemed completely oblivious to the world around her.

"Mary, did you hear what happened to Carson?" Ella asked.

The sharpshooter looked up with a frown. "No. Is something wrong?"

"He fell from a ladder while helping hang the banner. He was hurt badly and taken to the hospital. Alice went too, of course, with Lizzy. Lizzy asked me to work with you to get everyone ready for the show. There will be gaps without Alice, so you'll want to make plans for that."

"Of course." Mary finished with the rifle. "He will be all right, won't he?"

"They don't know. He has a bad head injury. He was bleeding a lot. And his back might be broken. He landed in an awkward position. He was barely conscious. In fact, I think he was probably in and out and didn't really know what was going on."

"This is terrible." Mary got to her feet. "Poor Alice. She must be beside herself."

"She was." Ella remembered the new men. "Oh, we have two new wranglers that will be helping out. They arrived right after the doctor left with Carson."

"What are they like? Do they have proper experience?"

Ella looked at Mara and then back to Mary. "They do. The older one has over twenty years. The younger one not as much, but they've worked together for a long while. Their names are Abraham and Half-Pack."

"Half-Pack?" Mary asked, putting her cleaning kit away.

"It was the amount he could carry when he was a little boy. Anyway, they both seem capable." Ella paused. "And they're both black."

Mary straightened. "Black? We've never had men of color working the show before. Do you suppose the other men will accept them?"

"I sure hope so," Ella replied. "We'll be in a real fix if not. If Carson is as bad off as I think, I doubt he or Alice will be returning anytime soon."

"Oh, goodness. I never thought of that," Mary said, shaking her head. "I've got to talk to the other girls. They aren't all that proficient in bow shooting. We may have to forgo having that in the act. This really does change things."

Ella looked at Mara and grinned. "In more ways than one."

"How's he doing?" Uncle Oliver asked Lizzy as he entered the hospital waiting room.

"The doctor hasn't returned from surgery yet." Lizzy had done her best to keep Alice from storming off to demand answers, but with every passing minute, it was becoming harder and harder not to do exactly that herself.

Alice's eyes were red from crying, which was startling against the pale white of her face. She was still obviously in shock from what had happened. Oliver sat beside her and took her hand in his. He just held it and said nothing. Lizzy thought it one of the most tender things she'd ever seen him do.

Finally, after another half hour, the doctor emerged from behind a large door. He looked as if he'd just come from the bank or a business venture. His three-piece suit looked immaculate, and his hair was carefully groomed.

"He's resting and stable in his condition," the doctor announced.

Alice jumped to her feet, tearing away

from Oliver. "Will he live? Is he all right? Can I see him?"

"Whoa now," the doctor said, motioning for her to slow down. His tone was much less severe than it had been at his initial announcement. "Your husband has a long road ahead of him. The extent of his injuries is completely unknown. We did explore his abdomen for internal bleeding. He had ruptured his spleen, so we had to remove that. He appears to have a great deal of swelling around his spinal cord, but we can't be sure about the injuries to it at this point. However, it's his head injury that is most concerning at this immediate juncture. His skull is fractured, and there's already some swelling. We'll have to watch him closely and hope he regains consciousness soon. His injuries are grave, Mrs. Hopkins. We are fortunate I was just coming to the hospital when your people approached the ambulance attendant."

Alice began to cry again, and Lizzy stood to embrace her. "We believe God orchestrated that, Doctor," Lizzy said, smiling at how faithful God had always been. "We are very grateful that you took the time to come with them."

"I have a feeling about this case. Mrs. Hopkins, I don't like to give false hope, nor do I want to motivate despair. The truth is, head injuries are tricky, and we never know for sure how it will go. The brain controls everything in the body, and when it is injured, it can be devastating. However, we will watch him closely and do our best."

"Is there anything we can do?" Uncle Oliver asked.

The doctor shook his head. "All any of us can do now is wait."

"I want to go to him," Alice begged.

"In time, dear woman. I'll have the nurse come for you as soon as possible. Until then, you must wait. It will be several hours, so I recommend you find something to busy yourself with. There's a lovely restaurant across the way. Something to eat will give you strength and help with the shock of all you've been through."

With that, he nodded in farewell and then walked back to a large desk, where a nurse waited for him with a clipboard of papers.

Lizzy wondered how she would cope with the same situation had the accident happened to Wes instead of Carson. It could just as easily have been her husband instead of Alice's. Wes was always helping out wherever he was needed, even when the job wasn't one assigned to him.

The thought of Wes lying unconscious in a hospital bed made her eyes well with tears.

She'd been so cross with him before he left. Now she wished she could take back every harsh word and just wrap him in her arms.

"You two are going to make yourselves ill if you just stand here crying all day. Come along. I'm going to take you to the restaurant the doctor mentioned. We're going to have something to eat, and then we'll hire a cab to take us back to the train so we can collect your things and Carson's. The troupe will move on tomorrow, and you'll need your clothes and personal items. Maybe we can find a hotel near the hospital for you. By the time we finish, hopefully Carson will be awake, and we'll know more."

"I don't want to leave," Alice said, shaking her head. "He might wake up and ask for me."

"You heard the doctor," Oliver countered. "It'll be several hours. Now, come along. Don't make me carry you out of here like a sack of grain." He smiled. "You too, Lizzy. Dry your eyes."

Lizzy sniffed back her tears and nodded. "Uncle Oliver is right, Alice. We should make sure you get something to eat. You might not have another chance for a while, and you need your strength."

Alice shook her head, refusing to move. "I couldn't eat. Not until I know what's going to happen."

"Carson is going to be fine. He has the very best of care, and there's nothing more we can do but pray. That's the very best thing we can do for Carson at this point." Lizzy looped her arm through Alice's. "Now, come on. You know Carson would be very upset if he knew you were out here fretting."

⇥⟳ TWELVE ⟳⇤

The performers reluctantly left Alice and Carson behind in Dallas. The prognosis for Carson was better than had been expected, but his recovery would be lengthy. Ella felt sorry for Alice having to stay behind with no one at her side for encouragement.

Ella had worried about the show itself, but fortunately, Oliver and Henry had been able to locate another mounted bow shooter. Angel Adams, a twenty-three-year-old woman of Cherokee heritage, had once worked with Pawnee Bill's show. She had quit to take care of her sickly mother, but now that her mother was again healthy, Angel was interested in rejoining a wild west troupe. Finding her was one of those situations that left no doubt about God's hand in the matter. Carson's doctor had tended her mother and knew all about Angel's performances. When he overheard Henry and Alice talking about how much she'd be missed in the show, the doctor told them about Angel.

"I know you'll enjoy being here," Lizzy told Angel as the performers gathered in the community car for a short meeting. The train was making its way to their next stop, and all the girls had been excited to meet Angel and learn more about her.

"Thank you. I've long heard about this show and thought it would be wonderful to work with you," Angel replied.

"Are you really an Indian?" Debbie, one of the Roman riders, asked, frowning.

"I am." There was pride in Angel's voice. "I am one-quarter Cherokee, and as such I like to perform as an Indian maiden." She smiled. "I go by the name Little Bird. It was my grandmother's name."

"Did she teach you to shoot?" Mary asked.

"No. I learned that from my father."

Mary smiled and nodded. "As did I."

"Angel has a great reputation for her shooting abilities, and we were very fortunate to find her," Lizzy declared. "I think it's wonderful that she is of Indian blood. When I was a girl, my father and uncle performed in Buffalo Bill's Wild West show, and he hired on hundreds of natives from various tribes.

I learned so much about Indian culture, and they were some of the nicest people I'd ever encountered."

Debbie seemed to understand she was being put in her place regarding any disapproval she might feel. She gave a slight nod and smiled at Angel.

Henry and Oliver entered the car and greeted everyone, but it was Henry who addressed the group. "I know you're all very concerned about leaving Carson and Alice behind, but I assure you they are in good hands. Also, we've arranged for Alice's sister to join her. They will stay at a hotel near the hospital for as long as is needed."

"Thanks to Mr. Adler's generosity," Oliver Brookstone interjected.

Henry smiled. "It's the least we could do. Carson and Alice were a vital part of the show and will always be welcomed back. Alice has promised to send us word on Carson's condition so that we know how he's faring."

There were murmurs of approval, and Ella wished Mr. Adler would hurry up with his announcements. She had asked to meet with Lizzy and Mary privately after this briefing, and she was anxious to be on her way.

"Most of you have met our newest addition, Angel Adams. Angel has a great reputation and quite a following. She's performed for several years and is extremely proficient in bow shooting." Everyone looked at the dark-haired beauty in a green serge suit. "Angel, why don't you tell us something about yourself?"

She folded her hands together. "I was just telling the ladies that I'm one-quarter Cherokee and my father taught me to bow shoot. I worked the Pawnee Bill show for several years but quit to take care of my mother. She's completely recovered now, and I want to return to work. I love what I do, and feel I can be an asset to this show."

"I do, as well," Henry said. "Now, do you have any questions for Angel?"

There were a few other questions, and Angel answered each, not seeming to mind the intrusion into her privacy. After that, Lizzy announced how things would go once they reached their next venue. Henry wanted to change things up a bit and make a special presentation of Angel's act.

"I think once we get into the routine, everything will go well. As you know, we have two more performances in Texas, and then we're off to Kansas." Lizzy turned to Henry and her uncle. "Did you have anything else?"

"No," Henry said, shaking his head.

"Nothing from me," Oliver replied.

Lizzy turned back to the troupe. "Well, I

want to encourage all of you to get to know Angel better. Our show is successful because we stand together as a family. Now, if you'll excuse me, I need to speak with Mary and Ella privately." She got up from the table. "We'll go back to my train car, however, so you can continue to get to know Angel."

Ella breathed a sigh of relief as she followed Mary and Lizzy from the car. Lizzy led them to the family car and motioned for them to take a seat. Then she checked each of the bedrooms. "We're alone."

"Why do we need such privacy?" Mary asked.

"I asked for it," Ella replied. "I have news from my brother. Carson's accident kept us all so stirred up that there has been little opportunity to tell you what I learned. But I know why August died."

Mary paled. "Tell me everything."

Ella leaned back in her wooden chair. "It's so horrible I can hardly believe it even now. Apparently, my family has long been in the business of selling slaves."

"Slaves? But that was abolished years ago," Lizzy said, shaking her head.

"So everyone thought." Ella was so ashamed of her family's practices that she could hardly bear to speak of it. She continued, however, giving all the details she knew.

She prayed that Mary would not hate her for her association with August's death.

"And August died because he wandered into one of these slave auctions," Mary stated sadly. "It's all so terrible to imagine. He wouldn't have begun to understand what was happening, and yet they killed him."

"No doubt so he couldn't ask questions and bring unwanted attention to their illegal trade," Lizzy added.

"What's to be done now?" Mary asked.

Ella shook her head. "I'm not sure. My brother intends to seek justice, but first he plans to confront our father. After that, Robert will get advice from friends in Washington, D.C. He hopes Father will be willing to give up all his wrongdoing and testify against Jefferson. The sad thing is there's no guarantee anyone will care about what they've done."

"Not care?" Mary said, her voice rising. "Slavery was abolished. Certainly people will care. What they've done is illegal and caused my brother's murder. Who knows what other innocent souls died at the hands of that monster."

"Yes, I know. But as Robert pointed out to me just before he left, there was a certain legality to it. The men and women involved signed documents committing themselves in return for room and board and necessities.

On the other hand, it was also fixed so that those same men and women could never hope to pay off their debt. There are lumber and mining towns that do much the same thing. Robert's hopeful that someone who has made the plight of the Negro their cause will take up the banner and demand justice."

"But there's no guarantee that anyone will," Mary murmured.

"No. Because despite slavery being abolished, you know very well how some white people look down on people of color. There are still laws against blacks voting and eating or drinking at the same establishments as whites." Ella shook her head. "There are a great many people, in fact, who would just as soon see people of color eliminated. You know it's true."

Mary sighed. "I do."

"This is horrible," Lizzy declared, "but now that the truth is known, I have to hope that something can be done. Your brother is a good man, Ella. I'm sure he'll do everything in his power."

"The sad thing is, this will forever divide our family. I'm certain Mother and Father will never speak to Robert or me again. Robert planned to talk to our sister as well, but there's no telling what she'll advise."

"Well, it certainly forever divided our

family," Mary said, her tone laced with anger. "My brother is separated from us by death."

Ella's eyes filled with tears. "I'm sorry, Mary. I didn't mean to imply my sufferings were equal to yours."

Lizzy put her hand atop both Mary's and Ella's hands and squeezed. "Both things are equally painful. We won't make it a competition. What's important is that we stand in support of Robert's attempts to get justice. We must do whatever we can to be useful should the need arise."

"I hardly know what we can do." Ella looked at Lizzy. "I've been vocal about what I overheard Jefferson admit doing. I'll speak to whatever legal authority will listen."

"I know you will, Ella. You've already tried your best to get them to hear reason. But with this added information, I'm hopeful that someone, somewhere will now be willing to hear your story and take action to help all those who were wronged. Only then will Mary feel that justice has been done for August."

Mary nodded. "Only then."

Lizzy started to get up, then sat back down. Ella's news had nearly made her forget her own. "I have something else I wish to discuss. I'm not at all certain what to do about it."

"What is it?" Ella asked. She would no doubt be glad to get the attention off of herself and her family.

"I just learned the other day that my uncle no longer owns any part of the show. No one in my family does. Henry Adler owns it all."

"How can that be?" Mary asked. She looked just as surprised as Lizzy had been.

"My father must have left the show to Uncle Oliver when he died. I don't know the details of it because I haven't spoken with my uncle. I intend to, but I've been deeply troubled by it and didn't know how to approach him. Especially since Amanda is around him almost constantly. Then Carson got hurt, and we needed to locate another performer and get her set up with the show . . . and, well, time just got away from me."

"That still doesn't explain how Henry Adler ended up owning it all," Mary countered.

"Apparently when Uncle Oliver was ill, he feared he would die. He asked Henry to buy him out. Henry already owned some stock, so I suppose Uncle Oliver felt it wise to sell him the rest. I don't know. It hurts me deeply that he would do such a thing without discussing it with Mother or me." She felt tears well up in her eyes.

"I would talk to him about it before you feel too betrayed. You don't know the circumstances." Mary grew thoughtful. "There may have been no other choice. Didn't you tell me that last year's tour was set up with unusual contracts that required all of the shows to be fulfilled or the pay would be lost?"

"Yes, there was a special arrangement with the portion of the shows we did in England. I agree that Uncle Oliver must have had his reasons. And I know it does little good for me to sit here and speculate. I need to speak with him, and I suppose now is as good a time as any." She drew a deep breath. "Pray for me. I don't want to be accusatory with him, but I feel terribly deceived." She wiped her eyes with the cuff of her blouse.

"You wanted to leave the show anyway," Mary reminded her. "You still have the ranch."

Lizzy shook her head. "Do I? What if Uncle Oliver sold that as well? I have no idea what's happened or where I stand."

"Then go talk to him. Ask him. I know your uncle. He'll tell you the truth."

"I suppose you're right. There's little else I can do."

Those words were still rumbling through Lizzy's thoughts as she went to Uncle Oliver's office and knocked on the door. There truly was very little she could do. She couldn't change her uncle's mind or heart where Amanda was concerned, and if he had sold the ranch as well as the show, her hands were tied.

"Come in," her uncle called.

Lizzy opened the door and found him sitting at his desk, paperwork all around him. Near his elbow was a whiskey glass holding a small amount of amber liquid. Lizzy didn't want to ruin her opportunity to find out about the show, so she determined then and there to hold her tongue about the alcohol.

"Can we talk for a moment?" she asked.

Oliver nodded. "Of course. Take a seat. What's on your mind? I hope you aren't here to tell me that you're leaving."

"No. Not yet anyway." She took hold of the rounded chair back but remained standing.

Her uncle watched her for a moment. "You look quite serious. Tell me what's wrong."

Lizzy decided to just come right out with it, but then Amanda waltzed into the office without so much as a knock.

"If you don't mind, we're having a private meeting," Lizzy said, turning to glare at her.

"No doubt you're here to convince Oliver to forsake me. Honestly, Elizabeth, you need to learn that some things are none of your business." Amanda went to Oliver and leaned down to put her arms around his neck. She planted a long, leisurely kiss on his forehead, then stood to smirk at Lizzy.

Lizzy lifted her chin. "I didn't come here to talk to my uncle about you, but if you insist on it, I'm happy to accommodate. I think the only reason you're trying to marry him is for his money."

Oliver protested. "That's ridiculous, Lizzy. Amanda isn't that way."

"You've hardly known her long enough to know what way she is or isn't."

Amanda gave a simpering smile. "He's known me long enough. True love doesn't require a long time."

Lizzy felt a growing sense of frustration. All of the issues that had come to light seemed to join together into one colossal ordeal for her. She had to get her uncle to see reason.

"Do you have any of your own money, Amanda? You surely don't, or you would never have taken on a sewing job with the show."

"It isn't important what I have or don't have, and it's none of your business."

"Really, Lizzy," Oliver interjected. "You mustn't worry about this. Amanda isn't marrying me for my wealth. I don't have any."

Lizzy glanced at Amanda, whose expression had sobered. "Have you told her that you sold the show to Henry Adler last year?

You certainly didn't tell me. I had to learn it from Henry."

Oliver looked down at the papers on his desk. "I didn't think it important."

"Not important?" Lizzy repeated. "It was something of my father's—something I presumed would always be in the family. Not only that, but I felt certain my mother had inherited my father's share. Instead, I learn that you owned the show in full."

"That was part of our arrangement. Your father knew that the show was important to me, and when he was on his deathbed, we made arrangements for him to take full possession of the ranch so that you and Rebecca would always have a home and income. I got the show, thinking it would be my livelihood for the rest of my life. Then when I grew ill, I felt I needed to sell it to Henry. He promised me I would always have a job. You, as well."

"A job?" Amanda questioned. "What are you saying, Oliver?"

He looked up at her and smiled. "I'm saying that I work for Henry now, which is why I know you aren't marrying me for my money. I don't have any."

"But you are Oliver Brookstone. The Brookstone show is your namesake. You can't be serious." Amanda sounded close to hysteria. "This must be a joke."

Lizzy folded her arms and shook her head. "Mother owns the ranch in Montana?"

Despite a worried look at his fiancée, Oliver ignored Amanda's comments. "Yes. The ranch is hers in full. Your father always preferred it there and wanted to make sure it stayed in the family. He knew you would want to live there when you left the show."

A heavy sigh escaped Lizzy's lips. She didn't like that she hadn't been consulted. After all, she was a grown woman, and the ranch and show were intricate parts of her life. But on the other hand, it was a relief to realize that the ranch belonged to her mother. They would always have it, because she knew her mother would never sell it.

"What about the money from selling the show?" Amanda asked. "Surely you still have that."

"Not exactly. When I thought I was dying, I told Adler to pay for shipping my body back to the States and then to give the rest of the money to Rebecca. When I recovered, we agreed he would pay me in installments so I'd have a monthly stipend. I get a comfortable amount each month. We'll do just fine, since our room and board is a part of our arrangement with the show."

"But I'm sure you can get the lump sum from Henry, and then we can leave the show,"

Amanda said, her tone returning to its sugary sweetness. "After all, we already talked about living in a grand house in California."

"Sure, we talked about it," Oliver said, "but no decision was made. I'm not ready to leave the show just yet, and besides, you told me you wanted to see the world. This is the ideal way to do it."

"No, it's not. I want to travel as a lady with beautiful clothes and the best of furnishings. Not as the seamstress to this lot."

"But, darlin', you don't have to work unless you want to," Uncle Oliver assured her. "I've already talked to Henry about it."

She put her hands on her hips. "You have ruined everything, Oliver Brookstone."

Lizzy raised a brow. "I thought you weren't marrying him for his money."

"Oh, shut up. You're both the stupidest people I have ever met. You had every opportunity to be a wealthy man for the rest of your life, and you let it slip through your fingers. Well, I don't intend to be a part of this nonsense. You can forget about the marriage, Oliver. I won't live the rest of my life in train cars going from town to town while you announce this ridiculous show."

Oliver couldn't have looked more stunned. "But wait, Amanda!" He stood to stop her, but she was already heading for the door.

"Please wait. I know we can have a wonderful life together. Amanda, please. . . ." His final word seemed to drain him of all energy. He sank to his chair as she stomped out of the room.

Lizzy was relieved that the truth was finally out, but she knew this wasn't going to be easy for Oliver to bear. She went and knelt beside him.

"I'm so sorry, Uncle Oliver. I knew she was up to no good, but I never wanted to see you hurt."

He shook his head. "How could I have been so blind? I thought she truly cared." His devastation was apparent.

"She's a good actress. No doubt she's done this before. The fault isn't with you."

"Of course it is. She fed my vanity and made me feel young again. I was no longer lonely and thought I had found . . . love." His voice broke, but he didn't fall apart.

"You'll always have love. Mother and I and Wes—we all love you, and you'll always have a home with us. We're family, and no one will ever turn you out."

He said nothing, just sat staring at the open office doorway. "I can't believe this is happening." He reached out and ran his finger along the rim of the whiskey glass.

"I know it's hard, but you can't let this

drive you back to drink," Lizzy begged. "It nearly killed you last time. I don't want to lose you."

"What is there for me now?"

She hated the despair in his voice. "There's the show. You love it. You love the crowds and the performances. You love being the master of ceremonies. Then there's your family and friends. Uncle Oliver, please don't give up on us."

He stared at the glass. It seemed to Lizzy that he had come to the same crossroads yet again. Which way would he choose?

⊸⊱ THIRTEEN ⊰⊶

Mara had never known the freedom she had with the Brookstone show. She had grown up with a clear understanding that everything she had was at the mercy of the Fleming family. Her mother had taught her from an early age that two things were most important. Love God and others, and keep your mouth shut.

"Nobody cares what you're thinkin', Mara, so you's just better off keepin' yo' thoughts to yo'self," her mama had said on more than one occasion.

But that had been hard for Mara. She had a great many opinions, and often she had shared them with Ella. She had been assigned to Ella as a companion and later as her maid, but as Ella had always declared, there was a strong sisterhood between them. Of course, it was a sisterhood that couldn't be shared with anyone else. Polite society wouldn't have understood or accepted their closeness. But whereas most white women ordered their black help around and kept them out of sight when not needed, Ella wanted Mara's company. They could talk for hours without anyone else in the room.

Better yet, Ella had never treated Mara as anything but her equal. And Mara had Ella to thank for the wonderful job she had with the Brookstone show. At least in part. Granted, her sewing skills were proving her worthy, but Mara would never have attempted to apply for such a job if Ella hadn't been a part of the show.

"I hope I'm not disturbing you," Abraham Green said from the open door to the costume car.

"You're not," Mara replied. She and Abraham had shared passing glances and a few words here and there, but this was their first time being completely alone.

"I wondered what you was up to and if maybe you wanted to accompany me to the mercantile," he said.

Mara smiled and set some mending aside. "I don't know you well enough to accompany you anywhere, Mr. Green."

He chuckled. "Call me Abe. That's what my friends do."

She nodded. "In that case, you can call me Mara."

"Means *bitter* in Hebrew. I learned that from readin' the Bible. But you don't seem bitter at all."

"You can read? How'd you manage that?"

He shrugged. "My daddy could read and write. He was raised up north. Fought for the Yankees when the war came. Afore that, he learned to lay bricks, and he was good at it."

"And did you learn that as well?"

"No. My daddy was killed in the last year of the war. I was just born, so I never got to know him. But since he could read and write, my mama was determined I'd learn too."

"My friend Ella taught me. I'm not real good. There was never much of a chance to practice, and Ella's folks would not have approved."

"Is Ella that little gal who rides those horses standing up?"

"That and the trick ridin'. She was born and raised on a horse farm in Kentucky. That's where my people were born and raised."

"Slaves?"

"Yes." Mara didn't bother to mention that the practice was apparently still going on. While she'd never felt truly free while working for the Flemings, she hadn't thought of herself as being in bondage. Now, however, those thoughts haunted her constantly.

"So your folks were free blacks?" she asked.

Abe turned a felt hat in his hands. "They were. Say, do you mind if I sit? You can get to know me better, and then maybe later you won't mind takin' a walk with me."

She met his dark brown eyes and nodded. "I think that would be acceptable. Ain't like we're hiding away so that folks can't find us."

Abe pulled up a stool and sat. He placed his hat upside down on the floor, then looked at her. "What else you want to know?"

Mara smiled. "Where'd you grow up after the war?"

"My mama took me to Chicago. She had an aunt there who worked for a big hotel and could get Mama a job. So we went. Mama worked in the kitchen, and I went to the school for Negro children. An old lady in the city was big on education for everyone, and she used her money to make sure children of color could go to school. That's where I learned to read and write. Come nighttime, I worked helpin' with the horses of the guests."

Mara couldn't help but notice the fine build of the man. He had powerful muscles that flexed beneath his threadbare shirt. She'd have to get him another made. Mr. Brookstone and Mr. Adler wouldn't want their wrangler going around without decent clothes.

"My mama died when I was ten," Abe continued, "and my uncle Saul took me west. I kept workin' with horses. We ended up spending a lot of time workin' for ranches."

"Sounds like you had a good life."

"I did." His expression warmed. "I can't complain about what God put on my plate."

She nodded, thinking about her own life. It might have been an illusion in part, but the love Ella and Mama showed her wasn't.

"So tell me about your family," he said.

"Ain't much to tell. My mama was a slave. My daddy died before I knew him, just like you."

"See there, we have something in common already."

"I suppose that practically makes us best friends," she said sarcastically.

Abe laughed in genuine amusement. "You got a smart mouth, girl. I like that."

Mara was glad he wasn't offended. "After the war, my mama stayed on the horse farm and worked for the Flemings, and I worked for them too. My mama was like a mama to Miss Ella, and she and I grew up close as two peas in a pod. Ella Fleming taught me to read and write a little. It didn't come easy to me, but since it was important to her, I tried."

"And now you're here with her, traveling around with the show. How do you like that?"

"Well enough. I ain't never seen the world, and this has me going somewhere new every day. What about you? You said you went west. You get very far?"

"We got to California and down to Texas and made stops every place in between. Uncle Saul was a cowboy—worked wherever he could get a job. We even tried our hand pannin' for gold once. It wasn't worth the effort."

He laughed, and Mara smiled. Abe had a way about him that made her feel comfortable—like she'd known him all her life.

He continued. "Uncle Saul taught me all about horses and said I had a natural way with them. Me and horseflesh get along real good. It's like we have a special bond."

"I's seen folks just like that. I think it's a gift from the Lord."

"I do too."

"So you know the Lord?" she asked matter-of-factly.

"'Course I do, woman. My mama told me Bible stories every night before I went to bed. When I was learnin' to read, that's what I practiced on. I'd read the Bible and practice copying down Scripture. Caused me to memorize quite a few verses. Then, not long before my mama died, I gave my heart to Jesus at a tent meeting." He chuckled. "There was singin' and dancin' and folks praisin' the Lord, and I just wanted me a part of that. Mama was mighty proud to kneel down with me when I prayed. I never saw her smile bigger than when I come up out of the water after gettin' baptized."

Mara felt such a strange connection with the man sitting in front of her. It was as if they were long-time friends and were just remembering past stories rather than sharing a first conversation. Everything about Abraham Green put her at ease, from his easygoing manner to his twinkling eyes.

"What about you?" he asked.

"Me?" Mara shook her head. "What about me?"

"How'd you come to know the Lord?"

"Same as you. My mama. She told Bible stories to Ella and me at night before bed."

"Something else we got in common." He grinned, and Mara felt her heart thud a little harder.

"We always went to church on Sunday," she said. "The family went to the white folks' church, and we went to the black folks' church. I always wondered if they had a different God than we did, but Mama assured me there was just one God. I prayed a prayer to get saved from my sins when I was about seven. I was afraid not to. I was afraid God might not let me come to heaven, and I knew that's where my mama was gonna go when she died."

"So you got saved to be with your mama."

"In a way that was my first thinkin'," Mara admitted. "Later, I got to know God better and wanted to be with Him too."

"Maybe you'll get to know me better, and you'll want to be with me," Abe said, but this time his expression was serious.

It dawned on Mara that he was just as struck with her as she was with him. It seemed silly to pretend otherwise. They were clearly taken with each other.

She gave him a hint of a smile. "I 'spect I know you well enough now to go with you on a walk."

He grinned and snatched up his hat as he stood. "I was hopin' you might see it that way." He held out his hand to help her from the chair.

Mara trembled as she put her hand in his. Somehow, she knew without a doubt that this was the man she would spend the rest of her life with.

───◆───

"This came for you," Lizzy told Ella as she came into the arena to observe the Roman riding practice. "I believe it's a letter from Phillip." She held it out. "I wish Wes was as considerate. I've heard nothing from him. I suppose he's much too busy to worry about my feelings."

Ella handed Lizzy the reins to a pair of matched black geldings and eagerly opened the envelope. She immediately recognized Phillip's poorly managed print. "I'm sure Wes is just busy trying to keep Phillip from drinking."

My dear Ella,

I don't have much to say, but that I miss seeing you every day. I've been spending most of my time breaking horses that we bought off a man in Miles City. I haven't had a drink since leaving Colorado, but I still want one. I don't know if that feeling ever goes away, but I'm praying it will. I hope you are doing well. Your promise keeps me going.

Phillip

There was no mention of love or flowery words of romance, but it gave her the most important information. He was well and working hard. And he hadn't been drinking.

"Is Phillip all right?" Lizzy asked.

Ella nodded. "He says he is. Says he hasn't had a drink since leaving the show, but that he still desires one. I know it can't be easy for him. I've heard such horrible things about alcohol." She handed the letter to Lizzy and took back the reins while Lizzy scanned the note.

"He mentions your promise." Lizzy looked up with a grin. "Did he propose, and you accepted?"

"Not exactly." Ella felt her cheeks warm. "He asked me to wait for him. He wants to make himself a better man—worthier of me is what he said. He asked me to wait for him so he could prove himself, and I agreed I would."

Lizzy smiled all the more. "I think that's very nearly as good as a proposal."

"Maybe." Ella knew she would have been fine with it had it been exactly that. But then her reason warned her that Phillip would be worthless as a husband unless he was able to lay his demons to rest. "He has to overcome alcohol first. I can't marry a man who's controlled by drinking."

"No. You can't. The liquor would always come first. But I know if anyone can help Phillip, it's Wes. There's a special bond between brothers, and that will give Phillip the extra strength to overcome. I remember my father helping Uncle Oliver stop drinking. It wasn't very easy, but that bond between brothers was what saw them through." Lizzy's expression grew fretful. "I worry he's going to start down that path again, and I don't know what I'll do."

"Amanda really hurt him, didn't she?" Ella hoped talking about Amanda would keep Lizzy's mind off Wesley's silence.

Lizzy sat on a bale of straw. "She did. He was so certain she truly loved him. I wish he could have seen her for who she was right from the start."

"I do too. Oliver is such a nice man."

"He is. He's kind and gentle and simple. There's nothing pretentious about him. He treats everyone the same—black or white, man or woman. He deserved so much better than what Amanda did to him." Lizzy twisted the note in her hand, not seeming to realize what she was doing.

Ella tied up the horses and sat beside her friend. "It's going to be all right. We're all here to help, but you know very well that Oliver has to want to stay sober. He has to want it for himself. Do you know for sure that he was drinking with Amanda?"

"I don't, but she was always giving it to him. I saw it on more than one occasion. Commented on it too. She didn't care. She said there was nothing harmful in a little drink. She just didn't care that Uncle Oliver couldn't handle it."

"Well, she's gone now."

Lizzy nodded. "Yes, and I worry that she took Uncle Oliver's resolve with her. If Wes were here I wouldn't worry so much. Oliver listens to him."

Ella could see Lizzy slipping into a melancholy mood. "I'm sure Wes will write soon. Come on. You're supposed to help me, and you can't do that if you're sitting here feeling sorry for yourself and worrying. I'm going to drive this team around the arena and jump the bar. You raise it for me after I make each successful pass. If we don't clear it, we'll do it again at the same height."

"I'm ready." Lizzy got to her feet while Ella retrieved the horses.

Smoothing out the pad on first one horse and then the other, Ella spoke in gentle tones. "There you are, Bart. Nice and comfortable." She turned to the horse at her left and rubbed his nose. "Buck, you are in fine form today."

The horse nuzzled her hand, looking for treats. When none were to be found, he pulled back.

"Treats come later," Ella assured him.

She mounted Bart and rode the team to the end of the arena where they would start their run. For Roman riding, she wore a thin-soled dance slipper. It helped her have better control on the horse's back when she could feel the movement beneath her feet.

Once she had the team in place, Ella stood and carefully took one set of reins in each hand. For her, the hardest part of Roman riding was keeping the horses close enough together that she didn't do the splits. Being short was definitely a disadvantage and probably the biggest reason she preferred trick riding.

"All right, the first bar's in place," Lizzy called.

"Move on," Ella called to the horses and gave the lines a little snap.

The matched blacks stepped forward, and Ella put them into a trot. She made one circle without jumping the bar, then urged the horses to gallop. She bent her knees as best she could to keep her balance and noted the rhythm of each horse. It took only a moment for them to match each other's stride.

The horses knew what was expected of them and easily cleared the bar in unison. Ella praised them and headed them around to do it again. They made passes for about fifteen minutes, and Ella's legs burned from the strain. She brought the team back around and halted them in front of Lizzy before sliding down to sit atop Bart.

"They have no hesitation," Ella declared. "I think we'll be just fine for the show."

"This winter we'll teach them to jump fire," Lizzy said, giving Buck a gentle pat.

Across the arena, Mara and Abe were walking together. They were caught up in talking and didn't seem to realize anyone else existed.

"I think Mara and Abe are sweet on each other," Lizzy said, taking the reins.

Ella slid from the horse and nodded. "I don't really believe in love at first sight, but I think that's what happened with them. I never saw Mara so much as look at any of the men on the farm. But then, maybe it was forbidden." She frowned. "Maybe she was afraid to fall in love for fear they'd be sent away."

"Did she know how things were?" Lizzy asked.

"Not exactly. We talked about it. She knew it was a matter of having an obligation and a contract. She knew they weren't allowed to go anywhere without special permission. Otherwise, there was no one around to tell them they were in a bad way, I guess."

She saw Abe put his hand at the small of Mara's back as they stepped over the threshold into the area where the horses were kept. Ella was happy for her friend. Maybe this was Mara's first chance to truly consider love.

"I hope they find happiness together," Ella said.

"Even if it takes her away from you? I know you're very close."

"I am, but when I left the farm, I knew I might never see her again. I always wanted to send for Mara but never felt I was in a position to do so. I knew my folks would never have agreed. Now I'm worried about her situation. If Daddy has papers that says she owes him and has to stay, then what if he sends the authorities after her?"

"Maybe you could write to him and offer to buy out her contract. I'd lend you any extra money I have. We could probably even appeal to Henry for help."

Ella's eyes widened. "I never even considered that. I don't know if Daddy has bothered to consider that she might be with me, but I could write and explain that I want to purchase her contract."

"But then he'd know that you understand what he's doing." Lizzy's brows knit together. "That probably wouldn't help Robert's situation. I hadn't thought it through when I mentioned buying her contract, but if you say anything, then your father will know that someone has figured out what he's up to.

The last time that happened, it got August Reichert killed."

Lizzy was right. Ella needed to remain silent. "I won't write to him. I'll just suggest to Mara that she not go out alone or make herself overly visible. We have to give Robert time to do whatever it is he plans to do."

"I agree. We'll all keep watch to make sure no one tries to steal her away. Your father may very well suspect she's here with us, so I'll let the boys know to be on their guard. If they see any strangers around, they can let us know."

Ella worried her lower lip for a moment, then sighed. "I'm really sorry for all the trouble I've brought your family. You've done nothing but help me and extend kindness from the beginning. I still remember how terrified I was at the thought of staying on the farm and being forced to marry Jefferson. You were so good to help me. I can never hope to make it up to you, and now here you are helping Mara as well."

Lizzy handed Ella the reins. "It's nothing less than what God would want. I wrestled at first, thinking maybe I was in sin helping you run away, but the more I prayed about it, the more it felt like the right thing to do. You know, sometimes in the Bible folks were called to do something that seemed foolish or even wrong, but it was for God's glory, and that made it right. I wanted to help you so that you weren't forced to marry that evil murderer who wants to keep mistresses and continue in his wicked ways. I figured it was rather like saving one of God's sheep."

"Well, I'll never forget your sacrifice and the way you risked yourself for me. If I can ever return the favor, I will."

"Your friendship has been reward enough. Besides, if things go as I think they might, we may well be sisters one day. And I always wanted a sister." Lizzy smiled and walked toward the gate. "Let's get these animals put away and get back to the train for some lunch. I'm famished."

"Lizzy!" It was Henry Adler. He looked excited about something.

Lizzy and Ella waited until he crossed the performance area to join them. "We were just going to get lunch," Lizzy said. "Would you care to join us?"

He shook his head. "No, but I have something important to ask of you, Lizzy."

She looked curious. "You have my attention."

Ella smiled. "I can go ahead with the horses."

"No, stay," Henry insisted. "I think you

might be able to convince Lizzy to do as I'm asking."

Now Ella was intrigued. "All right. Please continue."

"I didn't find out until this morning, but we have lost one of our trick riders. That new girl, Suzanna, just up and quit. Said she was homesick. She left me a note and not much else in the way of explanation."

"That leaves just Ella and Catherine," Lizzy said. "And Catherine is so new at this that her tricks are still very simplistic."

"Exactly. Lizzy, I'm begging you to consider helping out. Would you please perform again? At least here in America. I can manage to scale things down, maybe even pick up another rider, for Europe."

Ella gave Lizzy a smile. "It would be just the thing to keep your mind occupied. Why don't you say yes?"

"Wes wanted me to quit performing," Lizzy murmured.

"But Wes isn't here," Adler replied. "Besides, this is an emergency. We're losing so many performers that the show is going to suffer and the audiences won't be happy. Before you know it, word will get around, and no one will want to attend. I wouldn't ask if it weren't important."

Lizzy nodded. "I know." She shrugged.

"I'm terribly out of shape. I don't know if I can get my skills back to performance levels in time."

"Just do easy tricks for the first few nights," Henry encouraged.

"Yes, you know, the ones that are simpler but look difficult," Ella declared. "I'm sure you can manage it."

"I suppose I really have no choice if we're to have a decent show. Good thing the horses are trained for multiple riders." Lizzy considered the situation for only a moment longer. "I'll do it."

"It won't be much longer and you'll be Mrs. Christopher Williams," Chris said, pulling Mary onto his lap as she passed by.

She smiled, gave him a peck on the cheek, then jumped back up. "But I'm not yet, so I hardly think it's appropriate to sit on your lap."

"I suppose not," he said with a sigh. "How I do suffer."

Mary giggled and pulled up a chair. "How's your book coming along?"

He turned his swivel chair back toward his typewriter and laced his fingers behind his head. "It's coming along well. Adding Angel to the performers has allowed me to explore yet another side of things. I always figured I'd catch up to Bill Cody's troupe and interview some of the Indians who were hired on, but talking to Angel has me very excited about devoting an entire portion of the book to native people."

"You don't plan to leave me before the wedding, do you?"

It was his turn to chuckle. "Not on your life. We'll be near Bill when we're in Europe. He's touring extensively there this year. I'm sure it will be easy enough to catch up to him and interview anyone who's willing."

"So you really don't mind this life on the rails?" Mary watched his face, knowing that his expression would reveal the truth. To her relief, he remained all smiles.

"I find it invigorating. I enjoy being a part of your act and seeing you receive the applause and accolades you deserve, and I love the travel. Always have. I traveled constantly to write for the magazine before I quit to work on this book."

"Yes, but it can be grueling, and I know Henry has given you additional jobs."

"Writing jobs, which is what I'm happiest doing. It's not a problem to earn my keep by taking on Henry's requests, so don't fret about that. I suppose I would like to know, however, if this is what you want to continue doing. Or would you rather settle down somewhere with a house and a little picket fence and a garden? Or maybe an apartment in the city."

Mary scrunched up her nose. "That doesn't begin to appeal to me. The fact is, I don't know what I want, but I know I'm not ready to settle in one place. I hope that doesn't shock you or cause any problems regarding our future."

"Are you joking?" He leaned toward her and took her hand. "I couldn't be happier. I'm not ready to settle down either. I'm quite content to roam—at least for now. Once any children start to come, we can reevaluate the situation."

Mary felt her cheeks flush. "I've thought a lot about that too. I don't suppose there's any reason we wouldn't be able to . . . conceive right away." She looked at her hands, feeling embarrassed by the topic.

"And if we do, it will be wonderful. And if you want to raise them on the show—I will support that as well. We can have half a dozen little girls who look just like you. We'll call the act Mama Mary and Her Six-Shooters." He chuckled. "Of course, you can't have the play on words unless you give up that five-shot Smith & Wesson."

She looked up to find him smiling tenderly. "Truly? Do you think we could actually do that? Have a family and keep performing with the show?"

"Why not? We'll hire a nurse. She can watch the baby when we're performing and help with all our other needs, like making baby food and washing diapers. Then, when the children are old enough, we'll make them a part of the show. Maybe one day we could have our own family troupe."

Mary could see the possibilities. "It seems you've thought this all out."

"I'm a planner," he replied. "I look at all the possibilities and try to create a reasonable plan for each situation. No matter what happens, I love you, and I know we can make it work—if we work together."

"And are always honest with each other. I want no lies to save my feelings or ease my worry. Please promise me."

He nodded. "I promise, but you must as well."

Mary thought for a moment. It wasn't as if she would ever intend to keep things from him. "I promise."

"Then we should be the two happiest married folks in the world," he said, leaning close to kiss her.

"I don't know about that. Honesty doesn't

always equal happiness. Sometimes honesty is very hard and painful."

He stopped short of the kiss and straightened. "That's true, but I believe that even painful truth is better than lies. Don't you?"

"I do. I've always spoken my mind, as you well know, but I also always want to be aware of what matters most. I want us to have a great marriage—just like my grandparents and parents. I've never seen anyone love each other more than my oma and opa. You'll meet them when we get to Kansas for our performances. I know they'll come—especially since you'll be there. Oh, how I wish they could see us get married in Chicago."

Chris straightened. "Say, why don't we get married at the farm? It'll just be a couple of weeks before we get married in the show, and we don't have to tell anyone what we've done. We could have a small, private ceremony. Your sister and brother-in-law can stand up with us."

Mary grew very excited. "I never thought of that. It would be wonderful. Do you suppose we could really pull it off?"

Chris smiled. "Why not? We'll telegraph your grandparents at the next stop and ask them to arrange everything."

Mary got to her feet, then immediately plopped down in Chris's lap. She put her arms around his neck and planted a long kiss on his lips. His surprised expression made her smile.

He tightened his hold on her. "Maybe we should just get married at the next stop."

She laughed and got back to her feet. "Hardly. Two weddings will be quite enough."

⟡ FOURTEEN ⟡

August in Kansas was one of the hottest months. The humidity never seemed to ease, and with temperatures over one hundred, everyone suffered—man and animal alike. Mary didn't care, however. She was thrilled to have returned to her home state to marry and even happier to be back at the farm. Her grandparents were delighted to have her there, as well as to meet Christopher and get to know him.

The show had three days off for repairs, rest, and to see to anything else that was needed. Mary knew that when the schedule was planned, Lizzy had thought this a good place to stop. She knew Mary's family would be nearby and it would be important to Mary to see them. But also, the Reicherts had pastureland in which they'd let the show's horses rest. In addition, the railroad made getting supplies easy enough, and Topeka had large railroad shops where repairs could be made to the Brookstone cars.

Mary had explained her plan to marry Chris at the farm to Lizzy and Henry Adler, even though she had originally intended to keep things secret. Once the news got out, however, everyone wanted to be at the ceremony and do whatever they could to make it a beautiful event. It touched Mary deeply that her friends cared so much.

"Ve got the cake all ready," Oma said as Mary came into the kitchen. "Ooh, don't you look pretty."

Mary gave a twirl in her wedding dress. It was a cream-colored organdy gown with a high lace collar and crisscrossed lace bodice.

"Your mama vould have been proud to see you in her dress."

"I remember seeing it in the cedar chest and dreaming that I might one day wear it. I'm so glad that day has finally come." Mary ran her hand down the lacy sleeve. "It's almost as if she's here."

"Ja." Oma smiled and nodded. "Are you ready now? The minister is here, and your friends are keeping him company, but I'm sure everyone is anxious."

"No one more than I." Mary went to the

small mirror her grandfather had nailed up near the back door so Oma could check her hat before leaving for church or town. Mary used it to make certain her hair was done properly. Mary's sister, Kate, along with Ella, had fashioned the coiffure. Each curl was securely pinned, and a circlet of flowers—created from Oma's flower garden—had been placed upon Mary's head.

"Ve're ready for you, Mary," her grandfather said, entering the kitchen. "Everyone is gathered out under the villow tree just as you requested."

Her grandmother hurried to the door. "I'll go take my place. You come next."

Mary would have laughed if it hadn't been such a concern to her grandparents that everything be perfect. They had no idea that it didn't matter in the least to Mary. She only wanted them to be present—not to feel obligated to work.

She looped her arm through Opa's and gave him a smile. "I'm ready if you are."

"You look like an angel. I'm so happy to escort you to your man."

Mary gave him a kiss on the cheek. "And I couldn't be happier. Getting married here at the farm with you and Oma makes it perfect."

He led her out the back door and onto the lush green lawn. Opa's hunting dog, Red, was howling mournfully after being tied to the fence. Oma had been afraid he might jump up on Mary's dress, and so Red was confined. The dog, however, didn't understand and bayed on until Mary and Chris stood before the minister. Then Opa went to be with Red and calm him down.

"Not everyone has their wedding song sung by a hound," Chris whispered.

Mary giggled, and the minister smiled as he raised his hands. "Please bow with me in prayer." He waited only a moment for compliance, but even Red had the good sense to be quiet. "Father, we thank You for Mary and Christopher and their desire to wed in Your sight and under Your authority. Bless this union and the man and woman who come to You now to pledge their lives to each other. Bless their friends and family and show them how to be supportive of Mary and Chris as they embark on their new lives as husband and wife. In Jesus' name, amen."

"Amen," whispered those gathered.

"Who gives this woman to be joined to this man?" the pastor asked as a breeze made the hot day a little more bearable.

"Ve do," Opa declared. "Her grandmother and I." The pastor nodded, and Opa stepped back to stand with Oma.

"Dearly beloved, we are gathered here this

day in the sight of God and man to see this man and woman legally joined in holy matrimony."

He continued with the words that Mary had heard on many other occasions when her friends or other church members had married. She had always known they would one day be spoken for her, but she had no idea how much they would mean to her.

"Mary, wilt thou have this man to be your lawfully wedded husband, to live together after God's ordinance in the holy estate of matrimony? Wilt thou love him, comfort him, honor and keep him in sickness and in health, and forsaking all others keep thee only unto him as long as you both shall live?"

Gazing into Chris's blue eyes, Mary nodded. "I will."

"Repeat, then, after me. 'I, Mary, take you, Christopher, to be my lawfully wedded husband.'"

Mary repeated the words and let the pastor lead her through the vows that would bind her to this man for the rest of her life. It wasn't long before Chris was offering her the same pledge.

"I, Christopher, take you, Mary, to be my lawfully wedded wife, to have and to hold from this day forward, for better or worse, for richer or poorer, in sickness and in health, to love and to cherish until death do us part. This is my solemn vow before God."

Christopher slipped a ring on Mary's finger, then surprised her by drawing her hand to his lips, where he sealed it with a kiss. Raising his head to meet her eyes, he winked. Mary thought her knees might give way there and then. How this man could thrill her, make her feel both weak and strong.

"Then by the power vested in me by the State of Kansas and Shawnee County, I now declare that Mary and Christopher are man and wife." The pastor smiled. "You may kiss your bride."

Chris took hold of Mary's face and kissed her tenderly amidst the cheers and claps of their friends and family. Mary was sorry it was such a short kiss, but she knew it wasn't the time or place for a lengthier display.

Their friends threw wheat grains, just as they had done for Lizzy and Wesley's wedding, and a picnic celebration on the grounds of Mary's childhood home ensued. It was all she could have wanted for her wedding, complete with her happy sister and brother-in-law and their baby daughter, Johanna, who had been named for Mary and Kate's mother.

"Congratulations, Mary."

She turned to find Owen holding Johanna.

"Thank you, Owen. I'd ask if you're happy, but I can see for myself that you are."

He grinned. "I'm very glad you had the good sense to call off our engagement. It really is amazing when you love someone the way God intended for marriage."

Mary laughed. "Everything's better when we do it the way God intended. How's the farm?"

"The crops look to yield very well this year. Your grandfather and I went in together to get a hired man to help share the work. The wheat looks good, and the corn does too. There will be silage enough for all the animals, and I believe we'll make a profit this year if things go on as they have."

"That's good to hear. I pray it will be so."

Johanna began to fuss, and Owen took that as his cue to find Kate. Mary smiled, watching him weave through the crowd to turn the infant over to her mother. One day, perhaps, that would be Chris with their child.

"You look happier than I've seen you in some time," Lizzy said, coming alongside Mary with a cup of punch. "Here, I thought you might be thirsty."

Mary took the punch and drank it down in one long swallow. "I was parched. Thank you."

"You look cool and collected, despite the

heat. I don't know how folks live in this. I feel like every inch of me is sweating."

"This is just a good old Kansas summer." Mary knew others struggled in the humidity and heat, but she loved it.

The celebration continued until the sun began to slip beneath a golden field of wheat. Mary knew it was time to change her clothes and head back to town. The show was scheduled to hook up to a train and head north that evening around midnight.

She made her way inside and quickly changed back into the cotton dress she'd worn earlier. As she hung up her mother's gown, Mary thought of her mother and father. She was four when her mother had passed and not yet ten when her father died. Oma and Opa had taken in her and her siblings and lovingly raised them. As she grew up, Mary remembered hearing of other families in similar situations whose children had to be farmed out to various friends and family. She shuddered to think of how awful it would be not only to lose your mother and father, but also your home and siblings as well. What a blessing that her grandparents had cared enough to make sacrifices for the benefit of their grandchildren.

"Are you up here, wife?"

She smiled at the reference. "I am. Come on in."

Chris peeked in as he pushed open the door. "Everyone's ready to head back. We're just waiting on you."

She glanced around the room. "I think I'm ready. I was just hanging up Mother's dress."

"Your dress now, and maybe one day our daughter will wear it." He closed the distance between them and took Mary in his arms. "I have never been as happy as I am today."

She nodded. "Me too."

She couldn't say anything else because Chris had covered her mouth with his. He kissed her slowly and thoroughly, leaving her breathless when he pulled away.

His gaze met hers. "A promise of things to come. A lifetime of love and happiness."

She wished they could just remain there forever, but it was impossible. "Let's go before they send someone after us." She reached for her suitcase, but Chris took it from her.

"Allow me, Mrs. Williams."

"I'm so sore, I can hardly walk," Lizzy said days later. She had been practicing for the wedding show in Chicago. "Not only that, but all my timing feels off."

Ella shrugged. "You looked good. I couldn't

tell it from down here." She smiled up at Lizzy, who still sat atop Longfellow.

"Well, he certainly notices it." She patted the neck of the dappled buckskin. "I hope I can figure out what's got me off-center before Chicago. The tricks I've done at the other shows have been all right but certainly not at the level folks are used to seeing from me. I just feel fat and amateurish in every move."

"Well, you're not. You're the belle of the ball," Ella said, her voice full of admiration. "I've heard people talking, and they're in awe of you. Now stop worrying."

"I'll try. I'm sure fretting isn't helping my timing any."

"Exactly. Oh, by the way, you have to stop by the costume car and see what Mara's created for Mary. It's so beautiful. I hope she'll wear it often. The white skirt and vest are fringed, and Mara added silver buttons and red cording. It will look perfect with Mary's red hat."

"So she still plans to wear it for the wedding? No veil?"

"Yes. She said she feels the public will expect it. I think she'll look wonderful. It's not your average bridal ensemble, but Mary will look just right."

Lizzy smiled. "I'm sure she will." She looked over her shoulder at the practice area.

"I'd better get back to work. I've got to have this right before Saturday."

She needn't have worried. Saturday night arrived, and Lizzy performed better than ever. She thrilled the crowds with her dangerous drags and rapid series of tricks. By the time she finished, everyone was on their feet, cheering and calling out for an encore.

Then the wedding was announced, and the audience clapped and cheered even more. Lizzy hurried backstage to change into the attendant outfit Mara had made. It matched Ella's, with its dark blue split skirt and lacy white blouse that was long-sleeved and trimmed in ruffles. Mara had trimmed the waistband with silver medallions, and Lizzy thought it looked very smart.

She couldn't help but pine for Wes. He still hadn't written—not in all these weeks—and it hurt her to think he might not care. She had been so contentious when he'd left that she wondered if she'd driven him away forever. Maybe Phillip was just an excuse to be rid of her. Then again, Wes had gone to the one place he could be assured she would return. Lizzy had asked her mother about Wes, but even she had been silent. Lizzy had thought surely Mother would have sent a letter by now.

"It's not like they don't know the schedule," she muttered.

A melancholy settled over her. Her father came to mind. How she missed him. It was at times like these that he always had the best advice. She could almost hear him now.

"Don't fret about what you can't change, Lizzy darlin'. Think about the things you can change—the ones that really and truly matter— and give them to God. He'll show you what to do and when. He never fails to show us when we are willing to wait upon Him and listen."

She smiled to herself. "I will do that, Papa. I wish you were here, though. How I long to hear your voice and see your smiling face." She sighed. "How I miss you." She fought back tears. "Why did you have to leave me?"

"Lizzy, you ready?" Ella asked from the door to the dressing room. "Everyone's waiting, and the orchestra is about to start the wedding march."

"I'm coming." Lizzy grabbed her hat and secured it atop her head. She gave Ella a smile. "Let's go. I wouldn't want to hold up the wedding."

Lizzy went through the paces of the staged wedding, but as the event concluded, she felt only relief that she could soon disappear into her bedroom on the train and close the door to the rest of the world. She was more tired than she'd ever been, as well as sad. She could see the joy of Mary and Chris and knew that their marriage was on good footing, but her own seemed so questionable, and it hurt to watch others in their happiness.

When she was finally free to slip away, she gave Abe her horse. "If anyone asks about me, tell them I went back to the train. I'm not feeling all that well."

Abe frowned. "You want me to walk back with you, Miz Lizzy?"

"No. I'll get a hired cab. Don't worry about me."

She hurried to gather her things before anyone could stop her. Her emotions were all topsy-turvy, and she was certain she was on the verge of a long cry. Maybe it was time to go home. The show was nearly done performing in America. They would soon head to New York, where they'd give one final performance before heading to Europe. It was possible that she and Uncle Oliver could make their way to Montana now.

"Mind if I head back with you?"

She turned to find Uncle Oliver in the doorway of her dressing room. "Of course not. I would be glad for the company. How did you know?"

He shrugged. "I just figured you might be feeling as displaced as me."

"You didn't show that tonight when you were making announcements. In fact, I was impressed. The audience was too."

"The joy's gone from it," he said, shaking his head. "Everything's different now."

"Well, not everything." She picked up her suitcase and headed for the door, pausing just long enough to link her arm with his. "But I do understand what you're saying. A lot has changed."

"I miss your father."

"I do too," Lizzy said as they made their way outside. "In fact, I was just thinking of him earlier this evening. I long to sit and listen to his stories and advice. I don't suppose you'd like to offer me some."

There were several carriages for hire already waiting to take folks home from the performance. Lizzy got one of the drivers' attention, and they were soon on their way back to the station.

"You want advice from me?" Oliver half asked, half commented. "I'm surely not the man for that. I think I've lived too long. I'm not meant for the twentieth century. I'm too old-fashioned in my thinking. Henry has all these wild ideas and new plans for the show. Me, I'd just as soon see things go back to the way they were and keep things small."

"It was nice that way. We were more of

a family. But we'll always have each other, Uncle Oliver. No matter who else claims to love us—we know that our love is true. Family will always mean a great deal to me." She squeezed his hand.

"I agree," he replied. "I don't understand how I managed to get myself off track, but I think I'm going to be all right. I know you've been worried about me drinking, but I don't have that desire . . . this time."

"I did fear losing Amanda would make you lean in that direction," Lizzy admitted. "I'm glad to hear otherwise. You're so important to me and Mother. I don't want to lose you. You may think you don't belong in this century, but we need you. I know the ranch has never been your favorite place, but it is home, and it wouldn't be the same without you there."

He patted her knee. "Thank you. I suppose I need to focus on what's important. Your father would tell me to give it over to the Lord and wait for His direction."

Lizzy nodded. "That was exactly what I was remembering earlier this evening. So maybe that's confirmation to us both. We need to pray and then wait on the Lord."

The carriage halted, and soon the driver was opening the door. Uncle Oliver paid him and took Lizzy's suitcase from her. They made their way to the family car and climbed aboard. Oliver set the case down by Lizzy's bedroom door and covered a yawn.

"I'm heading to bed."

"Me too." She kissed his weathered cheek. "I love you, Uncle Oliver. Please always know that."

He smiled. "I do. I know that as well as I know Wesley loves you."

She frowned. How did he know she'd been concerned about that?

Oliver laughed. "I can see my comment surprises you, but I realize just how hard it's been on you not to have him here. I've seen you waiting for the mail and then walking away discouraged when nothing has come. Don't fret. Phillip's needs are no doubt quite a lot these days. It's a terrible thing to quit alcohol. You feel at times like you're going to die. Pray for them. Pray for them both. It's not an easy situation no matter how determined they are."

"I'm afraid I've been rather selfish in my thinking. It's hard, though. Wes and I didn't part company under the best circumstances. I was pretty upset with him."

Uncle Oliver touched her cheek. "Wes is a good man. He knows that you love him, and in time things will smooth out. In a few weeks we'll be home, and everything will be as it should be."

"I was going to talk to you about that. Maybe we could just leave from here and forget New York." She watched her uncle for any sign of approval.

He seemed to consider it for a long moment and then shook his head. "We've made a commitment, and the show must go on. It won't take much longer to see it through. We'll be in New York in a few days, and then the performance will be over before you know it."

"I'm not thrilled to return to the place where Jason tried to kidnap me. What if he's gotten away from the sanatorium and plans to come find me? What if he tries it again?"

Uncle Oliver shook his head. "You aren't really worried about that, are you?"

She felt as if he could see right through her. "No. I'm just tired and I miss my husband."

"Absence is good—once in a while. It makes folks appreciate what they have. Just bide your time, Lizzy. The show must go on and you must go on too, as must I."

He left her for his own bedroom. Lizzy found his words comforting. Her father had always said that seeing her commitments through to the finish was one of the most important things she could do in life. It built a reputation of trust, and if a person couldn't be true to the smaller commitments of life, how could they be trusted with the more important ones?

She sighed and leaned back against the paneled wall. She would see it through. The performance *and* her marriage. With God's help, she would carry on.

⊶⊱ FIFTEEN ⊰⊷

Phillip marked an X through the calendar. He'd gone another day without liquor. It hadn't been easy, especially when most of the ranch hands were heading to town for their regular Saturday night celebration. He had once been a part of that group, enjoying a few drinks and card games. He'd been one of the boys, but now, since giving up alcohol, he found himself strangely alone. What was a fella supposed to do for fun when having a drink couldn't be a part of it? The other hands knew the situation, and while they maintained a certain degree of friendliness, there was an awkwardness now that strained their conversations.

"Mrs. Brookstone invited us to join her for dinner," Wes announced, coming into the otherwise empty bunkhouse. He'd already washed up and changed into another shirt and looked a whole lot cleaner than Phillip. "Everybody else go to town?"

"Yeah." Phillip untied the kerchief he wore. "They left about fifteen minutes ago."

"It's just as well. They'd be jealous of us getting to eat Mrs. Brookstone's cooking."

Phillip glanced in Wesley's direction. "You go ahead. It'll take too long for me to get presentable."

"That won't work. Mrs. Brookstone said she wouldn't take no for an answer, so I'd just go ahead and get changed if I were you. You'll learn soon enough that Rebecca Brookstone usually gets her way."

Phillip could see Wes wasn't joking. "All right." He went to his trunk and pulled out a clean shirt. "I don't feel much like socializing."

"It's not like anyone expects you to entertain them. Mrs. Brookstone will just feed us some of her home cooking and bemoan the fact that Lizzy and Oliver aren't home yet. It's as much for her sake as ours. She misses her family, and she's lonely. The least we can do is give her some company."

When Wes put it that way, how could Phillip possibly refuse? After all, Rebecca Brookstone had been very good to him.

He pulled off his dusty shirt and went to the washbasin. The water in the pitcher was cold, so he took a dipper of water from the pot that always hung in the fireplace. After mixing it with the cold water, Phillip used the soap and a clean cloth to wash away the day's dirt. With that done, he donned the clean shirt and slicked his hair down before presenting himself to Wes. "Will this do, or should I change my pants?"

Wes nodded. "You look just fine. Come on, we don't want to keep her waiting."

Phillip nodded and followed his big brother toward the log house. "Weather's been mighty fine. I figure this is just about the best time of year."

"It has been nice," Wes agreed. "Be nicer once Lizzy and Oliver are back."

"It won't be much longer now." Phillip wished Ella were coming back with them, but he knew she was bound for Europe with the rest of the troupe.

They entered through the back door, which opened into a large mud porch, the walls lined with shelves and supplies. From there they stepped into the kitchen, where Mrs. Brookstone was standing at the stove.

She glanced over her shoulder. "You boys are just in time. I took the biscuits out of the oven a minute ago, and now I'm pulling the chicken from the skillet. Go take a seat, and we'll eat as soon as I finish here."

"Do you need any help?" Wes asked.

"No, I've got everything where I want it."

Mrs. B, as most of the hands called her, had set a very intimate table for three. She had positioned herself at the end with Wes and Phillip on either side of her. Phillip took his seat, but no sooner had he claimed the chair than he popped back up when Rebecca Brookstone entered the dining room with a large platter of chicken and biscuits.

"Sit, boys. We aren't going to be fussy around here." She placed the platter on the table and took her chair. Wes helped her, then took his own seat. Phillip was the last to join them at the table.

"Wes, will you say grace?" she asked.

"Of course." Wes bowed his head, and Phillip did likewise. "For what we are about to receive, make us truly grateful, Lord. Be with us here and with those far away and make us mindful of Your blessings. In Jesus' name, amen."

"Amen," Phillip murmured.

Mrs. B motioned for him to help himself. "There's potatoes and gravy, green beans, and of course the chicken and biscuits." She scooped up some of the beans for herself before handing the bowl to Phillip.

The meal was delicious, just as Phillip knew it would be. It wasn't the first time he'd enjoyed Mrs. B's cooking. Even so, he'd have preferred to be left to himself in the bunkhouse. He felt awkward sitting in his employer's house, sharing a conversation as if they were on equal footing.

"Phillip, you're as skinny as a rail. You need to eat more," she said.

He smiled. "Ma used to tell me the same thing, but I eat plenty. I guess I just work it off as fast as I put it in."

Mrs. Brookstone nodded. "I suppose you do. I've watched you out there working with the horses. You definitely use every muscle in your body just to stay in the saddle."

"That's a fact," he said, reaching for another piece of chicken.

"I had a telegraph from Oliver," she said unexpectedly. "The troupe is in New York, preparing for their departure to England."

"Why is Oliver in New York?" Wes asked. "Last I heard, I thought he and Lizzy were heading back after Chicago."

She gave him a sympathetic smile. "Henry begged Lizzy and Oliver to come to New York to close out the season there."

"Sounds like him. He won't be happy until he's worn everyone out completely," Wes muttered, shaking his head.

"Yes, well, apparently no one seemed to mind too much. I wasn't sure if you knew, but Lizzy is performing."

"What?" Wesley's expression turned dark. "Since when?"

"I'm not entirely sure, but Oliver mentioned her riding in the New York performance."

The news seemed to rob Wes of further appetite. "I thought we were finished with that." He pushed his plate away, but to Phillip's surprise, Rebecca Brookstone pushed it right back.

"Don't make this more than it needs to be. Eat your meal. Lizzy's a grown woman, and she knows what she's doing. It must have been important for her to agree to it." She didn't wait for Wes to reply but turned to Phillip. "I wanted to have you here tonight so I could see for myself how you were doing."

"I'm doing pretty good." Phillip gave a smile. He knew he could be charming when he needed to be. "I try to just take each day as it comes."

"That's always best. After all, we can hardly manage what hasn't yet come. Each day has enough trouble of its own."

"You can say that again," Wes muttered as he picked at his food.

Rebecca gave him a brief glance, then

turned back to Phillip. "I hope you know that I am proud of your endeavors. I know this hasn't been easy. I watched my brother-in-law struggle through the same thing. Alcohol is a difficult thing to put aside, but with the support of loved ones and prayer, coupled with your own determination, you can overcome. In fact, you are overcoming. I just want to encourage you."

Phillip was touched by her words. "Thanks, Mrs. Brookstone. It makes things kind of awkward with the boys, but I'll get by."

"Awkward in what way?"

He smiled at her and wished he'd kept his thoughts to himself. "Well, it's just that they want to go celebrate at the end of the work-week, and I don't feel like I can join them. I'm not strong enough to sit in the bar and not drink."

She considered this. "I can see why that would be a problem. I suppose all of the men are given to drinking?" She posed this question to Wes.

He nodded. "For the most part, yes. The ones who aren't big on it go along, but the temptation isn't the same for them as it is for Phillip."

She nodded. "I completely understand. Phillip, from now on, every Saturday night, you shall come here and be a part of our family activities until you feel strong enough to join your friends and not be tempted to drink. Wesley is family now, and that makes you family as well."

Phillip was touched by her generous offer. "Thank you, ma'am. I've never worked for anyone quite like you."

She smiled. "I'll take that as a compliment."

"Absolutely," he declared, a little flustered. "I meant it that way. You're a fine boss, and this ranch is the best I've ever worked for."

"Your brother tells me you've worked all over the country. Is that true?"

Phillip nodded. "I have. Been all over the West and into Texas. Never worked east of the Mississippi, though. Except with the show."

"Do you enjoy the ranch more than the show?" she asked.

He shook his head. "Not exactly. I enjoy the show because of who else is there. Otherwise, I might prefer the ranch. I think I've had enough movin' from place to place."

Rebecca Brookstone laughed. "Yes, I can well imagine. And I know from having watched you and Ella that you're rather sweet on each other."

"I asked her to wait for me." Phillip hadn't meant to blurt it out like that.

Mrs. B smiled. "You did? That's wonderful. What did she say?"

Phillip toyed with his fork. "She said yes. I told . . . well, it wasn't a proposal. I couldn't propose until I . . . knew whether or not I could master my love of alcohol. I didn't figure I'd be much good to her if I couldn't overcome drinking."

"That was very wise. I'm glad you were able to see things clearly in that way. It's never wise to move forward in marriage with something so daunting hanging over your head."

"That's how I figure it." He looked across the table at his brother. "I couldn't have done it without Wes, though. He's been there for me all along. I know it hasn't been easy for him either, what with me taking him away from Lizzy. I hated that I made her cry."

"It wasn't your fault," Wes said gruffly. "She was crying or angry most of the time. I've never seen Lizzy like that. She's usually so even-tempered. I don't think the show was suiting her, and she was all worried about Oliver and that Amanda Moore woman."

"Well, it sounds like Amanda is no longer a problem, from what Lizzy said in her letter. I suppose we should be grateful for that." Rebecca got up and motioned for Phillip and Wes to stay seated. "Are either of you up for some peach cobbler?"

Phillip grinned. "You bet."

They finished the dinner with dessert. Phillip had two helpings, then figured it was time to excuse himself for the evening. Wes, however, volunteered them to do the dishes.

"You wash," he said, pushing Phillip toward the sink.

Phillip rolled up his sleeves and got to work. He wished he could offer his big brother some sort of solace, but he didn't know what to say. Sometimes it was just best to be quiet.

"You go on back to the bunkhouse," Wes finally told him. "I'll finish up here. I need to talk to Rebecca before I head to bed."

Phillip rinsed the plate he held. "This is the last of them anyway." He handed the wet dish to Wes, then reached for a dry towel. "I guess I'll see you in the morning for church."

Wes waited until Phillip was out of the house before seeking out Rebecca. She had asked him to see her before he headed to bed. He found her in the living room, knitting.

"You wanted to see me?"

Rebecca looked up and smiled. "Yes. Come sit with me a minute. This talk is long overdue."

He wasn't sure what she had in mind, but

he did as she asked and pulled up the rocking chair.

He watched her finish her line of knitting, then put aside the yarn and needles to give him her full attention.

"I'd like to ask you to consider something. I didn't ask you before now because I wanted you and Lizzy to have some privacy in your first few months of marriage, but now that you've been together awhile and are about to reach your first anniversary, I'd like to pose a request."

"Of course, whatever you need."

"I wonder if you and Lizzy would agree to move into the house. It's such a big house, and you are family. I think it would be nice to have us all together here."

Wes had never given that possibility a thought. "I don't know. I've never talked to Lizzy about it. Do you suppose she'd like that?"

"I think she might. Especially now."

"Why especially now?"

Rebecca smiled. "Because given what you said this evening about her being angry one minute and crying the next, I suspect she may very well be with child."

Wes was glad he was sitting, because otherwise he might have fallen to the floor in shock. "A baby? You think that's what's going on with her?"

"I do. I was the same way. Just a mess."

Wes shook his head. "She never said anything about a baby."

"She probably doesn't know. And I could be wrong, but if I'm right, I'd love for you to move in here and let me help. A grandchild is something I've long looked forward to."

Wes could hardly think clearly. He had never supposed Lizzy might be pregnant. It was almost more than he could comprehend. Then a terrible thought crossed his mind: She was performing.

"What if she is . . . with child? She's out there performing. That'll risk the baby's life and hers." He felt a sudden chill. "I should bring her home. I should go now."

"Wes, she'll be home shortly. By the time you were able to reach her, she'd already be headed for home."

"I should at least telegraph her and tell her not to perform."

Again, Rebecca shook her head. "You aren't going to stop her, and you know that. Don't create more problems for yourself. Pray for her instead and give her to God. Then, while you wait for her return, move yourself into the house. You can have an entire wing to yourself, if you like. We can even redo the rooms to suit you and Lizzy."

He couldn't shake his feeling of dread, but

he knew she was right. He was helpless to stop Lizzy from performing. She'd already been performing in his absence, and if something was going to happen, it might have already happened. He clenched his hands in frustration. If only he'd been able to stay with her.

If only.

~✦= SIXTEEN =✦~

Ella received a note from her brother the same day the troupe arrived in New York City. Robert informed her that he was in town with their father and mother, and he wanted Ella to join them. He assured her Jefferson Spiby was not in attendance, but it still unnerved Ella to think that the last time she'd seen her father, he had been in strong support of that man.

"He says I may bring along anyone that I deem necessary for my protection," Ella told Mary and Lizzy. "And the meeting place is the Waldorf-Astoria."

"Right next door. That's convenient," Mary replied. "Chris and I would be happy to escort you. It's hardly proper for a young lady to go to a hotel by herself."

"I can come too," Lizzy declared, "but Chris and Mary are a much better choice."

"You could take Abe with you as well," Mara said. She was never shy about sharing her opinion these days, now that she realized the troupe considered her an equal. "I'm sure he'd be willin' to go." She paused and frowned. "'Ceptin' I don't know if they allow black folks in the Waldorf."

Ella nodded. "Thank you, all of you. I can't imagine what my family will do or say. I have no idea if Robert has explained what he knows to our father. The entire matter is overwhelming."

Lizzy put her arm around Ella's shoulders. "Don't fret. We won't allow anything to happen to you. Henry Adler would never let anyone take you from the show." She smiled. "You're far too popular. Those huge mail sacks full of letters to you are proof of that."

Ella gave a weak laugh. "I am so grateful for your friendship. All of you. This hasn't been an easy time for any of us, and now that we know the part my family played in August's death and the misery of so many people of color, I know I must see it through. I'm just afraid."

"We will be with you every step of the way," Mary encouraged. "You can count on that. I won't let anyone hurt you, even if I have to come fully armed."

Ella smiled. "I can just see you having an old west shootout in the middle of Fifth Avenue."

Mary grinned. "Well, why not? I could always tell the arresting officer that I was trying to drum up business for the show."

They all chuckled at this, and Ella found it relieved a bit of the tension. Of course, two hours later, as she made her way to the Waldorf with Mary and Christopher, that tension had returned in droves.

A clean-shaven bellman showed them to a room where large fireplaces were lit with welcoming fires. Ella spied her family in a far corner, completely isolated from the other guests.

She drew in a deep breath and glanced at Mary, who reached over and squeezed her hand.

"It will be all right," Mary whispered. "Don't show them any fear."

Ella tried to imagine the situation was nothing more than performing in one of the many Brookstone shows. She squared her shoulders and lifted her chin. Whispering one final prayer, she followed the bellman.

Robert saw her first and jumped to his feet. "Ah, here's our Ella."

Ella caught her father's glance and found she couldn't look away. He seemed to have aged twenty years since she'd last seen him and lost twice as many pounds. Her mother remained seated, but her expression betrayed her joy in seeing Ella after all this time.

"Oh, my sweet daughter. Come sit beside me." Mother held out her arms, and Ella went to her.

It was so good to see her mother again. Ella had missed her despite their not being all that close. Mother was reserved and kept her thoughts and feelings to herself, just as she had been taught. Still, Ella knew that she loved her children.

"Mama, it's so good to see you." Ella sat beside her mother and hugged her close.

"I feared I might never see you again, and when Robert suggested we could meet with you here in New York, I was so excited. And you know how I hate travel."

"I'm glad you made the trip, Mama." Ella glanced up at her father and forced a smile. "I'm glad you both came to see me. Will you be able to make our show?"

"It's doubtful," Robert said. "I've brought Father here to see a friend of mine. He's a lawyer who I believe can advise us."

"It's all a great mystery," Mother confided to Ella.

"You haven't explained to Mother why you need a lawyer?" Ella asked, noting her brother's grim expression.

She looked out across the splendor of the grand room, grateful that the other patrons seemed to respect her family's need for privacy. Had Robert truly avoided explaining the purpose of their trip?

Ella's father took up the explanation. "I deemed it better to wait. Your mother has never been a part of the business affairs at Fleming Farm. I never saw fit to tell her—especially about the matter that has brought us here."

Mother frowned. "Goodness, George, just tell me what's going on."

"I think it might be better if we adjourned to our suite. Would that be all right with you, Ella? You may bring your friends, of course."

Ella stiffened. If there was a possibility of someone causing her harm, it would be in the privacy of the hotel's rooms rather than here in the public eye.

Robert seemed to understand her apprehension and knelt down beside her. "I promise that no harm will come to you. Jefferson isn't here, and I won't allow anything to complicate our meeting."

She nodded. "Very well. Lead the way."

They quickly settled in the sitting room

of her parents' suite some nine stories in the air. Ella marveled at the view and swallowed the lump in her throat. She had prayed for strength to see this matter through and to support Robert as he explained to their mother what the secrecy was all about.

Mary and Chris had chosen chairs in the corner of the room to allow Robert and Ella a little confidentiality with their parents.

Robert took the lead and began a concise explanation of why he had arranged for their father to see an attorney. Mother paled as the truth was revealed. She grew teary when Robert gave her the briefest of details regarding August's death.

She looked at her husband as if seeing a stranger. "How could this be?" she asked. "How could you do such things?"

George Fleming shook his head. His remorse was clear. "It was an association I inherited from my father. I did my best to convince myself that it was something of a service that helped more than harmed, that I was employing people and caring for their needs. I suppose that's how I assuaged my conscience."

"But you know how I detest all that the war cost us. I lost so many people I cared about. It's as if you perpetuated it with this abominable act."

"As I said, Beatrix, I felt I had no choice.

My father had already established the business, and he expected me to do my part when I came of age." Ella's father shook his head. "I'm not proud by any means, but as time went by, I found myself more and more dependent upon the money I made. Our farm didn't generate enough for all that we spent. Had it not been for this peculiar arrangement, we might have lost the farm and all the comforts we had come to count on."

"It would have been better than forcing poor black people to sign away their lives," Ella murmured. "Or killing innocent young men who just happened into the wrong place at the wrong time."

She heard Mary sob and turned to see Chris had pulled her close while she cried. The sound of her heartbreak caused Ella's mother to weep. No one else spoke for several long seconds.

Finally, Robert took charge once again. "The situation is unpleasant, to be sure, but now we've come to the point where we hope to make matters right. Mother, I know this is difficult for you, but Father assures me he is ready to face whatever justice is required. It's important that he go of his own accord and declare his guilt, because then there may be leniency. But even if there is not, we cannot go on as if nothing has ever happened."

"What will happen to us?" Mama said, sniffing and dabbing her face.

"You will always have a home with Virginia and me," Robert declared, "no matter what punishment they require of Father. Virginia wanted me to make it clear that you will be welcome to live with us for as long as you need."

Ella felt sorry for her mother. Hers had been a world of beauty and elegance. She had only known the duty to stand as silent support to her husband and to mother her children, and where the latter was concerned, she'd had the help of others. Now her world was slowly crumbling, and Ella knew it had to be terrifying.

"When do you and Father go to see your friend?" Ella asked Robert.

He checked the time. "In an hour. Can you stay with Mother while we're gone?"

Ella thought of how much she'd prefer to wash her hands of the entire matter, but she nodded. "I'll stay with her." She looked over to where Mary and Chris sat. "You can go back. I'll be fine. I'll stay here, and then Robert can escort me to my room when he returns from his appointment."

"Are you sure that's wise?" Chris asked.

"I assure you that Jefferson has no idea we're here. As far as I know, he's not even in

Kentucky but rather New Orleans," Robert replied. "He has no idea my father has left the farm, so there is no risk of him taking any sort of action." He looked at Ella. "I promise you—you're safe."

She nodded. "Then go to your meeting, and I'll be here with Mother, anxious to hear what you learn."

———— ❖◦❉◦❖ ————

The hours went by slowly as Ella and her mother waited for Robert and Father to return. Ella managed to keep her mother talking about mundane things in order to prevent her from fretting.

"Did Mrs. Solomon have her annual summer picnic?" Ella asked.

Mother perked up at this. "Oh yes, and to my surprise, your father actually wanted to attend. You should have seen the turnout. The Merton sisters even came this year."

Ella fondly remembered the two elderly Merton sisters, who very rarely ventured out of their three-story Queen Anne home. They lived in the center of town and were old enough to have watched the town grow up around them.

"Mrs. Bouton had a garden party in June that they also managed to come to. I was truly surprised to see them make two events in one year."

Having paced for the last thirty minutes, Ella finally took a chair opposite her mother. "May I talk to you about something else?"

Her mother smiled. "You should know by now that you may speak to me about anything."

"I'm in love."

Mother's eyes widened in surprise. "In love?"

Ella nodded. "With a young man who worked for the show. Well, actually he started out at the Brookstone ranch. He breaks wild horses and does other work but also helped with the horses in the show."

"I see. And you met him at the ranch?" her mother asked.

"Yes. He was there when I arrived, and he was always very kind. He has such a gentle nature."

Her mother smoothed her skirt. "Will we get a chance to meet him while we're in New York?"

"No, I'm afraid not. Phillip is in Montana. He left the show a few weeks ago and went back to the ranch." Ella bit her lip.

"What has you worrying your lip?" her mother asked, smiling. "You've always had that habit, no matter how hard we tried to break you of it."

Ella smiled. She had no idea her mother knew her well enough to know about her bad habit. "I remember Lucille chiding me about it. She said it would ruin my mouth."

"I'm sure she did." Mother shook her head. "Still, there's a reason for it, so tell me what has you troubled."

"You must promise not to be too critical of Phillip."

Her mother frowned. "Do you think me overly critical?"

"There have been times that I felt . . . well, certain issues always seemed to bring out your disdain in a way that belittled others. I don't want you to belittle Phillip, because he's had a very difficult life and is working hard to overcome his mistakes."

Mother gave a slight nod as she looked down at the floor. "I suppose that judgment of me is well earned. I never thought of myself as being harsh and severe in my thoughts, just pointing out the truth. But rest assured I will endeavor to think kindly of your Phillip."

Ella knew the truth had hurt her mother, but rather than stop and apologize, she continued. "He has a problem with alcohol. That's why he went back to the ranch. He and his brother left the show so that Phillip could stop drinking." She braved a glance at her mother, who was now watching her intently.

"It's a hard habit to break. Much harder than biting your lip."

"I've heard very little from him, and I'm worried about him. I know I can never be anything more than a friend who loves him from afar unless he's able to stop drinking. I've helped him on several occasions when he was drunk, and I know that's no life for me."

"No. It would be a disaster. I speak from a certain understanding. You see, my father imbibed quite regularly. It was always a grave concern to my mother."

Ella stilled. "I didn't know."

"No. I never wanted you to. My father died young, although I don't know for sure that alcohol caused it. The doctor said it was his heart. Nevertheless, I remember my mother suffering greatly because of his drinking."

"Grandfather was cruel to her?"

"No," her mother said, shaking her head. "He was the most loving of drunks. I doubt there was a harsh word ever said when he was under the influence of the bottle." She paused a moment and grew thoughtful. "Sadly, I thought him far more pleasant to be around when he'd been drinking. He would play games with me and my siblings and tell us such stories. No, my mother suffered because of the judgment of others. Her church friends were vocal, as were others.

She never felt she could attend parties without having to explain why things were as they were. Finally, she gave up social outings unless they were absolutely necessary. She told her friends her health was compromised, and indeed she had a delicate constitution that often left her fatigued."

Mother took Ella's hand. "I only tell you as a cautionary note. Alcohol can tear at a family in many ways. Perhaps if I'd been honest with you sooner, you wouldn't have given your heart to this young man."

"You don't have to be afraid, Mother. I won't marry him unless he is able to prove himself. And I don't think he would ask to marry me unless he was able to overcome. It was, after all, his idea to quit. He knew how I felt about it, to be sure, but he finally saw some value in himself. His brother helped him better understand God's love for him. I'd like to think I helped him in that as well."

"You speak with a great deal of sense. I'm so proud of you. I can't say that I understand your desire to perform in public, but perhaps my past is part of the reason I disdain attention. If you are happy, then I am determined to be happy for you."

Ella hugged her mother close. It was so wonderful to have this moment—to share these thoughts and feelings. All her life she had turned to Lucille and Mara while her mother acted as hostess for Fleming Farm. There never seemed time for intimacy except in the most extreme of moments. She would cherish this time with Mama for the rest of her life.

The door to the suite opened without warning, and Robert and Father entered. Robert looked grave, and Father walked as if he had the weight of the world on his shoulders.

"How did your meeting go?" Ella asked, jumping up. "What will happen now?"

"There's no real way of knowing until we bring it to the attention of the authorities. However, that's what we plan to do in the next few days. My friend will accompany us to Washington, D.C., where we will speak with another good friend. Both will act as legal counsel and represent Father. It's our hope that we can arrange for the truth to be told at that level so the authorities who have covered up this egregious sin won't have a chance to hide the proof. Father will share what he knows and his part in it, and with his help, Jefferson will pay for the murder of August Reichert."

"And the people they enslaved?" Ella could barely pose the question.

"Yes," her brother replied. "And them."

"And will you have to go to prison, George?" Ella's mother asked.

"It is difficult to know." Father helped Mama to her feet. "But no matter what happens, it is the right thing to do."

Ella went to her brother. "Thank you for what you've done. I know this hasn't been easy."

"No. It hasn't, but as Father said, it is the right thing to do."

Ella turned back to face her father. "I am grateful."

"And I am sorry. So very sorry for ever trying to force you to marry Jefferson. He had me cornered against my will in all of this, and I couldn't refuse him. The welfare of my family and finances were so intricately entangled with his. He will stop at nothing to get what he wants, as you unfortunately have witnessed. I still do not trust him to refrain from hurting you, which is one of the reasons I agreed to do this." He heaved a sigh. "Besides, it's taken its toll on me, and I fear I can't go on much longer."

Mama took his arm. "Don't say that, George. Things will be better now that the truth is coming to light. You'll see."

Father reached inside his coat and pulled out some folded papers. He handed them to Ella. "These are Mara's. You'll see they are marked *Paid in Full* and she is free."

Ella clutched them to her breast. "Thank

you, Father. I know it will mean the world to her, because it means the world to me. I hope you will set the others free as well."

"I have already seen to it, with Robert's help. We may well end up losing everything, but I will die with a clear conscience, having made a decisive attempt to right the wrongs I've committed."

❖❖ SEVENTEEN ❖❖

Now direct your attention to this death-defying trick," Oliver Brookstone announced as Lizzy prepared for her final run. She adjusted one of the saddle belts that had been added for her stunts and secured her foot.

She had been practicing the trick for weeks, but there were still problems. She considered just forgetting about it and doing something that she felt more secure in, but she hated to disappoint. She whispered a prayer, chided herself for her fears, and then put Longfellow into a gallop.

Things went well at first, but then just as she began the most difficult part of the maneuver, the strap that held her foot loosened, and Lizzy slipped. She knew she was falling and heard the screams of several viewers.

Only this time the danger was more real than they knew.

Lizzy stretched to grab the saddle or Longfellow's mane, but her hand met only empty air. She saw the sleek body of the horse move past her as she went down head first, and then everything went black.

———◆◆◆———

"Lizzy. Lizzy, please wake up."

She heard the voice as if it were coming from far away. The voice was familiar, yet she couldn't clear the fog in her head. Nor could she seem to open her eyes. What was going on? What was wrong with her?

"Please come back to us, Lizzy," the voice said. "I can't bear the idea of losing you, and I could never hope to explain it to your husband and mother."

This time the familiarity was strong enough that Lizzy realized the voice belonged to Uncle Oliver. She couldn't understand his desperation, but she concentrated as hard as she could and forced her eyes to open. At first things refused to focus, but she blinked a few times, and the room started to right itself.

Oliver came into view. "Oh, thank God!" He hugged Lizzy tight. "I was so afraid."

"What . . . happened?"

The last thing she remembered, she'd

been performing. Now, as she looked around, it appeared she was in a hospital bed.

"You took a bad fall. The strap broke, and you lost your hold," Uncle Oliver explained. "You fell on your head. The doctor said you have a concussion." He patted her hand. "You scared at least twenty years off me."

She closed her eyes again. "I fell?" She tried to remember. *I was performing, but no . . . I quit.* She shook her head and opened her eyes. "It's all scrambled in my memory."

"Never fear, my dear. It will all come back in time. I've had a concussion on several occasions," Uncle Oliver assured her. "It tends to give you a headache and cause some confusion for a while, but it passes."

"I'm so sorry, Uncle Oliver." Lizzy struggled to sit up, but Oliver pushed her back down.

"Doctor's orders. You're to stay flat in bed for the next twenty-four hours."

"But why?"

He smiled. "Well, for a couple of very good reasons. One is your health. You need time to heal."

"And the other?"

"The health and well-being of your unborn baby."

Lizzy's eyes widened at her uncle's amused expression. "Baby? I'm going to have a baby?"

"Yes."

She thought of Wes's protests and fears regarding her performing. She put her hand to her abdomen. "Is the baby . . . all right?" There was a catch in her throat.

Oliver nodded. "The doctor says the baby is just fine. No sign of any problems. You mustn't fret." His smile broadened. "I'm surprised you didn't know."

"I had no idea. I mean, Wes and I hoped to have children right away, but no, I didn't know." She remembered something her mother had said about her months carrying Lizzy. "It certainly explains a great deal of my moodiness. I felt like crying one minute and yelling the next. I thought I was losing my mind. Not only that, but I was getting so thick-waisted. I had to have Mara let out the band on my skirt."

"Well, if your mother had been with us, she could have explained. She probably would have known right away what was going on."

Lizzy relaxed and shook her head in wonder. "A baby. I can scarcely believe it. Oh, I wish Wes were here with us."

"I do too, but you know the next best thing is that you and I make our way home. As soon as the doctor clears you to travel, I intend to see to it. I've already told Henry."

She frowned. "You didn't tell him about

the baby, did you? I mean, Wes really should hear it before everyone else."

"No, I didn't mention it. I felt exactly the same. This is news that the papa deserves to hear before the world. I just told him that the doctor felt you should go home and rest, and he agreed. He felt horrible about you getting hurt. In fact, that huge bouquet of flowers by the window is from him. You should have seen the argument that ensued between the delivery boy and nurse. The nurse thought the bouquet was a menace and didn't want to let him leave it."

Lizzy glanced past her uncle at a massive bouquet of pale pink roses. The roses were mingled with an arrangement of sweet peas, baby's breath, and other delicate blossoms. "It's beautiful."

"You know Henry. Money is no object. Anyway, there are some others who've been quite worried about you. Mary and Ella have refused to leave the hospital until they know you've regained consciousness, and Henry is beside himself, because the troupe is scheduled to leave tomorrow for England."

"By all means, assure everyone that I'm fine. But say nothing of the baby." Lizzy smiled. "I still can hardly believe it." She looked at her exhausted uncle. "I hope you know that we'll need you now more than ever."

His bushy eyebrows came together as he frowned. "Why would you need me?"

"Because someone has to take on the role of grandfather. You'll be the closest thing we have, and I know you'll do a better job of it than anyone else. The boys at the ranch will try to fill in and do what they can, but you're family. You're the one who can tell this baby stories about the old days, about the move to Montana, and all about my father."

Oliver took her hand. "I'll do whatever I can, Lizzy girl. I haven't been a very good uncle the last couple of years."

"We've had a lot to endure. Losing my father was nearly the undoing of us both." She hated even remembering how hard it had been to accept her father's death. "But God has gotten us through. We've had our ups and downs, but we're family, and as such we are stronger together."

"I agree, and I want to apologize for ever losing sight of that. I'm afraid Amanda completely distracted me from what was important."

"The only thing that matters is that you saw the truth in time. You're going to be all right, Uncle Oliver. We're all going to be just fine. We have to be. This baby is going to need us."

He chuckled. "If this baby is anything like

you, we're going to need all the help we can get."

"I'm so glad you're all right, Lizzy." Ella gave her friend a complete visual examination from head to toe. "Are you sure you're feeling up to the trip home? I'm positive Mr. Adler would put you up in a hotel for a few more days."

"I'm fine." Lizzy was packing the last of her clothes in her trunk. "Uncle Oliver will make certain that I don't overdo it."

"He's been very protective," Mary agreed. She and Ella had come to help Lizzy prepare to leave.

"He finally has a purpose that is worth his effort. I know he's happy to return home, the same as me." Lizzy folded a long wool skirt.

"But I thought he loved the show. You once told me he hated ranch life because he thrilled to the audience's applause," Mary recalled.

"He does." Lizzy looked thoughtful. "But I think he's starting to grow weary of it as well. He knows family is far and away more important, and no matter what happens in life, he knows the value of being there for one another. I don't think the show holds near as much appeal for him now that the family is gone or leaving it for good."

"That makes sense. He thought it was the show, when in fact it was the family. Your family was at the ranch as well, but maybe the busyness just separated rather than pulled everyone together."

Mary's conclusion made sense to Ella, but she was still worried about Lizzy. "I hope you feel better soon. I hate that you were hurt. I thought we'd lost you when you fell and didn't move."

"You know as well as I do that accidents happen, and usually they aren't that severe."

"Severe enough that my father died," Mary reminded them.

"I know." Lizzy gave her a sympathetic nod. "I didn't mean to suggest it doesn't happen, but it is rare. Usually we just end up with bruises or stiff muscles. That's by far the worst accident I've ever had, and it was my own fault. I should have checked the straps." She smiled, hugging the folded skirt to her chest. "Let's change the subject. You two are off for Europe and all the excitement and fun that comes with traveling abroad. Are you looking forward to the journey?"

"I felt so green last time. I pray that won't happen again." Ella glanced around the room to see if Lizzy had forgotten anything. "I'm going to miss you terribly. It won't be the same without you."

"No, it won't," Mary agreed. "I know it's better for you to return home, but I wish you were coming with us. We've become such a close family that I don't know what I'll do without you."

"You'll still have each other," Lizzy pointed out. "You'll be just fine."

"Will you promise to write and tell me how Phillip is doing?" Ella pleaded. "I've had no other word, and I'm so worried about him."

Lizzy put the skirt in the trunk, then took Ella's hands. "Of course. I'll write, and I'll make Phillip write too. I'm sure he's just been very busy. Try not to fret."

Ella nodded. "I keep praying and praying that he'll be able to forget about alcohol."

"Well, he has you to think on, so maybe that will be enough to replace thoughts of drink," Lizzy offered. "I think the love you two share will give you each strength to endure the separation."

"I just care so much about him. I even told my mother that I was in love with him."

"You did?" Mary asked in disbelief. "What did she say? Was she disappointed that you had fallen in love with a lowly cowboy?"

Ella shook her head. "If she was, she didn't tell me. I'm sure she originally had plans for me to marry a man of means, although I know for certain that she never wanted me married to Jefferson. I heard her talk to Father about it once, reminding him that Jefferson was closer to his age than mine. But as an obedient Southern wife, she probably only spoke to him the once."

"I'm sorry that things are about to change so drastically for your family, Ella. But you should know that you will always have a home with us. Don't ever worry about being thrown to the wolves," Lizzy declared. "Mara too."

She added this as the slender black woman entered the room, carrying a stack of blouses.

"These are mended and ready to pack, Miz Lizzy."

Lizzy took the blouses. "Thank you, and I hope you heard what I said. You will always have a home in Montana at the ranch. Don't ever worry. If you need us, you have only to wire us, and we'll do whatever we can to help."

"Thank you, Miz Lizzy. I 'preciate your kindness."

"Well, as I've said before, this troupe is a family. Some of us are closer than others, but the same is true of all families. Some members just work better together than others. Nevertheless, Brookstone's Wild West Extravaganza has always been a family, and I hope it always will be."

"It won't be the same without you and your

uncle," Mary replied, "but we will endeavor to carry on with the heart of your family at the center of all we do." She waited for Lizzy to put the blouses in the trunk, then embraced her friend. "I'm going to miss you."

"You'll be so busy shooting at Chris that you won't give me a second thought. And just think, maybe this time next year, you and Chris will have added to the family."

Mary smiled. "And maybe you and Wes will have as well."

Lizzy blushed and nodded. "I hope so."

The parting was bittersweet, but Ella managed to say her good-byes without tears. She thought for a long time after the ship had sailed and Lizzy and Oliver had taken the train west about how she was embarking on yet another new journey in her life. Her brother and father had returned Mother to Robert's farm in Kentucky and then made their way to Washington, D.C. Her father might well be sent to prison. Meanwhile Ella traveled all over Europe, performing on horseback to the cheers and applause of strangers.

And then there was Phillip. Their separation had given her so much time to think about him and the future. She knew that her girlish attraction and romantic notions weren't enough to make a solid marriage, but she also knew there was more between them. They both loved God and were seeking His direction. They had a lot to learn about each other, but Ella felt confident that they belonged together.

The door to her ship cabin opened, and Jessie entered with Angel Adams close behind. They were Ella's roommates for the trip over.

"Why are you hiding in here?" Jessie asked. "There's an amazing party going on upstairs. You really should come. Henry Adler has spared no expense."

Ella smiled. "I'm tired and figured I'd do better to just enjoy the quiet of the cabin. But you two go right ahead and have fun."

"We had to come back for our shawls," Angel explained as if Ella had asked. "But I intend to dance and feast all night. I figure there will be plenty of time to rest when I'm old."

Ella laughed. Angel was older than Ella but acted years younger. Ella supposed the weight of her family's problems and Phillip's drinking had aged her somewhat.

She was relieved when the girls were gone and she was once again left to the quiet of her cabin. But her solitude was not to be. A knock sounded on the door not five minutes later.

Ella opened the door to find Mary on the other side. She held out a plate of food like an offering.

"I thought you might be hungry."

"Not really, but come on in."

Ella stepped back, and Mary entered the cabin. She crossed the room to put the plate on a small side table.

"You're not seasick, are you?"

"No. Just not hungry."

"Are you going to stay in the cabin and mope the entire trip over?" Mary asked in her brazen manner.

Ella shrugged. "I might. I do have a lot on my mind."

Mary's expression softened. "I know you do, but I'd hate for you to be swallowed up in it. It's not worth it. I speak from experience. I know that times are hard and that facing the future and what might happen to your family is daunting. I also know my part in all of this."

"Your part? You simply wanted justice for the death of your brother. And I'm glad we're moving closer to that."

"I am too," Mary replied, "but as much as I've wrestled with that desire, I know it won't bring him back."

"No."

The word hung heavy between them. Ella sighed. She wished that she could go back in time and change the outcome of the night Jefferson killed August Reichert. But to change that would change everything, including her falling in love with Phillip. Would she also change that?

"I know you're worried about your part in all of this, Ella, but you shouldn't be."

Ella looked up to meet Mary's compassionate gaze.

"It was never your fault," Mary assured her, "and even the fact that you kept what you knew to yourself wouldn't have changed anything. I want you to know that I love you like a sister, and I'm grateful for our closeness. I hope in time you can find peace of mind despite what's happened and what your father and Spiby did." She paused and gave a slight shrug. "I just wanted you to know that. I want us always to be close. Like Lizzy said, we're a family."

❖❂ EIGHTEEN ❂❖

Lizzy strained to see out the filthy train car window, looking for any sign of Wes or her mother. The depot platform was unusually busy. People and porters were crowded together, making her task all the harder.

"They should be here," she murmured.

"Don't get yourself worked up. Of course they'll be here." Oliver stood and reached overhead to get their smaller traveling bags down from the storage rack.

"I'm just so anxious to see Wes and Mother." Lizzy smoothed her wrinkled suit coat. She had dressed in a burgundy outfit trimmed in black piping and matching buttons. Wes had once declared it his favorite. The small hat she wore was an older one she'd found at a secondhand store. It suited her better than the large, elaborate hats of the current fashion. "Do I look all right?"

"You've asked me that a dozen times. You look beautiful. You're all radiant and glowing, as an expectant mother should be."

"Uncle Oliver, hush." She looked around, afraid someone might have overheard.

He chuckled. "Your secret will be out soon enough."

"Yes, but I want to be the one to tell it." She picked up her black purse. "Let's hurry and see if we can't be first off."

They followed the porter down the steps and onto the platform. Lizzy looked first one way and then the other. She finally spotted Wes, whose height allowed him to stand slightly above the crowd.

"Wes!" She hurried down the platform, nearly tripping over her own skirt.

She threw herself into her husband's arms, delighted by the grin he wore. He wasn't angry at her for all her bad behavior. Or if he was, he was hiding it well.

"I've missed you so much." She showered his face with kisses despite the inappropriate display it made.

Wes held her snug against him, raising her up so that her feet didn't even touch the ground. "This is quite the welcome," he murmured.

"I feel like we've been parted for a dozen years."

"What about me?" Mother asked.

Lizzy stopped kissing her husband and turned to where Mother stood next to Uncle Oliver. "I missed you too. It's just that I treated Wesley rather badly before he left with Phillip. Speaking of which, is he here?"

"No," Wes said, lowering her to the ground. "He's not strong enough to deal with town just yet, especially with us staying overnight."

"Overnight?"

"Yeah. It's already late afternoon, and we figured it'd be better to wait till morning. Your ma and I got rooms at the hotel for the night."

"Oh, that's wonderful." Lizzy was relieved to know they would be able to rest before the long drive home. "How thoughtful. I know Uncle Oliver will appreciate that. He's feeling rather stiff after the train."

"Indeed." The older man put a hand to his back. "I'm afraid years of physical labor are catching up with me, not to mention days of travel. I'm tired, but also famished. What say I treat us to the best steak we can find?"

"That sounds delicious," Mother replied.

They made their way to the baggage car. Wesley suggested Uncle Oliver and the ladies go ahead to the restaurant and order his steak medium rare while he collected the trunks.

Lizzy didn't want to be parted again so soon, but neither did she want to start arguing with her husband. She owed him more than a simple apology for her poor behavior and agreed without a word.

It wasn't long before he joined them at the restaurant. He took his seat at their table for four and covered her hand with his. Lizzy met his smile and felt her heart beat a little faster. She had loved this man nearly her entire life, and now she was carrying his child. The thought of it fascinated and terrified her at the same time. A baby was growing inside of her. A gift from God.

They passed the supper hour eating and discussing all the news from the show. Lizzy answered her mother's questions about her fall, and while she wanted to blurt out the news about the baby, she knew she needed to share it with Wes first. In private.

Finally, everyone had eaten their fill and Uncle Oliver gave a yawn. "I'm afraid," he said, pushing back from the table, "that I am completely spent. My back and hips are begging for a bed."

"I believe we should retire, then," Mother said, putting her napkin aside. "Not only did Wes and I have the long drive into town this morning, but we saw to our shopping before you two arrived. I think a good night's sleep is in order for all of us." She pushed a key toward Uncle Oliver. "You have room twenty-one, I'm in twenty-four, and Wes and Lizzy have fourteen." She stood. "I don't know about the rest of you, but I intend to sleep late."

Everyone laughed at this, having never known Rebecca Brookstone to indulge in that luxury.

They made their way to the hotel and bid each other good night. Lizzy felt almost shy, slipping off to one of the rooms with Wes. They had spent more than one night as man and wife in hotel rooms, but for some reason this felt far more intimate after their time apart.

Once behind closed doors, Lizzy pulled the pins from her hat and set it aside. She glanced at Wes, who had taken a seat on the edge of the bed.

"The cases and trunks are behind you," he said casually. "Do you need me to open any of them?"

"No. I have my overnight things in the small case. I can manage perfectly." She slipped out of her jacket and hung it over the back of a wooden chair.

She glanced at the iron bed and then around the rest of the room. There was a small dressing table and washstand, but little else. She turned back to Wes, who was watching her with a strange look on his face.

"What?" she asked.

He shook his head. "I just can't believe we're finally together . . . alone. I've missed you."

Lizzy nodded and began to pull the pins from her hair. "I've missed you too. I'm so sorry for the way we parted. Sorry for the way I behaved. You were only doing what God had laid on your heart, but my feelings got in the way. Then, when I didn't get any letters from you, I figured you were really angry with me."

"No." He shook his head. "Just busy. I knew I should have written, but every time I started to, something happened. You can see the letter I kept trying to write when we get home." He chuckled. "I think I managed to get three lines down."

"It doesn't matter now." She put the hairpins aside and ran her fingers through her long dark hair. She let the waves tumble down over her shoulders. It felt so good to have her hair free. "I know Uncle Oliver sent a telegraph about the accident." She met her husband's gaze. "You haven't asked me about it."

He nodded. "I didn't ask on purpose. I didn't want that to be the focus of your homecoming. Besides, your mother asked enough questions for all of us."

Lizzy had to agree with that. "Still, I'm surprised. I figured you'd want to chastise me." She smiled, not wanting the situation to get too serious.

He shrugged. "Everyone has the power to change. Your mother convinced me it wouldn't do any good to reprimand you for doing the things that you love . . . the things that make you who you are."

"My mother can be very wise," Lizzy said, smiling. "But just so you know, I'm perfectly fine, and I have no intention of ever performing again. You were right. That time of my life is done. I'm ready for a new time."

He watched her, never once looking away. She knew he felt the same longing for her that she felt for him. She knew now was the time to share her news.

"I have a surprise for you," she said, coming to stand directly in front of him.

His left brow rose in question.

Lizzy touched his cheek. "I'm going to have a baby."

"I know." His simple response was followed by a grin.

She was stunned. "You know? Who told you? Did Uncle Oliver say something in the telegram?"

"No." He shook his head and pressed his hand over hers. "Your mother figured it out. I told her how things were between us before I left. I told her you weren't at all like yourself, and she told me she was the same way when she was expecting you. Of course, I couldn't be sure that you were with child, but I was hoping."

She smiled. "Then you're glad."

He looked at her in disbelief. "How could you even question whether I'm glad or not?" He wrapped her in his arms and pulled her close. "Of course I'm glad. I'm beyond glad. I've wanted to shout to the heavens, but I knew I needed to wait to hear it from you."

Lizzy laughed as her eyes filled with tears. "I'm so happy."

"So am I." He kissed her tenderly, running his hands down her arms. When he pulled away, he reached out to touch her abdomen and grinned. "You're already growing."

She held his hand in place and nodded. "And soon the doctor says we should be able to feel him moving."

"Him?"

She shrugged. "I figured you'd want a boy first."

"I'll take whatever God gives us. A little girl just like you would be grand."

She cocked her head. "Just like me?"

Wes laughed and pulled her back in his arms. "Exactly like you."

"I couldn't believe you had already guessed about the baby," Lizzy told her mother as they drove home in the wagon. Wes and Uncle Oliver chose to ride on horseback, leaving Lizzy and her mother to share a long conversation.

"You were acting just as I did. Your poor father was beside himself. He told the doctor he was sure something was desperately wrong with me, because I was always crying and I'd never once cried since we were married." Mother smiled and shrugged. "When Wes mentioned what had happened, I just knew it must be for the same reason."

"I'm so happy, I can hardly stand the thought of having to wait another four and a half months. It seems like it will take forever."

"The time will pass more quickly than you can imagine. Believe me. Oh, I took the liberty of buying several bolts of white flannel for diapers and material for outfits. We'll have plenty of sewing to do."

Lizzy looked out across the rolling hills and sighed. It was so good to be home, to be with the people she loved. Then she remembered that the ranch now belonged to her mother.

"Uncle Oliver told me about the ranch. That you own it in full."

Her mother kept her eyes on the team as she drove. "I know. He told me last night what a shock it was for you to find out about the show. I'm sorry about that. I wasn't trying to keep it from you."

"I didn't mind that. It was just that I thought we owned half of it. When I learned there was some sort of trade between Uncle Oliver and Father, I didn't mind at all. In fact, I was relieved."

Mother finally looked at her. "I'm so glad. I didn't want you hurt. I know the show is important to you."

"But the ranch is more important. I always wanted to settle down and stay there, or at least be close by. Father loved the ranch more than the show and it makes me think of him. I feel his presence when we're there."

Her mother nodded. "I'm glad you feel that way, because I've deeded it to you and Wes."

"What?" Lizzy shook her head. "But it's yours."

"I want you two to have it. I know your father would have wanted it that way. It's too much for me to manage alone."

"But you'll never be alone. Wes and I would never leave you unless you asked us to."

"That will never happen, especially now." She looked at Lizzy and smiled. "I'll soon have a grandbaby to play with. Maybe even more than one, in time. The ranch is yours, my

Christmas present to you both. I took care of the paperwork when we were in Miles City."

"Does Wes know?"

"No. I wanted to tell you first. But I did ask him to move into the house. I want you to make your home there, and I want to have you close by so I can help you." She patted Lizzy's leg. "And play with my grandchild."

"Well, I hope you know you'll always have a home with us. Uncle Oliver too. And anyone else who needs a place."

"I love that this is your heart. You would make your father very happy."

Lizzy couldn't keep the tears from coming. "I'm sorry," she said, sniffing. "I'm just so happy. I can hardly believe how God has blessed me. I wish Father could be here with us. Then everything would be perfect."

Mother nodded. "I feel the same way. But even with him gone, I feel certain we're going to be amazingly blessed."

That evening as Lizzy slipped into bed and Wesley's waiting arms, she marveled at the day and all she had to be thankful for.

"Can you handle another surprise?" she asked, snuggling close.

"Another surprise? Are you having twins?"

She laughed. "Not that I know of." She planted her chin on his chest. "Mother has deeded us the ranch."

"What?" He frowned and shook his head. "I thought she and Oliver owned it together."

"No. He and Father had an arrangement that I knew nothing about. When Father was dying, Uncle Oliver turned the ranch over to Father in full so that Mother and I might always have it. Uncle Oliver wanted the show, and then he sold it to Henry Adler when he thought his days were few."

"I'm sure he regretted that."

"No. On the train ride here, we talked about it. He said he was actually relieved. He's tired, Wes. Worn from travel and life's cares. He wants to take life easy, and I told him our baby will need him to act as grandfather, since our fathers are gone." She smiled. "I figured you'd approve."

"Of course I do, but why would your mother deed the ranch to us? I mean, she'll hopefully be around a long while yet."

"I think she did it because she knows we'll always let it be her home, and she feels we'll be better at managing it. She says it's far too much for her."

"But we wouldn't have left her to manage it alone," Wes countered.

"No, but I think she knew it was important for you to own it. You need to step into the position of being the man of the house and owner of the ranch. It'll bring a new respect for you, and the men will approve. I know they will. And if they don't, then you'll let them go and find new workers."

"I don't know what to say. I never expected this, even if I did marry the boss's daughter."

Lizzy frowned. "Did you plan to move away?"

"No, but I certainly never figured to own a big place like this."

"Papa always said that if he could have a son, he'd want you. He loved you a great deal, and I know he'd be proud as a peacock to know we married."

"I loved him too, but I love his daughter even more."

Wes buried his fingers in her hair and pulled her to his lips. He kissed her with a warmth and passion that matched her own for him. She sighed against his mouth and smiled. If ever she doubted this was where she belonged . . . all doubt was gone.

"A baby?" Phillip said in wonder. "When?"

Wes grinned. "Doc says January. Just when all the cows are calving and we'll be so busy we won't know what to do with ourselves. Probably in the middle of a blizzard too, if I know Lizzy."

Phillip laughed. "Probably. That's really somethin' though, big brother. Congratulations."

"There's more," Wes said. "Lizzy's ma has given us the ranch. Apparently she's held the full deed since her husband died, and now it's mine and Lizzy's."

"For sure and for real?" Phillip asked. He couldn't imagine anyone just giving someone such a gift.

"Yup. She wanted to make sure it stayed in the family and that she had plenty of time to play with her grandchild." Wes looked happier than Phillip had seen him in a long time. "And in turn, that means you will always have a home if you want one. I'll need you to take on more responsibility, but as the owner's brother, you'll be in a position of authority. Leastwise, I'd like to put you in that position."

"I don't know what to say." Phillip shook his head. The news was more than he could have ever anticipated. "I spent so many years wandering and feeling alone that I'd happily stay on even as the hired help."

"Like the prodigal son, eh? Well, just like that story, I'm not relegating you to that place. You are family, and we need you. I'm proud of you for working to give up liquor, Phillip. You're a truly changed man, and I want you to know that you'll always have my support and love. I know God is going to give you the strength to beat this."

Phillip nodded. "I want that. More than anything else. Well, it goes right along with wanting to marry Ella. But one hinges on the other, so they really are like the same thing."

"I understand that."

"Do you think she still cares about me?"

"Why don't you ask Lizzy? If anyone would know, it's her."

"Would you mind if I go speak with her right now?"

Wes laughed. "I'd be disappointed if you didn't. She's in the barn. She wanted to check on the horse she got for Christmas last year."

Phillip didn't bother to reply but took off for the barn. He found Lizzy there just as Wes had said. She was stroking Emerson's face and talking to him in that pretty way only a girl could do. She glanced up at the sound of his approach.

"I hope you don't mind my interruptin'," he said.

Lizzy smiled and gave the horse something from her pocket. "I don't mind at all. How are you?"

He shrugged. "Pretty good, but I'd feel a mite better if we could talk about Ella."

She nodded. "I wondered when you'd get around to asking me about her. Ella sent this for you." She pulled a letter from her pocket. "She felt a little frustrated with you for not writing, so I promised I would make sure you wrote to her while she's gone."

"When we first got back," Phillip began as he took the letter, "I wasn't in any shape to write to much of anybody. Then I was just really busy. Wes seemed to think keeping me exhausted was the best way to keep me from wanting to drink." He looked at the small envelope and smiled. "She isn't too mad, is she?"

"No, I don't think so," Lizzy replied. "But I know she'd feel better if she could hear from you. She wants to know how it's going and if you're managing to stay away from liquor. Not only that, but she has some real burdens of her own to bear."

"She isn't sick or anything?" He hadn't considered that Ella might have gotten hurt. "She didn't have an accident, did she?"

"No. I would have told you right away." Lizzy put her hand on Phillip's arm. "She's just fine, but it has to do with her family. Her father and that man who wanted to marry her. I'm sure she's explained it in the letter, but if you have questions, you can ask me. I'll tell you what I know."

He nodded. "Thanks, Miz Lizzy."

"Just Lizzy. I'm your sister now, remember?" She smiled. "And you're my ornery little brother and my baby's uncle. I have always been close to my uncle Oliver. He held a very special place in my life, and I know you'll hold an equally special one in the life of my baby."

He felt his chest tighten. "I never thought of it that way. It makes me feel . . . well, like I finally belong."

She hugged him. "Of course you belong. You belong to us and us to you. We're family." She looked into his eyes for a moment, then kissed his cheek. "Forever."

⊰⊱ NINETEEN ⊰⊱

FOUR MONTHS LATER

lla shivered. She looked out the hotel window and watched as the snow fell and blanketed New York City. It was New Year's Eve, and the town was in a celebrating spirit. The tour in Europe had ended two weeks ago, and now the troupe was safely back in the United States. Henry Adler had declared this their best year ever, and he felt confident that the Brookstone Wild West Extravaganza would continue to grow in popularity. Ella hoped for his sake that this would be the case, but she missed Phillip and the others who'd left the show. Without them, nothing seemed the same.

True to her word, Lizzy had written long letters, and Phillip had added his own shorter missives to keep Ella informed as to his progress. But it was never enough and only made her miss him all the more.

It had been difficult for the show's mail to keep up with them in Europe, and after a time it had stopped coming completely. Once they returned to England, however, Henry found bags of letters for the Brookstone show forwarded to his estate. Ella had sorted through fan letters to find a few envelopes from Montana and even two from her sister-in-law in Kentucky. Phillip was well and keeping sober. He missed her and was counting the days till he could see her again. This brought a smile to Ella's face. A part of her had worried that once Phillip battled through his demons, he'd no longer need her.

At a knock on the hotel room door, Ella dropped the drapes. She made her way across the room, fighting a wave of dizziness. "Who is it?"

"It's me, Mara."

Ella opened the door. Mara extended several newspapers. "I got these like you asked."

"And did you get the telegram sent to Robert?"

"I did." Mara nodded and followed Ella into the room. "You think Mr. Robert will come here to see you?"

Ella suppressed the urge to cough. "I'm

not even sure where he is. The letter I had from Virginia said he was very busy with Father and the lawyer. That hotel in Washington was the last place I knew them to be, so hopefully they're still there and Robert will get my telegram."

She took the newspapers to the table, where the breakfast dishes still awaited the hotel staff. Mara helped her push the dishes aside so she could spread out the first of three newspapers.

Twenty minutes later, Ella put the last of the papers aside. She'd seen nothing regarding her father and Jefferson's slave trade. In her letter, Virginia had said that the reaction of the authorities had been mixed. Jefferson's lawyers argued that the Negros had signed on to work of their own free will and that no law had been broken. However, there was the issue of August Reichert's murder and the fact that Jefferson had told more than one person that it wasn't his first. Virginia penned that Robert hoped that between their father's testimony and that of a few other witnesses, Jefferson would be sent to prison.

"I wish I could read something about what's happened." Ella stood and grabbed her handkerchief as she coughed. Again a wave of dizziness washed over her, forcing her to reach for the back of the chair to steady herself.

"That cough done got worse overnight, and you look terrible pale," Mara declared. "I'm gonna order you some tea with honey and lemon."

"I'm sure it's just a cold. The ocean air was hard on me." Ella tucked the handkerchief in her sleeve. "I don't like the idea of returning to Kentucky, but I must go see my mother. I know she's afraid of what the future holds."

"Abe and I will come with you," Mara said, surprising Ella. She smiled at the younger woman. "We wanna get married, and my old minister Brother Johnson will be happy to do the deed."

"Aren't you afraid of returning? I am. There are people all over that county who knew what was going on and turned a blind eye. Or they were forced by Father and Jefferson and would hold us a grudge."

"I got the Lord on my side, and so do you," Mara declared. "And He don't never turn a blind eye. He's watchin' over us all the time. We can count on that."

"Indeed." Ella gave another shiver. "I think I'm going back to bed. I'm chilled to the bone. I'm going to write a note for Henry Adler. Would you be willing to take it to him for me?"

"Of course, and then I'll be back to see that you're takin' proper care of yourself."

Ella nodded and found some hotel stationery. She quickly wrote a note explaining her desire to see her mother before returning to join the troupe. Once she was finished, she folded it in half and gave it to Mara.

"When that's done, would you mind sending Abe to purchase the train tickets for us? I'd like to leave yet today."

"I'll see to it, but only so long as you get back to bed. If you don't rest, you won't be fit to travel anywhere."

Lizzy grabbed her stomach and frowned. She looked at the others across the table. No one seemed aware of her discomfort as they dug into breakfast. For days she'd been having what her mother deemed "getting ready" contractions, but the ones this morning seemed different—stronger. Thankfully they weren't all that close together.

"So the troupe isn't coming back to the ranch anymore?" Mother asked.

"That's what Henry's letter said," Oliver explained. "He's found a farm in Virginia where the weather is temperate year-round. He believes it will be a better headquarters. He plans to break the news to the troupe at a New Year's Eve party he's throwing."

"That's tonight," Phillip said, as if they'd forgotten.

"Exactly so." Oliver nodded. "Henry felt that this would be a better arrangement for everyone. He plans to hire on a new crew, although he said that Phillip and I were welcome to return."

"And do you think you'll take him up on the offer?" Mother asked.

"Not me." Oliver shook his head. "I gave it a lot of thought, and my place is here. Lizzy said the baby needs a grandfather."

Lizzy smiled, happy to hear he'd decided to stay. She knew the show had been his lifeblood at one time, but he was getting old and worn, and he'd fare better staying in Montana with the family who loved him.

Phillip shook his head. "I don't like that they aren't coming back here." The look on his face said it all. "I was counting on seeing Ella soon."

"She may still come, Phillip," Mother said. "After all, this has been her home, and the troupe will take a break for a few weeks, I would think. Everyone will want to go home to see their loved ones."

"They daren't take too much of a break." Oliver slathered his biscuit with jam. "Henry said their first performance will be in March."

"Well, the absence of the show will be

quite a change for us." Mother looked at Lizzy. "Did you know anything about this?"

Lizzy straightened and shook her head. "No, he never said anything to me. I suppose it does make sense. The winters will be much milder and the rail lines more accessible."

Mother nodded. "I never knew the show to have any trouble getting trains out here, but I suppose this is better for them." She smiled and offered Phillip the plate of biscuits. "Do you plan to rejoin the show?"

"That'll depend on Ella," Phillip replied. "If she wants to keep performing, then I would like to be with her. I hadn't figured I'd leave the ranch so soon—at least not until March when the show starts its tour. But if they aren't coming back, then maybe I'll need to go sooner."

"Ella and Mary have become the foundation of the show," Oliver declared. "I think Henry would do almost anything to keep them. Oh, but he did add in the letter that our Lizzy was welcome to return." He smiled her way.

"Our Lizzy can scarcely climb the stairs," Wes countered, "much less climb into a saddle."

Uncle Oliver's smile widened. "But doesn't she look pretty. I swear she looks more like you every day, Becca."

"I don't know about that, but I'm glad to have her here with me," Mother replied.

"Phillip, we definitely need you on the ranch," Wes threw out. "If Ella doesn't want to continue with the show, then maybe you could convince her to marry you and live here in Montana."

Phillip paused with his coffee cup halfway to his mouth and nodded. "I think she'd like that well enough." He took a long drink and smiled. "Good coffee, Mrs. B."

Lizzy's mother smiled. "Glad you like it. I feared it might be a little strong, but given the cold weather, I figured we could use it that way."

Lizzy jumped and grabbed her swollen abdomen. This time everyone noticed. She looked at her husband and saw the concern in his eyes.

She said the first thing that came to mind. "I don't want to worry anyone, but these contractions seem much stronger than before."

Mother frowned. "Are they coming regularly?"

"Yes." Lizzy shrugged. "I know it's just New Year's Eve, but I think the baby may be on the way."

The men all paled, and only Mother maintained her composure. "Phillip, ride to town and bring back the doctor. Wes, I'll trust you to get Lizzy upstairs. Help her change into a nightgown and build up the fire in your room." She rose from the table and smiled as if she were arranging for nothing more important than a game of checkers. "Oliver, you come with me."

Lizzy looked into the worried face of her husband. "Looks like we're soon to be parents."

He nodded and helped her from her chair. "Should I carry you?"

She laughed. "I was beginning to think I should ask you the same question. Try not to worry so much. Women have been having babies for thousands of years."

"Yes, but not my woman." Wes put his arm around her and added, "And not my baby."

By the time Ella reached her hometown, she was quite sick. She hated to expose her nephews and niece to whatever she had, so she ordered the driver to take her to Fleming Farm. She knew it had been closed up and maintained only the most minimal of staff, but Mara and Abe assured her they could take care of anything she needed.

Walking into the foyer, Ella longed for her bed. "Be sure to send word to Mother," she told Mara. "We'll need someone to cook and a couple of maids. I know there are still groomsmen and other outside workers, but ask Mother to send the others." She put her hand to her head and fought off a wave of dizziness. "It's freezing in here. We need a fire," she murmured.

"Don't you be worryin' about nothin'. Abe and me will set things right." Mara put her arm around Ella's waist. "Come on, let's get you to your room."

Abe quickly had a fire going in Ella's old bedroom, while Mara helped her change her clothes in the dressing room. A series of coughs racked Ella's body. Her chest hurt something fierce, and Mara told her it looked to be pleurisy or pneumonia. Both could be deadly.

The last thing Ella remembered as she faded off to sleep was wondering if she would die and never see Phillip again. It saddened her to think she might never have a chance to be his wife and spend her life with him. Such thoughts made her sleep fitful.

When she awoke, Ella was surprised to find her mother sitting beside her bed. "Mama, what are you doing here?" Speaking caused a long round of coughing.

"Mara sent word that you were ill. I couldn't stay away." Mother felt Ella's brow. "You have a fever, and I've sent for the doctor."

"I'm sure it's just a cold gone bad." Ella tried to sit up, but the room tilted first one way and then the other. Dizzy, she eased back against the thick pillow. "I guess sitting up isn't a good idea."

"No," her mother agreed. "You need to rest."

Ella shook her head. "I could feel my strength slipping away as the train moved south. I probably should have stayed in New York. Now I've exposed you to whatever is wrong with me."

"I'm not worried," Mother replied. She got up and went to the water pitcher and bowl sitting atop a small table. She poured a bit of water into the bowl and then wetted a cloth. Returning to the bed, Mother sat beside Ella and placed the cloth on her forehead. "This should help bring down the fever."

Ella couldn't remember ever feeling so miserable. She coughed and felt the tightness in her chest threaten to cut off her breath. Wheezing, she struggled to clear her lungs. Once the spasms ended, she was even more exhausted than when they'd started.

"Mara has gone to get some rosemary and oregano. We're going to put it in the water over the fire. The steam will help you breathe easier."

The doctor arrived, but Ella didn't know

him. He listened to her heart and lungs, then drew a bottle out of his black bag. "Give her a teaspoon of this every four hours. Keep her in bed and give her plenty to drink. She'll either be better in a week or worse. If she's worse, send for me again."

While Mara showed the doctor to the door, Mama looked at the bottle and read the label. "It contains heroin. I've never heard of that." She frowned, shaking her head. "I can't imagine it works as well as rosemary and oregano." She put the bottle aside. "I think we'll stick with remedies that I know work."

For several days Ella was in and out of sleep. At times her chest felt heavy and her breathing was labored, making her wonder again if she would die. She didn't ponder it long, however. She simply had no strength.

When her sleep was less tortured, Ella dreamed of Phillip. She could see him riding wild horses, breaking them for the saddle. Sometimes in her dreams, she and Phillip walked hand in hand, talking about the future—their future. How she yearned to have him near.

"When will I be better?" she asked her mother after a particularly fierce round of coughing.

"Soon," her mother encouraged. "But you need to cough this stuff out of your lungs."

Ella could hardly draw a decent breath, much less find the strength to cough, but Mara and Mother insisted she do so. Three or four times a day, they forced her to sit and breathe deeply over a steaming pan of water and herbs. It always brought great relief and worked to break up her congestion, but it took every last bit of strength she possessed. When would it ever end?

Finally, after what seemed to be weeks, Ella awoke to feel her head and lungs a little clearer. She actually smiled when her mother approached the bed with hot tea.

"I think I'm better," she told her mother.

"Yes, your fever broke yesterday. Mara and I feel certain you have turned a corner. You still have to keep your lungs clear, however. You're not out of the woods yet."

"I feel like I've been living in the woods and sleeping on the ground. I ache all over. When can I get out of bed?"

"You need to regain your strength first."

"I have to recover soon." She looked at her mother and then at Mara. "I can't lie about in bed forever. The show needs me."

"The show's takin' a break," Mara reminded her. "You ain't missin' a thing."

"Except that I planned to go back to Montana during the break. I want to see Phillip. I need to know how he's doing."

"You've been very sick, Ella." Her mother's tone made her concern clear. "You must rest in order to get well. You can hardly expect to perform in your condition."

Ella knew her mother was right, but she still wanted to be back on her feet—and not just because of Phillip. She also needed to know what was going on with Father, but she didn't want to risk upsetting her mother. There was no choice but to bide her time.

After a week, Ella felt more like her old self. She knew it would be some time yet before she felt like traveling to rejoin the troupe, but she could at least sit in a chair for a while each afternoon. Mara brought her books to read and an occasional newspaper, but still there was no word about what was happening with her father and Jefferson. There were also no letters from Phillip or Lizzy.

"Don't be worryin' none," Mara told her as she brushed Ella's long blond hair. Until that day, the routine brushing had hurt and Ella hadn't enjoyed it at all, but today the pain was absent and she didn't mind Mara's tending. "What with Mr. Henry settling the show in at the new place in Virginia, he's probably too busy to write to you."

"I should be hearing something from someone. Lizzy or Mary at least. Of course, Lizzy's due to have a baby soon, so perhaps she can't write. And I know Mary and Chris planned to visit her grandparents, so maybe they're too busy." Ella sighed. "Henry could at least let me know when practices will begin."

"You need to stop frettin'."

Ella rolled her gaze heavenward. "I suppose I have no other choice. I wish Robert would at least let us know what's going on. Poor Mother. She must feel completely beside herself without any news."

"I 'spect so, but she knows that Mr. Robert will be tellin' her what he can when he has the time. You should follow her example." Mara gave her a smile. "But I know patience ain't never been your virtue."

Ella couldn't help but smile in return. "No, I suppose it isn't."

"I don't know that she looks like Lizzy or Wes," Phillip declared as he inspected his niece. "She just looks like a baby to me."

Mother laughed and handed the infant to Lizzy. "She looks just like Lizzy did when she was a baby."

Lizzy smiled down at her daughter. "I think she's perfect no matter who she looks like. What amazes me is how much she's grown in just a few weeks."

"How are my favorite ladies?" Wes asked,

strolling into the front room. He went to Lizzy, who sat in the rocker, and kissed the top of her head. "I came to see if you needed more wood in here. That snow is really comin' down. Phillip and I need to get out there and check on the herd. No doubt those cows will be dropping calves like it's a contest."

"We have plenty of wood, Wes. You and Phillip did a wonderful job. We'll be set for some time," Mother replied.

"I wish you didn't have to go out in this weather." Lizzy cradled the baby closer. "I worry about you both."

"We'll be fine." He kissed her head again, then reached down to run his finger along the baby's cheek. She immediately turned her head toward his finger as if to latch on.

"You boys check in periodically so we won't worry," Mother instructed. "What with the cows being in the nearest pastures, you shouldn't have too much trouble, but it's good to know you're all right just the same. And that way you'll know that we're fine as well."

"That's more important to me," Wes declared. He reached into his coat pocket and pulled out his gloves. "Come on, Phillip. We got work to do." He gave Lizzy one last glance. "Behave yourself."

She smiled. "I might say the same, but I

know my request will fall on deaf ears. You'll do just as you please."

He pointed at himself and raised his eyebrows in mock surprise.

Lizzy laughed. "Yes, you. Don't try that innocent act with me."

Wesley laughed and headed out with Phillip.

Once the men were gone, Lizzy looked at her mother and sighed. "I don't know when I've ever been happier. The only thing that could make it better would be to have Father here."

Her mother sat on the footstool by the fire and nodded. "I know. I was thinking much the same. He would have been so proud of you . . . and her." She nodded toward the baby.

Lizzy shifted and held her daughter up directly in front of her. The baby looked at her with dark blue eyes that seemed to take in every inch of Lizzy's face.

"Cora Anne, you are a beauty, and no matter what anyone says, you look perfectly like yourself." The baby yawned, and Lizzy laughed. "I don't think she cares one way or the other."

TWENTY

Are you sure it's the right thing for you?" Wes asked as he and Phillip cleaned up for supper.

"Ella's the right thing for me, and Ella is going to stay with the show." Phillip dried his face on a towel and shrugged. Henry Adler had shown up at the ranch to pick up additional stock that he'd arranged to buy. It seemed like a sign from God, as far as Phillip was concerned. He would return with Henry and help with the animals and equipment.

"And you don't think it's too soon?"

"No." Phillip turned to Wes and met his concerned gaze. "I'm fine. God has freed me from my desire for liquor. I don't even want to drink anymore."

"But neither have you been around it much, and certainly not without someone there to support you. I worry that once it's there in front of you—"

"Stop worrying," Phillip interrupted. "Like Mrs. B says, worry is a sin. You're doubting that God can manage things."

Wes unrolled his sleeves and secured the cuffs. "I'm not doubting God."

"So you're doubting me, and I guess you have a right to do so. I made a real mess of my life, but I'm lookin' to God for help now. You have to admit, I've done real good so far. I was even in town with the boys last weekend and didn't have a drop of alcohol. I figure that should prove somethin'."

"You've done a great job," Wes said, pulling on his coat. "I just don't want you to backslide."

"I don't want that either, and I don't intend to let it happen. You and Lizzy will be prayin' for me, and I know that with God and Ella's help, I'll be able to keep from drinkin'." He pulled on his own coat and slapped his brother on the back. "Now, come on. They're waitin' supper on us."

They left the barn and made their way to the house. Phillip knew his brother would continue to worry about him, but hopefully in time he'd see that Phillip was strong enough with God's help to stand firm.

Everyone was already taking their place at

the dinner table when he and Wes entered the dining room. Wes went straight to Lizzy and kissed her. It made Phillip feel a little envious, but he immediately repented and tried to focus on something else as his brother helped Lizzy with her chair. One day he and Ella would be together, and he'd have the right to kiss his wife.

"When do you want to head back, Mr. Adler?" he asked, taking a seat opposite the older man.

"I figure tomorrow. Is that soon enough for you?" Henry Adler grinned. "I know you're anxious to see your girl."

"I am." Phillip grinned. "And you will be glad to know that I intend to ask for her hand. I'm sure she'll even be willing for us to have the engagement be a part of the show."

"That's marvelous," Henry replied, rubbing his hands together. "Everyone has come to expect the engagements and weddings. I heard there is even some wagering taking place as to which shows will feature these events."

"People will wager on anything," Oliver Brookstone said, pouring himself a cup of coffee. "A fool is always willing to be parted from his money."

Henry laughed. "It serves the show well, so I suppose I don't mind."

"Gentlemen and Lizzy," Mrs. B stated, coming into the room, "I hope you're hungry." She placed a huge platter on the table. A large pork roast accompanied by baked apples covered the dish.

Phillip couldn't have been more delighted. There were also potatoes and gravy, as well as a variety of other side dishes. They were feasting quite well tonight.

Oliver offered grace and then began to slice the roast. The bowls and platters were passed around until everyone's plate was heaped with food. Phillip smiled. He felt like part of a family—something he hadn't had since running away from home at sixteen.

The room was void of conversation for the first few minutes of the meal while everyone sampled Rebecca Brookstone's cooking. Soon enough, however, the compliments began to flow.

"Mother, no matter how many times I try to follow your recipe," Lizzy said, shaking her head, "I never seem to be able to make gravy that tastes like this."

"I do have a few years on you. When you were performing and learning new tricks in the saddle, I was cooking and learning new tricks at the stove," Lizzy's mother reminded her.

"Well, I can see I have my work cut out

for me if I'm ever going to be anywhere near as good as you." Lizzy glanced at her husband. "You'll just have to be patient with me and enjoy Mother's cooking for the time being."

"I don't mind at all," Wes said with a forkful of pork halfway to his mouth.

"Lizzy, I wish you and Wes would change your minds and return with me to the new farm," Henry said without warning. "We could make arrangements for the baby, and you two—well, *three*—wouldn't have to travel with the show."

"Now, Henry, that is hardly very nice of you," Oliver declared. "My sister-in-law gives you this wonderful supper, and you want to take her granddaughter away."

"I don't appreciate that at all, Henry," Mrs. B said, waggling her index finger in admonishment. "Now, eat your supper, and no more talk of trying to steal my family away. You're already getting Phillip, and he'll be sorely missed." She gave Phillip a loving smile. "Hopefully you and Ella will return here soon."

"Thanks, Mrs. B. I hope so too."

The dinner continued, filled with pleasant conversation. Phillip ate until he was stuffed and still found room for some of Mrs. B's applesauce cake. As far as he was concerned, it was the perfect meal to end his time at the ranch. Tomorrow he and Henry would head out early for the East Coast. It would take at least a week to reach the Virginia farm, and then hopefully Ella would be waiting for him.

The next morning, Wes drove Henry to the train station in Miles City with Phillip following behind, leading a row of horses. Phillip knew his big brother was worried, but there was little he could do to convince Wes that things would be all right except to stick to his word and convictions and remain sober. Once a few months passed and Wes got word that Phillip was doing well, he was bound to relax. Until then, however, Phillip would no doubt be a constant cause of worry.

Wes and Phillip unloaded the wagon onto the platform baggage area, then waited for Henry to return with the train tickets. Wes was clearly uncomfortable, and Phillip tried his best to make the situation a little more lighthearted.

"Well, big brother, when I return to the ranch, I fully intend to challenge you to a bronc-bustin' contest. Of course, you'll probably be too worn out and old for such things."

"Oh yeah? You really think I'd let my baby brother beat me?" Wes countered. He smiled and seemed to know exactly what Phillip was trying to do.

"I don't figure you'll have much of a chance. You're an old married man now, with a baby to boot. Who knows—by then another one may be on the way."

"Whoa!" Wes said, holding up his hands. "Let me enjoy Cora first."

They saw Henry returning with tickets in hand. "The train is due in twenty minutes. If you like, I'll treat us all to coffee and whatever else you'd like at the nearest café."

"Sounds good to me," Wes said. "It's a bit too cold to be standing out here on the platform that long." He motioned for Henry to follow him. "Right this way."

Henry handed Phillip his ticket, then started after Wes. Phillip glanced down and noted the destination wasn't Virginia at all, but rather Kentucky.

"Hey, wait a minute, Mr. Adler. I think there's been a mistake." He easily caught up to his brother and the older man. "This ticket only takes me as far as Kentucky."

Henry nodded. "That's right. That's where Ella is. She's been there all month, re-covering from a bad case of bronchitis." He frowned. "I thought you knew that."

Phillip shook his head. "No. No one said a word to me. Is she all right?"

"She was pretty sick for a while, but I've been assured that she's on the mend and plans to be in Virginia on the first of February. I thought you'd like to stop there first and travel with her. But she has Abe and Mara with her if you'd rather just stick with me."

Phillip shook his head. "No, sir. This suits me just fine."

Henry and Wes both chuckled.

Ella stretched in bed and put her book aside. She was feeling much better, and Mother and Mara had both declared her past any point of concern. They insisted she still spend a good part of the day in bed, however, which was more than a little frustrating. Ella was soon expected in Virginia with the wild west show, and she needed to strengthen her muscles.

"I can't tell them, but I'm still weak as a kitten and hardly able to perform," she muttered.

"Are you grumblin' in here?" Mara asked as she entered the room with a steaming cup. "I made this here cocoa for you, but maybe I should just take it back."

Ella smiled. "I'm just anxious to be up and about."

"I know you wanna be out there ridin',

but it'll come soon enough. Now, here's some cocoa, and when you're done with it, your mama and Abe and I are going to town for supplies. We're also gonna check the schedule for the train to Virginia."

"That's wonderful. Thank you."

Mara handed her the cup. "But you need to rest and take a little nap while we're gone. Do I need to stay behind and make sure you do that?"

Ella sipped the cocoa, then shook her head. "I'll be as good as gold. I promise." No need to mention that she intended to do a few of her strengthening exercises prior to napping.

"See that you are," Mother said, coming into the room. "We won't be long. Is there anything in particular you would like us to bring back?"

"Phillip." Ella sighed. "I know he'll be at the farm when we all get together in Virginia. At least I pray he'll be there. But I wish I could see him now. I just want to know that he's all right."

"Well, if there was a way," Mara said, straightening the thick down comforter over Ella, "I'd see he was here."

"As would I," Mother replied. "But for now, you'll just have to wait."

Ella nodded and sampled the cocoa again.

It was rich and creamy, just the way she liked it. She looked across the room at the window. "Did it snow last night? Everything seems awfully bright. In Montana, when it snows and the sun comes out the next day, it can be blinding."

"No snow, it's just a clear, cold day," Mother replied. "Now, you be a good girl. We need to be on our way, Mara. Let's leave Ella to rest." She kissed Ella's forehead. It was an unusually affectionate action for her, but Ella didn't say a word. She smiled and wondered if her sickness had given Mother a reason to feel more maternal, or if all the family troubles had caused her to revisit her feelings. Whatever the reason, Ella found it comforting.

"Now, promise me you'll stay in bed."

"I give you my word, Mother."

"Very well. We'll be back as soon as we can."

She headed out the door, and Mara paused only long enough to give Ella a little smile before pulling the door closed.

Ella finished the cocoa and set the cup aside on the nightstand. She considered getting up to do her strengthening exercises, then thought better of it. She was awfully tired. Snuggling down under the comforter, she closed her eyes.

It wasn't long before she was asleep, and with sleep came dreams that soon turned dark and nightmarish. Ella found herself lost, wandering in a forest. She had no idea where she was or why she was there. She turned down one path and then another, but no matter where she turned, nothing seemed familiar. She called for Phillip, but no answer came. Never had she felt so alone.

When she woke with a start, Ella had to fight the desire to scream. Instead, she drew in a deep breath and blew it out.

"You seem rather startled. Did something frighten you, Ella darling?"

Her blood seemed to freeze in her veins. Ella prayed that she was still dreaming.

"Have I surprised you?"

She turned to find Jefferson Spiby sitting in the far corner, watching her. Ella blinked hard, then glanced toward the door to her room. It was closed, just as it had been when Mara left to go to town.

"How did you get in here?" she asked. Surely this was just a nightmare.

"I've been watching this place since learning you were here. I knew I'd get an opportunity to see you." He grinned in his leering fashion and got to his feet. "You see, I have never given up on my plans for you, my dear, and now that I am dealing with some rather peculiar difficulties thanks to your father, I figure you are my salvation."

Ella didn't know what to say. There were only a few people working at the house, and no doubt Mother, Mara, and Abe were still gone. Otherwise Jefferson would never have risked entering.

"I thought you were arrested . . . in jail."

He chuckled and took a seat on her bed. Ella tried to scoot away, but Jefferson put his hand down and kept her from moving.

"Now, now, my dear. You really shouldn't play so coy with me. After all, I still intend for you to be my wife."

"I will never consent to such a thing. No minister would ever marry us."

He shrugged. "Then we won't use a minister. I think true love is a matter of the heart, anyway. Wouldn't you agree?" His dark eyes seemed to bore right through her defenses.

"I've been sick," she blurted, not knowing what else to say. Jefferson had never tolerated sickness very well. He was something of a worrier when it came to illness.

"Yes, I know. It's the only reason I haven't kissed you. I don't want to expose myself to whatever has laid you low."

"The doctor said I'm quite contagious. I've been near death for a good part of the month."

He smiled. "But doing so much better, as I hear it. I spoke to the doctor just the other day. He's new to the area and doesn't know who I am. We happened to cross paths, and I asked after you."

Ella frowned. She had no idea how she was going to get out of this predicament. Her chest tightened, and she began to cough, causing Jefferson to jump to his feet. Good. He was still leery enough of whatever disease she might have to back away. Coughing would serve her well.

"I apologize, but I can't help it. My lungs are full, and the doctor said I must cough it out." For good measure she held her handkerchief to her mouth and coughed again.

"Well, be that as it may, you will have to leave your sickbed and come with me."

She looked at him, her eyes widening against her will. "I can't go anywhere. I'm much too weak."

"Then I'll have to carry you."

"You might catch my disease." She gripped the handkerchief so tightly that her fingernails dug into her palm.

Jefferson ignored her and yanked back her covers, letting them fall to the floor. He eyed her bare legs with a disgusting grin. Ella quickly pushed down her nightgown, but that only delighted him.

"Oh, my dear Ella. You are such a child in so many ways. I look forward to growing you up in my own leisurely fashion once we're well away from here. Now, get up and get dressed. We're going to be long gone before your mother returns."

Ella refused to move. "I can't, Jefferson. I haven't been out of bed in weeks." It was a lie, but she figured God would understand.

He considered this for only a moment before stalking over to her wardrobe. He opened the wooden doors and began rummaging through her outfits. Finally he pulled out a pink woolen gown and threw it on the bed. "Put it on, or I'll dress you myself."

Ella wasn't about to let him have that privilege. She slowly moved to the edge of the bed. "Go outside, and I will dress."

He laughed. "I'm not going anywhere. Put it on, or I'll put it on for you. Now!"

The tone of his voice left no doubt that he meant business. She nodded and glanced down at her nightgown. She wasn't about to shed it in front of him, so she used it for her undergarment. She thought for a moment about asking for her corset, then decided against it. This dress had been a bit large on her anyway. She would forgo the corset and hopefully have plenty of maneuverability. It might very well mean the difference between being able to escape successfully or having Jefferson catch her.

She slipped the dress on over her nightgown while Jefferson watched. He shook his head and rolled his eyes as if to mock her childish shyness.

"My boots are at the back of the wardrobe, and my stockings are in the drawer. May I get them?"

"Of course. The quicker the better," he said, giving her a sweeping bow.

Rather than let Jefferson watch her intimately tie her stockings high on her thigh, she secured them just below her knee and laced up her boots to keep them somewhat in place. She hoped a moment might present itself later to fix them properly.

Once this was done, she went to her vanity table, where her hairbrush and pins lay, and started to fix her hair, but Jefferson was having none of that.

"We haven't the time. Where's your outer coat?"

"I'm not certain. If it's not in the wardrobe, then perhaps it's downstairs."

"Check the wardrobe," he ordered.

Ella found her gray wool coat freshly brushed. She took it from the hanger and held it up to offer proof of its existence.

"Put it on. If you have gloves and a warm hat, get them."

She went back to the drawers of the wardrobe and selected gloves and a woolen scarf. "Why are you doing this, Jefferson? You can't hope to get away with it. Even if you force yourself on me, you're still a wanted man. This will only add to your charges."

"Not if I work it right. You see, my dear, none of this would be happening but for your father opening his big mouth. Once he realizes I have his precious daughter, he'll whistle a different tune. I intend to send him a letter and instruct him as to what he will do. If he cooperates with me, then you will live. Without his testimony, they have no evidence of me committing murder, and I'm confident the charges will be dropped. And if he doesn't cooperate . . . then he'll pay. First with your life and then your mother's and then his own."

A cold wave of fear washed over Ella. Jefferson was truly without regard for her life or anyone else's. He only wanted what would benefit his needs.

"Where . . . where are we going?"

He grabbed her arm. "You're coming with me. That's all you need to know."

"But I'm sick, Jefferson." Ella began to cough violently. Part of it was purely for show, to remind him of the possibility of catching her illness, but there was an equal amount of honest need in it.

He held her at arm's length but refused to let her go. "It's to my benefit that you are. You're too weak to try to do anything foolish. Now move." He pushed her toward the door.

⊰⊱ TWENTY-ONE ⊰⊱

Mara came into the silent house with a strange feeling of apprehension. She untied her scarf and listened for any sounds of life. There was nothing. She walked into the kitchen and found it completely deserted. There wasn't even a pot on the stove. Making her way back to the entryway where Mrs. Fleming was unbuttoning her coat, Mara frowned.

"Miz Flemin', did you give everybody the day off?"

"No. Why do you ask?" Mrs. Fleming glanced around.

"Ain't nobody in the kitchen. Nobody and nothin' cookin'. I didn't see nobody outside neither. Guess we can ask Abe when he comes back. I'll go upstairs and check on Ella."

Mara didn't wait for Mrs. Fleming's reply but headed upstairs. She felt a sense of dread as she caught sight of the open bedroom door. Ella's door had been closed when they left.

"Ella, you awake?" She looked into the room and found the bedcovers thrown aside and the wardrobe doors open. Had Ella tired of staying in bed? She had been complaining the last couple of days about not being allowed to get up and go to the table for her meals.

But something didn't sit well with Mara. It wasn't like Ella to promise one thing and do another. She had assured them she would stay in bed.

Mara made her way back downstairs just as Abe came in from the back. He was shouting—calling her name.

"Mara! Mara! Miz Fleming! Come quick."

Mara reached the bottom step, and Mrs. Fleming looked completely baffled. "Whatever are you shouting for, Abraham?" she asked.

Abe came into the room with the Fleming cook and two housemaids. All three women looked terrified. Abe stopped abruptly and pulled the women in front of him. "Tell 'em what you done told me."

The older of the three women spoke up.

"It was Mr. Jefferson Spiby," she said, shaking her head. "He come to the house just after you left. He didn't knock or nothin', just opened the door and came in like he owned the place. I was so scared 'cause I knowed he was under arrest and I thought maybe he escaped."

"Oh no!" Mrs. Fleming's hand went to her throat. "What about Ella?"

"She ain't upstairs." Mara looked at Abe, who nodded.

"He done took her," the cook replied before anyone else could speak.

"What?" Mrs. Fleming looked pale. "He took my child?"

"Yes'm. We was hidin', but we saw it. He took her and made her ride in front of him on his horse. They took off down the road, and I sent one of the boys to follow after."

"Where is he now?"

"He ain't come back yet. It's been pert near two hours."

Mrs. Fleming bit her lip. Mara would have smiled at the similarity to Ella if the situation hadn't been so grave.

"Should we send for the sheriff?" Mara asked.

"Of course!" Mrs. Fleming nodded. "Abraham, would you please go back to town and bring him?"

Abe nodded. "I'll take a horse, if that be all right."

"Yes. Take the fastest. One of the boys will know which."

Abe gave another nod before heading back through the kitchen. Mara looked at the other three dark-skinned women. They were all clearly afraid. They knew from past experience what Jefferson Spiby was capable of. He'd no doubt hurt them as he had hurt Mara. How she prayed for God's retribution to rain down on that man.

"You best get some supper on," Mara said, nodding toward the three women. "Gonna need to keep up our strength." She would never have presumed to order the Fleming help around, but it was clear that Mrs. Fleming was beside herself.

The three women took off in a hurry. No doubt they were glad to have nothing more to do with the matter.

"What are we going to do?" Mrs. Fleming asked, looking at Mara. "He's taken her. She's sick and weak, and he'll no doubt do horrible things to her."

"Now there, Miz Flemin'. You won't do nobody no good to go imaginin' all sorts of things we can't know for sure. Let's wait for that boy to come back from followin' them.

We'll know better what's what when we hear what he has to say."

It was about forty minutes later when the cook returned with the young groom in hand. Mara and Mrs. Fleming were in the front room, warming themselves by the fire Mara had built.

"I followed him, ma'am," the boy said, twisting his hat in his hand. "I stayed in the brush so he couldn't see me."

"Did he go back to his farm?" Mrs. Fleming asked.

"No, ma'am. He done took to the south road. The one what goes into the woods and down along the river."

Mrs. Fleming said nothing for a few minutes, then turned to Mara. "His family had a hunting lodge not far from the river, but it was on the very farthest reaches of their property, at least ten or fifteen miles from here." She pressed her fingertips against her head. "I can't remember. I was never there, but Robert and George were. They would know exactly where it's located."

"Would the sheriff know too?" Mara asked.

"I don't know. It's possible. Oh, I do wish he would get here. I feel so helpless. It'll be dark soon." She turned back to the boy. "Is there anything else you can tell us?"

The boy shook his head. "I don't know nothing more than he went south. Miss Ella was riding in front of him on the horse, and she was coughin' a lot."

"My poor girl." Mrs. Fleming began to weep into her hands.

"You can go, boy. That's good enough. When the sheriff gets here, we'll call for you to tell him all of this. Tell Cook I said to give you a half-dozen cookies."

He nodded with a big grin, then took off like a streak.

Mara handed Mrs. Fleming a handkerchief and patted her shoulder. "My mama used to say that when things look the worst, that's when God shines the best. We need to keep prayin', Miz Fleming. God gonna shine down on Miss Ella. You wait and see."

Ella's throat felt raw from her continual coughing, but still she persisted. She could tell by the way Jefferson stiffened each time she began hacking that he was more than a little disturbed. At one point he even got down and walked the horse to avoid close contact with her. She had analyzed the situation, thinking maybe she could maneuver the reins from his hold, but she could see that it would probably be impossible.

The light was growing dim when Jefferson stopped and remounted. The path split into two, and he chose the one to the right. It would keep them closer to the river, no doubt. Ella had no idea where he was headed, but the damp, chilly air was starting to permeate her clothes.

"Are we not going back to your farm?" she asked.

"You'd like that, I'm sure. There's probably Pinkertons and other law officials looking for me there." He tightened his hold on her waist, pulling her back against him.

"Pinkertons?" she repeated, hoping to sound ignorant of the entire affair.

"Your fool of a father turned against me, and now the world has done the same. In time, however, I'll make him pay. I'll make your entire family pay."

Ella grimaced but was determined not to fight. If he saw that she was too weak to resist, then he might not be concerned about her running away. She slumped against him and coughed.

"Will we ever rest? I don't feel very well, Jefferson."

He only growled in reply and kept the horse moving. Ella knew she should pay close attention to their surroundings, but as night closed in, that became impossible. The temperature began to drop, and Ella shivered so hard that her teeth chattered.

Overhead the skies were a dusky hue of gray and dark blue. The light was nearly gone when Jefferson finally stopped the horse and dismounted. He pulled Ella down, holding her in his arms like a baby. She closed her eyes, knowing that if she saw his face, she'd be unable to control the urge to fight him. Instead, she pretended to faint and went limp in his arms.

For several seconds he did nothing but stand there, holding her. Then, just as she thought she'd have to feign waking up, he moved to the right and lowered her to the ground. Ella stayed put. She didn't so much as open her eyes. She heard Jefferson moving around and realized he was unsaddling the horse. He came near again and draped the saddle blanket over Ella. After he moved away, she cracked open her eyes just enough to see his shadowy form shift around in the darkness. Eventually she opened her eyes in full.

Jefferson soon had a fire going, and without thinking about his reaction, Ella crawled closer.

"I see you're awake."

"Sorry. I've been given to fainting since I took sick. My body is just too weak." She spoke in a hushed tone to emphasize her words. Then, just for good measure, she gave another cough.

"I thought you were doing much better. That's what the doctor said."

"I *am* doing much better. I nearly died." She didn't know if that was true or not, but it didn't matter. Jefferson needed to believe she was too ill to fight him or escape. "Where are we going?" she asked, holding her hands out to the flames.

"My family has a hunting cottage about ten miles from here. I didn't figure we could find our way in the dark."

"So we're just going to sleep out here in the wild?"

"Unless you happen to know of a hotel nearby." His remark was thick with sarcasm.

Ella shook her head. "I know nothing about this territory. I've never been this way before. My father kept me at home except for those times we traveled abroad. I suppose he didn't want me anywhere near your operation." She coughed several times for good measure.

Jefferson was strangely silent. It wasn't like him not to be goaded into snide comments. Ella thought perhaps he was too tired or too worried. She hoped for both. If he fell asleep, she might have a chance to escape him.

"Did you bring any food?" she asked,

wondering exactly how much he had planned ahead.

"No, but there will be food at the cottage. I laid in a supply. Taking you was an accidental benefit. I just happened to see your mother and the others headed to town and knew you'd be alone. I didn't have time to plan out our escape." He put another piece of wood on the fire. "We just need to get through the night. Now, get over here."

Ella looked across the fire at him. She wasn't sure what he had in mind, but she found it almost impossible to move. "I'm too weak. I barely managed to crawl to the fire."

She let go another round of coughing and heard Jefferson give an exasperated sigh. He got up and grabbed the discarded saddle blanket, then came to her. She thought perhaps he intended to cover her again, but instead he threw himself down beside her and pulled her against him. She tried to get away but remembered her plan to convince him that she was too weak to fight and gave up.

He laughed and tightened his hold on her, then pulled her down as he threw the saddle blanket over them. "Lie still and go to sleep. I'm not about to let you slip away in the night. Just remember this: I'm a very light sleeper, and if you so much as consider leaving, I'll know it."

Ella nodded and didn't try to loosen his hold. His very touch, however, stirred an anger deep inside her. Jefferson had forced his will on so many people, and someone needed to stop him. Perhaps that was why this had happened. Perhaps Ella was the one who would finally put an end to Jefferson Spiby's horrendous deeds.

She looked around the camp without raising her head or even daring to draw a deep breath. She needed a weapon, but there was nothing. Even a quick glance at the fire was no help. Jefferson had found large pieces of wood that Ella would never be able to lift from the fire, much less wield. Did he have a revolver? She hadn't seen one.

"Go to sleep," he demanded, "or I might be forced to give you more attention than you desire."

She stiffened, knowing in that moment that if she had a gun, it would take very little effort to use it against him. She'd never wanted to kill another person before, but just contemplating Jefferson's plans for her made Ella more than willing to do so.

"What do you mean, the sheriff refused to come?" Mrs. Fleming asked.

Mara could see the disbelief in her expression. She knew Ella's mother had counted on the law being able to bring her daughter home safely.

"He said this family done caused him too much trouble already. Said if Flemings were in trouble, then Flemings could get themselves out of trouble." Abe looked at Mara and shook his head. "There's a lot of hateful folks in that town."

"They blame us for the end to their commerce. George told me a lot of people benefited from what he was doing." Mrs. Fleming reclaimed her chair by the fire. She looked completely defeated. "My poor child. That man will stop at nothing to hurt her. He blames her for everything. I heard him tell George that if she hadn't overheard him and run away, none of this would have happened."

Mara knew the truth of it. She could still remember the night she'd helped Ella escape to join Lizzy Brookstone at the train.

"Miz Fleming, you said Mr. Fleming and Mr. Robert know how to get to that hunting lodge. We could send them a telegram and ask about it. Maybe Abe and I could go after Spiby and bring Miss Ella back," Mara said, looking to Abe for affirmation. She knew it wouldn't sit well with him for her to go along, but it was the best she could come up with.

"That's right," the older woman said,

nodding. "They would know. We could get their help. If Jefferson has taken Ella there, they could tell us the way." She got up and went to her writing desk across the room. "I'll write out the message to send."

Mara went to Abe as her former mistress wrote the note. "I didn't mean to volunteer you for another job," she said, smiling apologetically.

"Ain't no way I'm lettin' you risk your life goin' after that girl. I'll go, but you're stayin' here," he said in a barely audible voice.

"You're gonna need help."

"Maybe so, but not from you. The good Lord will figure out who to send."

"Maybe He already done figured that out," Mara replied, hands on her hips.

Mrs. Fleming came back to them and handed Abe the note and some money. "This should cover the expense. I suppose you should wait for a reply."

"Ain't no reply gonna come yet tonight, Miz Fleming," Abe replied. "I could come back and go in at first light."

Ella's mother looked at Mara as if hoping she might say otherwise.

"He's right, Miz Fleming. Fact is, the telegraph office already be closed. We're gonna have to wait till morning just to send it."

This sent the older woman into another

fit of tears. Mara put her arm around Mrs. Fleming's shoulders and looked at Abe. "I'm gonna get her to bed. Would you ask Cook to bring up some tea and maybe somethin' to eat? It's gonna be a long night."

✦⸗ TWENTY-TWO ⸗✦

Ella found herself roughly awakened the next morning. Jefferson was in a hurry to get moving.

"If you need to relieve yourself, do so over there where I can still see the top of your head," he said, pointing to some heavy brush and vegetation near their campsite.

It was impossible for Ella to escape. She knew that as well as she knew her own name. Rather than protest or argue, she did as he instructed, all the while trying to figure out what she could do.

He had the horse saddled and ready when she returned, and Ella could see that he was agitated.

"Didn't you sleep well?" she asked as he motioned her toward the horse. She walked slowly and gave a light cough.

"Shut up and hold still." He lifted her in his arms and put her atop the animal. Then, without pausing, he followed her up. After arranging his coat, he pulled Ella back against him. He yanked the reins hard to the right and guided the horse onto the narrow trail.

Ella didn't recognize the territory but did note that the river was always on their right. If she managed to escape, she'd know to keep it on her left in order to make her way home. Glancing up, she took in the thick layer of gray clouds. They made everything gloomy and muted the light. Perhaps it would snow.

"Sit still," he ordered.

"Sorry. I was just wondering if it was going to snow."

"With my luck, it will."

Ella hated being in Jefferson's arms but tried to refrain from movement. She had to put his mind at ease to keep him from thinking she was any kind of threat. She continued her occasional cough and allowed his touch. Things were going well until he buried his face against her hair and she nearly jumped out of the saddle. He only laughed and tightened his hold on her.

"Glad to see you're feeling better."

"You startled me." She didn't offer further excuse. Instead, she focused on keeping her anger at bay. She knew Jefferson well enough to know that everything he did was in order to strike fear in her. He wanted her so afraid that she couldn't function.

Well, I'm not the frightened little girl he once knew.

After several hours they reached the hunting cottage, and Ella felt both relief and dread. She wanted so much to be in out of the cold, but at the same time the house represented imprisonment with Jefferson as her jailer.

Jefferson surprised her by bringing the horse only to the edge of the clearing. "Don't make a sound or it'll be your last," he warned her.

He climbed down from the horse and considered the cottage for a moment before tying the horse to a nearby branch. It was obvious he feared someone had already discovered his hideout. After several minutes, he seemed satisfied that no one else had disturbed the grounds and yanked Ella from the saddle.

Walking toward the house, he kept Ella in front of him like a shield and drew his pistol. She might have laughed at his efforts had the situation not been so grave. Jefferson was at least a foot taller than she was. Ella hardly offered him much protection.

She coughed, and he squeezed her arm in a viselike grip. "Be quiet, you fool."

The two-story cottage was larger and

more rundown than Ella had expected. She remembered her father and brother's stories of coming here with the Spiby men to hunt. It was a place where they could escape the cares of the world. Her father had been quite fond of it and sometimes wished for a place of his own just like it. She doubted he'd feel the same if he could see it now. The wood siding was in sad need of paint and the front porch was sagging. The entire property was overgrown.

As Jefferson pushed her forward, Ella tried to memorize the surroundings and come up with ideas for places to hide. When they were finally inside, Ella strained to see in the dim light. The cloth-covered furniture rose up like ghostly specters from long ago. She shivered and hugged her arms to her body, but Jefferson didn't seem to notice or care.

He left her standing alone while he checked out the first floor. Ella thought about making a run for the door, but Jefferson was quickly darting from room to room. She still felt certain that her best chance was to convince him she was too weak to be a threat. With that in mind, she feigned a spell and collapsed to the ground. Just that brief movement had Jefferson at her side in a flash.

"What's wrong with you?"

"I'm afraid sleeping in the cold last night

has brought on a relapse. I feel quite faint." She curled up and closed her eyes.

He gave a growl and left her where she was as he finished his exploration. She heard him pulling covers off the furniture and wondered if he would also get a fire going. As far removed as they were from civilization, surely he wouldn't worry about the chimney smoke being seen.

After several minutes he returned and without warning picked Ella up off the floor. She remained limp in his arms, surprised that he was gentle as he placed her on a sofa.

She looked up and coughed. "If . . . I die . . . please tell Mother that I love her."

He shook his head. Ella didn't know if he disbelieved how sick she was pretending to be or if he was genuinely concerned. She had a hard time believing this callous, unfeeling man cared about anyone or anything. Still, if she could stir a bit of pity in him, it might be to her benefit. She coughed and gave little gasping breaths as she had done weeks ago when she'd first taken ill. She couldn't be certain, but she thought it seemed to urge Jefferson toward making a fire a little faster.

With a fire ablaze in the hearth, the room began to warm, and Ella felt her body begin to thaw. She was grateful to be able to rest on something soft, but her mind wouldn't allow her to let down her guard and sleep. Her anger gave her a strange sort of energy. This man had killed innocent people and would harm her family if he got a chance. She had to find a way to beat him at his own game.

Jefferson continued to pace from window to window, keeping watch for anyone who might have followed them. He made Ella more than a little nervous, and finally she couldn't take anymore.

"Jefferson, you said there was food. I feel so weak. Might I have something to eat?"

He stopped mid-step and looked severely at her. She wasn't sure if she'd angered him or if he was still lost in his thoughts of what to do next.

"Figure it out for yourself. There's food in the kitchen. But don't get any ideas about running from me. Even if you were in your best condition, I'd have you back in a matter of minutes . . . and I'd make sure you never considered doing something so foolish again."

Ella sat up. "Do you plan to stay here forever?"

"Hardly. The authorities will eventually find out about this place. We'll be long gone. I have friends in California. A pretty town called Riverside. You'll like it. We'll leave here and catch a train west. Once we're there, I'll have money and all the help I need to completely disappear from the authorities and start my new life. With you."

"Why haven't we heard anything from Robert?" Mrs. Fleming questioned, pacing the room.

Mara shook her head. She didn't like the situation any better than her former mistress, but without Robert to tell them where the hunting lodge was, Mara knew they would be hard-pressed to find it. They'd even asked among the few remaining workers, but none of them had ever gone with Mr. Fleming or his son on any of the hunting trips.

Twice a day, Abe went to town to check for telegrams from Robert, but nothing had come. It had been two days since they'd returned to find Ella gone. Mara feared Jefferson might have done a great deal to Ella in that time. She knew exactly how cruel he could be, and if he felt inclined to make a person suffer, he would do so. Still, Mara didn't feel she could be honest with Mrs. Fleming about such things. She doubted Ella's mother knew about the rape Mara had endured at Spiby's hands. Women of her social standing were shielded from such things, and while Mr. Fleming knew full well what was going on, he would never have told his wife.

"What if we send Abraham to Washington, D.C., to find Robert and bring him back?" Mrs. Fleming suddenly asked. "It surely would not be that difficult. We have the name of their hotel. He would simply have to go there and wait for Robert and then bring him here. George might also be free to come." She looked at Mara with such hope that the younger woman could only nod.

"I 'spect he could go, but what if Mr. Robert is makin' his way here?"

Mrs. Fleming frowned. "I hadn't considered that. I suppose he could be, but surely he would have telegraphed us to say as much."

Mara heard the sound of an approaching rider on the long gravel lane. "Somebody be comin'." She went to the window and saw a single rider racing hard up the drive. "Maybe somebody be bringin' us a telegram."

She made her way to the foyer with Mrs. Fleming close on her heels. Mara hadn't even reached the door when it flew open and Robert Fleming rushed inside.

"Mother! I came as soon as I could. Have you had any word from Ella?"

Mrs. Fleming fell into her son's arms. "No. No word at all. Jefferson took her. That's all we know."

"And you feel certain he went to the family hunting cottage?"

"Yes." She pulled back just enough to see his face. "One of the stable boys followed him for several miles. He took the old river path—the one that you and your father took to the hunting lodge. I had Abraham go to the Spiby house, but no one there had seen anything of Jefferson." She tried to look around Robert's broad shoulders. "Is your father here with you?"

"No. The authorities wouldn't allow him to leave, but it's all right. I remember the way, and I'll bring Ella home safely."

"But you can't! Not without help. He's a madman." She looked to Mara for confirmation.

"My Abe will go with you." Mara and Abe had discussed the idea of Abe going. He had already intended to head out by himself once he learned the whereabouts of the lodge. "He's just been waiting to know where to go."

Robert nodded and led his mother to the nearest chair. "We're wasting time. Let me go change my clothes. I'll wear something of Father's if you don't mind."

Mrs. Fleming nodded but said nothing. She pulled a handkerchief from her sleeve and dabbed at the tears that flowed freely down her face. Mara wished she could offer the older woman some comfort, but they had never been close, and she feared it might be seen as an intrusion. Still, something inside her urged her to cross that line.

Mara went to Ella's mother and took her hand. Giving it a squeeze, Mara glanced up to see Mrs. Fleming give her a questioning look.

"Times have changed, Miz Flemin'. I figure God would have us pray together and encourage each other even if our skin be different colors. Your Ella is precious to me too."

Beatrix Fleming considered this for a moment, then nodded. "God is our only hope—Ella's only hope. I know what that man is capable of doing. I've heard the talk." She looked away. "I try not to allow such thoughts into my mind, but I'm tormented by them. Jefferson will ruin her—perhaps even kill her."

It was clear that Mrs. Fleming had already imagined the worst. Mara held her hand tight. "Mr. Jefferson is an evil man, but our God—He be good, and He's more powerful than Mr. Jefferson and the devil he serves."

Mrs. Fleming sniffed back her tears. "Yes. Yes, He is."

◆━◆━◆━◆━

Phillip looked around, hoping he might be able to get directions to Fleming Farm. The depot platform was abuzz with people, given a westbound train had come in moments before his train's arrival. Phillip asked one of the depot baggage handlers, but the handler had never heard of the Flemings. He suggested Phillip try the depot master, but the master was busy with an old woman who declared her luggage was missing. Phillip glanced around and spotted the post office. That was probably as good a place to start as any. He hoisted his trunk on his shoulder and made his way to where the postmaster was receiving mail from the train.

The old man eyed him curiously as Phillip made his way into the small building. He gave a smile as he pulled off his Stetson. "Howdy. Are you the postmaster?"

"I reckon I am," the man replied. "What can I do for you?"

"I was wonderin' if you could point me in the direction of Fleming Farm."

The postmaster frowned. "You family?"

"No." Phillip shrugged, putting on his guard at the tone in the old man's voice. "I'm just a friend." He lowered his trunk to the wood floor.

"Well, they don't have too many of those these days. If I were you, mister, I'd be mindful of that."

Phillip frowned. "Sorry. I didn't know I was stirrin' a hornet's nest. Fact is, I know the daughter and came to escort her back to the Brookstone Wild West Extravaganza." He did his best to work his boyish charm. "If you've never seen her trick ride, you should do your best to make one of the performances. I'm just a wrangler, but I've never seen anything like it."

The postmaster relaxed a bit and refocused on the mailbags. "I haven't got time for such things. Fleming Farm is out the north road about seven miles—maybe a little more. There's a big gate at the end of the drive. You can't miss it—says Fleming Farm. If you don't have a horse, you can rent one from Charles Meyers at the farrier shop on the west end of town."

Phillip gave a nod. "Much obliged." He grabbed his luggage and headed back outside, pausing only to resecure his hat and lift the small trunk to his shoulder.

The town was busy for its size. Main Street bustled with horse and buggy traffic, as well as riders. It was still rural enough, however, that there wasn't a motorized car in sight. Phillip preferred it that way. He'd seen many an automobile in the cities but had no hankering to own one or even try them. They were smelly and undependable. He'd take a good horse over a car any day. A horse wasn't likely to break down, and fuel was readily available in just about any field.

He rented a mount at the farrier's and

left his trunk as assurance that he'd be back within a day or two. He told Meyers that if he failed to show up, he could always find him at Fleming Farm. The farrier grunted but seemed disinterested as he went back to work at the forge. Phillip thought his behavior strange, but he didn't care. He was so excited to see Ella again. See her and propose.

The ride out of town was quiet and pleasant enough, despite the cold. Phillip imagined Ella growing up in this part of Kentucky. He wanted to believe she'd been happy for most of her childhood. From what little she had told him, her life on the farm had been one of privilege and ease.

Phillip pulled his collar close before reaching into his coat pockets for his gloves. The air was damp and had turned quite cold. It looked like they could expect snow or at least an icy rain. Hopefully he'd be at Fleming Farm enjoying a warm fire before that happened.

In no time at all he saw an ornate wrought iron and stone gate. Overhead it read *FLEMING FARM est. 1845*. He smiled and urged the horse to pass beneath. "Get on up!"

The horse picked up its pace, doing a fast trot up the long fence-lined drive. Pastures stretched out on either side. Phillip could imagine them full of horses. Ella had told him about her father's passion for Morgans.

He wondered where the animals were now. The fields were strangely empty.

Phillip turned his attention back to the well-kept gravel drive. Someone had gone to a lot of trouble to keep it in perfect order. When the large three-story house came into view, Phillip slowed his mount. The same meticulous care had been given to the columned white mansion. Beyond it there were stables and barns, fenced pens and pastures, but all were empty. The house, although regal in appearance, seemed almost ghostly and deserted. He frowned and made his way to a small hitching post, where he dismounted and tied up the horse.

He looked toward the house and then the barns. He'd never been a front door sort of man, but he was calling on the daughter of the house. He wrestled with his choices a moment longer and then breathed a sigh of relief when a tall black man came from around the side of the house.

"Can I help you?" he asked.

"I sure hope so," Phillip replied with a big smile. "I'm here to see Miss Ella Fleming. I'm Phillip DeShazer."

The man smiled. "I've heard you mentioned. They hired me on to be a wrangler with the Brookstone show after you left." He held out his hand. "The name is Abraham, but my friends call me Abe." They shook, and before Phillip could speak, Abe continued in sober tones. "You're a welcome sight, I must say. We've got problems."

Phillip frowned. "With Ella?"

"'Fraid so."

"Is she sicker? Henry Adler said she was on the mend."

"She is . . . or at least was before—"

"Before what?" Phillip interrupted. He looked toward the house. "What's happened?"

"Mr. Jefferson Spiby is what happened. Do you know about him?"

Phillip nodded. "He tried to kill Ella when he was in Montana."

Abe gave a nod. "Best I know, he escaped the law and came back. He found out Miss Ella was here alone, and he took her. We figure he's taken her to his family's hunting place on the river."

"Why are we wasting time standing here then?" Phillip untied his horse. "Let's go get her back."

Abe nodded. "Her brother and I was just about to do that very thing. Guess God figured we needed more help. I'm sure Mr. Robert will be glad to have you along."

Phillip had a sketchy memory of seeing Ella's brother in a hotel lobby. He had seen a man kiss Ella and feared he was a beau. Other than that, he couldn't remember much at all, because he'd been drunk.

"You'd best go on up to the house and pay your respects to Mrs. Fleming. She's half-sick with worry, but it'll do her good to know we've got another man on this hunt."

Phillip retied his horse, and Abe led the way to the house. Phillip paused in the foyer, gazing at the grandeur. Ella had grown up with so much more than he could ever hope to give her. The gilded mirrors alone were more than a year of his salary.

"Mr. Phillip!" Mara declared, coming from one of the side rooms.

Phillip met her dark-eyed gaze. "Ella's been taken by Spiby?"

She nodded to Abraham. "You done talked to Abe about it?"

"I did. Abe thought I should introduce myself to Ella's mother before I head out with him and Ella's brother."

Mara nodded. "Come on in here and meet 'em both."

She led the way to a pale woman sitting in an overstuffed chair. A man who looked to be in his mid to late thirties knelt beside her. He looked up and assessed Phillip in silence. The woman turned to see Phillip. Neither spoke.

"Miz Fleming, Mr. Robert, this is Ella's beau, Mr. Phillip De . . . De . . ." She shrugged.

"Ain't never been able to say that boy's last name properly."

Phillip smiled. "DeShazer." He stepped forward as Robert got to his feet. "Abe told me what happened, and I intend to help. I'm a good tracker."

Robert nodded. "You're a godsend."

"I just arrived on the train."

"The westbound?" Robert asked. "I was on that train myself."

"No, the eastbound that arrived about ten minutes later. The westbound was just leaving when I got here," Phillip replied. "Made for a lot of folks comin' and goin'."

Again Robert nodded. "Well, I'm glad you're here. I know the general location of Spiby's hunting cottage. It's deep in the woods not far from the river, but quite a ways to the south. The trail won't be easy. It's not generally traveled, what with it being mostly on Spiby's land. I'm sure it's overgrown."

Phillip squared his shoulders. "If they went that way, I can track 'em."

His confidence brought a smile to Robert's face. "Then let's go. The sooner we do, the sooner we can get Ella back."

✦═ TWENTY-THREE ═✦

Robert put them on the trail to the Spiby hunting lodge but made clear his concern that too much time had passed.

"Surely Spiby would have moved on by now. He knows the Pinkertons are after him. He's a murderer, and the law isn't going to just let him go."

Phillip said nothing. He hated thinking of Ella being in Spiby's control. He'd heard her talk about her former fiancé and knew from when Spiby showed up at the Brookstone ranch just what a threat he could be. Phillip remembered seeing bruises on Ella's neck after Spiby tried to strangle her. The memory only stirred his anger and urged him forward. He would see that Spiby suffered for taking her.

Robert rode up even with Phillip while

Abe fell behind. "What do you see? Did they come this way?"

Phillip had been paying close attention to the trail for tracks and signs of Spiby's leaving the path. "Yeah, just like you thought. Spiby didn't do anything to cover his trail."

"He probably figured no one would remember how to get there. We haven't gone to the lodge in over ten years. I wasn't even sure the family still kept it. It was starting to fall into disrepair the last time I was there."

Phillip only nodded. He kept his gaze glued to the trail in case something changed.

"You do know that Spiby isn't an honorable man."

Robert's comment surprised Phillip. Why would he bring up something like that now? Phillip threw him a quick glance. "I know enough. I was at the ranch when your pa and Spiby came to take Ella home. Spiby tried to kill her."

"Yes, but unfortunately I was thinking of other things he might well have done to her by now. They've been together at least two nights."

Phillip frowned as he began to understand Robert's meaning. The thought of that man touching Ella left Phillip with little doubt that he could commit murder. The very idea of Spiby forcing himself on a helpless woman—

much less Ella—was more than Phillip could bear.

When Phillip didn't respond, Robert continued. "Jefferson Spiby takes what he wants. He's never concerned himself with his reputation or that of others. He's been known to have multiple mistresses and to impose his will on women no matter their walk of life. He may well have . . . forced himself on Ella."

Phillip's gloved hands tightened on the reins. He didn't even try to hide his anger. "Why are you telling me this?"

"Because I want you to be aware of the kind of man you're dealing with, and because . . . I know you are in love with my sister."

"I am." Phillip drew in a deep breath and nodded. "And nothing will change that."

"You can't know that," Robert replied. "You may find Ella so changed that you won't want to continue the relationship. I'm just saying these things in order to help you prepare yourself for what might be."

Frowning, Phillip turned to Robert. "I don't like to think of that man taking Ella and tormenting her in any fashion. I pray to God she's still alive and that she's unhurt, but no matter what has happened, nothing is going to change my love for her. If Spiby has forced himself on her, I won't love Ella less. I will, however, most likely kill him."

They rode in silence for several minutes, and then Robert cleared his throat. "I didn't say those things to make an enemy of you. I just want to be sure you truly care for her. After all, I don't know you. Ella's gone through so much, and this is no doubt worse than anything else. She's going to need a strong and powerful love to see her through—especially if she's been used in such an ugly fashion."

"I understand," Phillip said, having already considered this might be Robert's angle. "I keep thinking about something Ella once told me when I was drunk. She said that God didn't expect us to clean ourselves up before we came to Him. He just wanted us to come. She said we're all broken and dirty and sinful, but God loves us so much that He looks past all that and sees what we could one day be with His help. God is the only one who can take the ugly things and make beauty out of them. I can't make Ella whole or take away the bad that's happened to her. Only God can do that. But"—he glanced at Robert—"I intend to look past the ugly things that may have happened and see only the beauty that she is."

Robert's expression softened. "I think I understand why my sister loves you."

Phillip looked back at the road. "There's nothing of myself to recommend, but God in me changes everything. I love Ella, and no matter what happens I'll still love her and want her as my wife."

"Well, I must say you are an admirable man. I think I can speak for our father as well when I say that I can't imagine anyone worthier of Ella's hand. I shall look forward to the day when I can call you brother."

Robert's words were filled with admiration, but Phillip knew that while he'd never think less of Ella for what might have been done to her—he would most certainly see to it that Jefferson Spiby paid for his crimes.

———❖———

Ella awoke and stretched as well as she could against the confines of the ropes Jefferson had used to tie her to the bed. He had been so preoccupied making sure no one had followed them that he paid her very little attention. Throughout the night, Ella heard him pacing and checking doors and windows. He was no doubt exhausted, and for this Ella was grateful. Without sleep, Jefferson wouldn't be able to think clearly. Hopefully that would give her an edge.

She tested the ropes just as she had the night before. They held fast. The bed creaked and groaned as she pulled against the bindings. Unfortunately, the noise brought

Jefferson to the room. He looked haggard as he made his way to the bed.

"I see you're awake. You didn't cough as much last night, so I presume you are better for having spent the night indoors."

"Yes, I'm sure the warmth was beneficial. Now if I can just regain my strength." She tried not to sound too excited or too morose. Jefferson was no one's fool. He might be momentarily uncertain, but that wouldn't last. "I hope you'll untie me and allow me to use the facilities." She forced herself to look him in the eye. "I really must go."

He didn't question her but undid the ropes in silence. When he'd finished, he surprised her by lifting her from the bed and standing her up beside him. She tried not to grimace or show any fear, but in truth she was terrified. Jefferson was a murderer and an abuser of women. It was only a matter of time before he decided to have his way with her. Ella knew that if he tried to take liberties, she would die defending her honor.

"Is it far?" she asked, hoping to break the tension she felt.

He shrugged. "No farther than any outhouse. Come on." He headed for the back door.

Jefferson had put her in the downstairs bedroom off the main living area. He'd not attempted to join her there but did keep the door open as he took up his place in the front room. Ella hadn't thought it possible to sleep, but her own exhaustion soon overcame her, and she had woken only when Jefferson's pacing disturbed her. Now, amazingly enough, she felt more like her old self.

Jefferson led the way through the kitchen and out the back door. He pointed to the outhouse. "I'll be right here," he promised, "so don't try anything stupid."

Ella nodded and made her way to the small two-door contraption. For people with money, it was surprising that the Spibys hadn't built better facilities. Maybe it was because only men came here.

She opened the door and realized that with the door open, Jefferson couldn't see if she stepped inside the outhouse or went around to the back of it. She could use that to her advantage later, she decided. She tended to her needs, then made her way back toward the house. There was a pump just off the back steps, and she stopped there as Jefferson watched her. "Is there water in the house?"

He nodded. "I've heated some over the fire. You'll have more than enough unless you want to take a bath." He gave her a leer. "I'll gladly heat more if that's your desire."

"No." She shook her head. "It's much

too cold. I simply wish to wash my face and hands."

He shrugged. "Suit yourself."

Ella let him take her by the arm and lead her back through the house to the front room. He pointed to the water and then to a stack of towels. "I found those in the chest. Use what you need. There's a bowl on the shelf."

"When are we leaving?" she asked, trying to sound disinterested. Her heart was pounding so hard, however, that she was certain Jefferson knew how important the answer was to her. She spotted the bowl and reached for it, but it was too high for her petite frame.

Jefferson saw the dilemma and came to her aid. "Soon. We can't waste time. Your people will be looking for you, so it's best to get you out of here as soon as possible. With you sick, it was difficult, but now that you're better, we can move more quickly." He handed her the bowl and then reached out with his other hand to touch her hair.

Ella shivered and gave a cough. "I'm not completely well. You can hardly expect me to heal overnight. Especially after all you've put me through." She stepped away and reached for the ladle. She didn't know what Jefferson might be thinking, but she prayed for God's direction and filled the bowl with hot water.

She took the water to the table and then grabbed one of the folded towels. All the time she looked for anything that might suggest a weakness on Jefferson's part. He was clearly nervous. He knew that his situation was grave and that not only were the authorities looking for him, but Ella's people as well.

As she cleaned up, Jefferson paced from window to window. He seemed to be trying to figure out what they should do. Ella decided to offer her own thoughts. She would have a better chance of escape once they were back in civilization.

"I suppose Lexington isn't all that far. People would be less likely to notice us in a big city like that," she suggested.

He grunted but said nothing. Ella watched him as if keeping track of a snake. She was wary of making sudden moves to draw his attention but also knew the importance of keeping him in her sight at every moment. All the while, she tidied herself.

"Do you suppose there might be a brush in the house?" she asked.

"I doubt it," he said, glancing up at her. "The women we had here weren't overly concerned with such things."

Ella could only imagine. "I can hardly show up in town looking like this. People would definitely notice. Perhaps you could ride ahead and bring back a brush and clean clothes. These are filthy."

He laughed. "You could just shed them and give them a good washing. I know I wouldn't mind. I'll even build up the fire so you don't chill."

Ella decided to try another tactic. "Why are you doing this, Jefferson? You know it's going to be harder to travel with me. People are looking for me. You'd have a much easier time of it on your own. Why not just kill me and be done with it?"

He seemed surprised by her question. "I'd much prefer not to kill you."

"I presume, given your past record, you'll kill anyone who interferes in your plans."

"And you figure to interfere?" He grinned and moved closer.

Ella chose her words carefully. She still wanted him to believe her too weak to be much of a threat. She shrugged. "I can't help but slow you down. That in and of itself will be an interference."

"My dear Ella, I plan to disappear into the wilds of the West. I will disappear for a long time, until folks have forgotten about me. I will change my name and appearance, and Jefferson Spiby will cease to exist. Such an ordeal could be quite lonely without someone to keep me company. I figure you'll do nicely.

In the meantime, folks might do what they can to find you, but they'll do it very carefully, because they know if they push me too hard, you will pay the price."

"I'll pay the price no matter."

He had reached out to take hold of her but stopped. For a moment all he did was look at her, and then without another word he marched back to the window.

To Ella's relief, he ignored her until late in the afternoon, when he instructed her to fix him something to eat. Otherwise he seemed completely lost in his thoughts and plans.

Ella found crackers, canned meat, and fruit in the kitchen. From the way Jefferson had talked earlier, she figured he'd made arrangements for this escape a while ago. Perhaps he knew there was a possibility he would be imprisoned prior to her father going to the authorities. Even so, the provisions weren't that good, so chances were better than not that he'd had no real plan in mind.

By the time evening came, it was raining. Ella knew it might very well turn to snow, given the temperatures, and wondered if she could use the weather to her advantage. Jefferson would never expect her to make a run for it in these conditions. She'd given him no reason to think she was anywhere near strong enough to escape.

Then again, she felt certain it would be easier to escape him once they were in the city. With other people around, she could plead for help or at least demand someone send for the authorities. But that might get an innocent bystander killed if Jefferson felt desperate enough.

Ella wrestled with her thoughts all evening, and by bedtime she had convinced herself to do nothing until they attempted to get to a train. But Jefferson changed all that with a single statement.

"I believe I'll share your bed tonight."

Her blood went cold. She looked up to find him watching her with that same leering smile she'd come to hate. She knew there was no argument she could make to change his mind.

"Do what you will. You know I'm too weak to fight you." She hoped the matter-of-fact statement would put him at ease.

He chuckled. "I'm really not so very bad, my dear. I can make things quite pleasant for you."

"Might I use the facilities before we retire?" She kept her gaze fixed on his.

"But of course."

Ella got to her feet and went to where her coat hung by the fire. She started to slip it on, but Jefferson took it from her. "No. Leave it here. Your boots too. That way you won't be tempted to run away."

"You're right here where you can easily stop me," Ella said. "How could I possibly run away?"

He gave a soft chuckle. "Nevertheless, I figure this will be proper incentive for you to obey. You'll be so cold by the time you return, you won't mind my warmth at all. In fact, you'll beg for it."

She bit her lower lip to keep from throwing a sarcastic reply back in his face. It wasn't going to be easy to go on the run in pitch-black night without coat or shoes, but Ella wasn't about to wait around and be Jefferson's bedmate. Not so long as she had breath in her body.

Jefferson followed her to the back door. Ella could hardly see for the darkness and rain. She turned to her captor. "Might I have a lantern?"

"There's no need. The outhouse is at the end of the path. Just go and get back."

Ella gave a curt nod and headed out into the rain. Icy drops pelted her face as she squinted to better see. She reached the outhouse just as Jefferson shouted to her.

"Hurry up!"

"I am. I can hardly see."

She drew a deep breath and opened the

door. Hopefully he wouldn't be able to tell that she'd left it open. Without rethinking her plans, Ella slipped around the back of the outhouse and made her way to a line of trees that she knew stood at the edge of the clearing. She sighed with relief as her hand touched one of the trunks. For a moment she stood perfectly still. The darkness allowed her to see only in shadows. The house was across from her to the south. The forest led off to the north, and that was the direction of the river.

"Hurry up, Ella. It's freezing out here."

She cringed at the sound of Jefferson calling to her. He was still much too close. Ella moved deeper into the trees.

Pain coursed through her as she stepped on a jagged rock. She rarely ever walked in her stocking feet, and the rocks and roots felt like daggers against her frozen flesh. It couldn't be helped. She had to hurry and get as much distance between her and Jefferson as she could.

"Ella! Where are you? Get back in this house!"

He'd realized she was gone. Now there was no turning back—not that there ever was. Ella whispered a prayer and moved through the trees.

⇥ TWENTY-FOUR ⇤

Phillip awoke with a start. He sat up and looked around the camp. Abe and Robert slept soundly under the canvas lean-to they'd made for protection. At least, they had been until Phillip stirred everyone to life. The fire had long ago burned out, and although the rain had stopped, everything was waterlogged. Phillip pulled his blanket close and struggled to see in the darkness beyond the camp. He thought he'd heard something, but now there was only silence.

He prayed again for Ella and that God would give them insight to find the lodge and save her before Spiby could take off for parts unknown.

"What time is it?" Robert asked.

"I don't know, but I figure we ought to get moving if we're going to try to surprise them while it's still dark." Phillip rubbed the sleep from his eyes.

They had pushed on through the daylight hours until the rain made it impossible to see. Robert had suggested they retire early for a few hours' rest and then attack the lodge at night while Spiby and Ella slept. Catching Spiby off guard would be key.

"How much farther you figure, Mr. Robert?" Abe asked, sitting up.

"No more than a mile or two." Robert got to his feet and began to pack up his bedroll. "At least I don't think so. It's been a long time."

Abe and Phillip rolled up their blankets without waiting for Robert's instructions. They all knew the plan and their roles.

"A hot cup of coffee would be good about now," Robert said as he made his way to his horse.

"And a thick beefsteak." Phillip's voice carried his amusement. He remembered often commenting about wishing for one thing or another as a child. Ma always said he was wishing for what he couldn't have rather than being grateful for what he did. He reached into his pocket and pulled out a piece of jerked venison. "But I guess dried deer meat will have to do."

Abe laughed. "Couldn't get much of a

fire going even if we could catch us a cow to butcher."

Robert and Phillip saddled the horses while Abe took care of the canvas they'd used for shelter. Within a few minutes they were ready to head out. Phillip knew the going would be slow in the darkness. He felt confident that as long as they pointed the horses in the right direction, their mounts would choose the open path rather than venture into the trees.

"Since you said the trail leads right to the clearing where the lodge sits, I suggest we move in as close as we can while maintaining cover," Phillip said.

"I agree." Robert mounted his horse. "I'll lead the way."

The trio eased along the path, anxious for dawn. Brush and trees made ghostly figures, and when the wind stirred, it was as if the branches beckoned them forward. Otherwise there was no sign of life—no sound to suggest anyone was nearby. The darkness and cold were their only companions. Chilled to the bone, Phillip pulled his collar up and his hat down to stay as warm as possible. Mostly, he prayed.

———————

"Ella! You can't get away from me. I know this land better than you!"

Jefferson continued to call out after her, but Ella refused to give in to fear and turn back. She could hardly feel her feet. They were so cold—and probably bleeding from the debris-covered forest floor—but she didn't care. She kept her hands up in front of her face in order to feel her way through the thickets and brush, but otherwise she prayed and tried not to think about the man who was closing in behind her.

After a time, Jefferson stopped hollering. Ella wasn't sure if that was good or bad. At least when he was yelling at her, she had some idea of where he was. Now, however, there was no telling. He could have worked his way around her and be waiting just ahead. She paused and listened. Nothing could be heard but the remnants of rain as it dripped through the trees. She thought of finding one of the full pines and crawling beneath it to hide until light, but as tempting as that thought was, she feared she'd freeze to death. She had no coat, no shoes, and her stockings were ripped to shreds.

She tried to keep her mind fixed on home and Phillip. She didn't want to give in to despair. Not now. Not when there was a chance she might make her escape. She remembered once, after her tutor had told her about Lewis and Clark's exploration of the West, she had asked her father if they could go on an exploration and sleep outside under the starry skies. It sounded like such a grand adventure. Her father had quickly informed her that such things weren't for the likes of refined women. Ella thought that very disappointing. Why did men get to have all the fun?

Now, however, she would gladly have traded the danger of the woods at night for her warm bed and restricted life. The next time she enjoyed such luxuries, she would be extra grateful for them. If there was a next time.

She didn't really fear death, but she longed to see Phillip again and tell him how much she loved him. Her time in Europe had left her without doubt on that count. Even now, the thought of seeing him again was what pushed her on. It gave her strength as her reserves quickly gave out. Several times she found herself starting to cough and suppressed it as best she could. If she made too much noise, Jefferson would find her.

The snapping of branches sounded from somewhere behind her, and Ella froze in place. Was it Jefferson? An animal? Branches breaking as they froze?

Please, God, help me.

She pressed on as quietly as she could manage with her stiff limbs. She couldn't be sure of where she was or if she'd even managed to maintain a northerly course, and exhaustion was quickly overtaking her. Every step she took was sheer misery. Her hands and feet were frozen, and her legs were like lead weights as the wet wool material of her skirt clung to them. Twice she'd caught her hair in the branches of a tree or bush and thought for sure Jefferson had found her. Now, as a hint of dawn added light to the skies, Ella couldn't fight a deep sense of fear. The darkness had kept her hidden, but now she would be visible to Jefferson. This was his land, and he had already proven to know it well.

Ella staggered toward an opening in the brush. She could see on the other side that there was a bit of a trail, but whether it had been made by man or animal, she didn't know. Was it safe to follow it? It wasn't yet light enough to see where it led.

Tears slid down her cheeks. She crumpled to the ground in defeat. Where was she to go?

Lord, I have no idea where I am or where I can go to be safe. Please help me.

She wiped her cheeks with the hem of her skirt, but it did little good. The fabric was soaked from the rain. She couldn't give up now. She just couldn't. Yet she felt so helpless and hopeless. It was hard enough to face the first, but the second made her feel even worse. She knew God was with her. There was hope in that, but she also knew that she might well lose her life in this course.

Drawing a deep breath, Ella studied the area around her. Maybe she should find a hiding place and wait until it was once again dark. Maybe she could tear strips from her gown and pad her feet. Maybe she could take pieces of bark and use them to make soles to walk on. Maybe—

Something darted out at her from the side. Ella let out a scream, confident that Jefferson Spiby had found her. Instead, a deer rushed past, giving a leap as it suddenly spied her.

If Jefferson was nearby, she'd just given away her location. Her decision was made. She'd have to keep moving. Perhaps she should take the path and see where it led.

With great effort, she forced herself to stand. The pain she felt was no comparison to the fear. She forgot about tearing pieces of cloth or stripping bark and instead hurried as best as her bruised and bloodied feet would allow.

"It came from that direction," Phillip said, pointing. He'd heard the scream and knew it was Ella. "Take my horse. I'm going on foot."

Before Robert or Abe could protest, Phillip had jumped from his horse and headed toward the brush. He was confident that Ella was just beyond the trees, close enough to get to without the horse. No doubt Jefferson Spiby was the cause of her distress. Phillip felt his belt for the knife he kept there. He'd rather have a gun, but the knife would have to do. He pushed aside the brush and looked for any sign of a path or of Ella. It was only now getting light enough to see by, yet in the tight weave of trees, shrubs, and dead vegetation, Phillip had difficulty making his way.

"Lord, please help me find her. Help me know which way she's gone."

The toe of his boot caught on a root, and Phillip fell headlong onto the leaf-covered forest floor. He had started to get to his feet when he spied something pink. He plucked a piece of cloth from where it had torn off and stuck to a thorny bush.

Ella! Mara had told them Ella was wearing a pink dress. It was the only one missing from her wardrobe.

Phillip jumped up and looked around. He listened, intent on hearing even the slightest movement. She had come this way. She was close. He decided that even if Spiby were in pursuit, he would call for her. Maybe his presence would frighten Spiby into leaving her alone.

"Ella! Ella, it's Phillip! Where are you? Ella?"

There was no reply.

Phillip tried not to despair. She might not be able to speak. The scream may have indicated Spiby had her and was causing her pain.

He pressed on, watching the area carefully for tracks. He picked up her trail easily. Thankfully the forest had shielded her tracks from the heavier rain, so her progress was easily seen. He followed as quickly as he dared. When he reached the edge of a small clearing, he could see that she had actually taken a rest here. The brush was beaten down in a small circle. There were also deer tracks and a small animal trail that no doubt led to water. In the wet, muddy ground, he saw what looked to be a human footprint.

Good grief, was she barefoot? Phillip knelt and ran a finger along the small print. It had to be Ella's.

Now he felt even more frantic to reach her. She was barefoot, and who knew how long she'd been exposed to the cold and damp without proper attire. What if she'd run from the house without any clothing at all? Then he remembered the piece of cloth in his hands. At least she was dressed.

Phillip seethed. Whatever Spiby had done to her, he'd pay. Phillip drew a deep breath and pushed his anger aside. Now wasn't the time to think on those things. Right now he needed his wits to find Ella.

He followed the deer trail, seeing additional footprints. She was running, at least a short distance. He could tell by the stretch of space between the prints. And then just as the path bent to the right, Phillip spotted her ahead. She had fallen and lay in the path, unmoving.

"Ella!" He rushed to her and lifted her in his arms. Was she dead? "Ella! It's Phillip. Wake up."

Her eyes fluttered, and for a moment she stared blankly at him. Then, as she seemed to register what was happening, she reached up. "Phillip?"

He grinned. "Yes. It's Phillip. I've come to rescue you."

"That's a turn of circumstance," she murmured. "Usually I'm the one rescuing you."

"Not anymore," he said, hugging her close.

He headed back the way he'd come as quickly as he dared with Ella in his arms. He wasn't sure what Robert and Abe had done when he'd taken off, but hopefully they were close enough that he could reach them without too much effort.

Ella had closed her eyes, but whether she was just resting or had fainted, Phillip didn't know. He didn't want to waste his energy on trying to talk to her when she was clearly spent. She had no coat, and her exposed skin was icy to the touch. Worse still, her bare feet were in bad shape, the soles cut in multiple places.

Phillip reached the place where he'd entered the woods. It wasn't easy to pick his way back to the road while balancing Ella and keeping her from further harm, but he managed it. When he came into the clearing, he was glad to see that Robert and Abe were still there.

"Ella!" Robert cried, jumping down. "Is she alive?"

"Yes, but nearly frozen. Quick, get some blankets so we can wrap her up and get her warm."

Abe and Robert untied their bedrolls and worked the blankets around her as Phillip continued to hold her.

"Did you see Spiby?" Robert asked.

"No. He may be out there still, looking for her," Phillip replied.

"Most likely he made his way back to the house when he heard you calling for her," Robert said. "My guess is that he knows we've found him and he'll hightail it out of here."

"We have to get Ella warmed up. His hunting lodge is the only thing nearby. Do you suppose we dare go there? If he's still there, we have three of us to his one." Phillip looked to Robert for his thoughts.

"I don't like the idea of meeting the enemy in his camp," Robert replied. "He knows this area better than we do, and he definitely knows the house better."

"But it's imperative we get her warmed up. I think we have to take the chance. A couple of us can stand guard while the other one tends to Ella."

Robert glanced down the trail. "I agree. We'll just have to take our chances and pray for the best."

Ella awoke to warmth and the smell of coffee. She smiled, and for a moment she thought perhaps her abduction was nothing more than a nightmare, but then she opened her eyes. Her heart nearly stopped as she recognized her surroundings and realized she was back in the hunting lodge. However, the man standing at the window wasn't Jefferson.

She moved her legs and cried out as pain radiated up from her feet. The man at the window turned. It was Phillip.

"Am I dreaming?" she asked.

He was at her side in two long strides. "Lie still, Ella. Your feet are pretty torn up. We wrapped them as best we could, but you need to rest. We plan to head out in the morning, but for now you need to stay put."

She shook her head. "How did I get here?"

"What do you remember?"

She thought a moment, then opened her eyes. "I was running from Jefferson."

Phillip's brows came together as he frowned. "He managed to get away. Do you remember where he planned to take you? Where he was heading?"

She was hesitant to believe that Jefferson was really gone. "He told me we were going to California." She rubbed her temples. Her fingers still felt cold, but at least they didn't hurt as they had. "I knew I had to get away, and when he let me go to the outhouse, I ran."

"I found you collapsed on the deer trail."

"Oh, Phillip, I can scarcely believe you're here." She held out her hand. "Are you sure this isn't a dream?"

He smiled. "It's real enough. I came to your house to surprise you and instead found out that Spiby had stolen you away. I've never been more afraid."

She patted the mattress beside her. "Sit with me."

He sat and took her hand. Ella gazed into

his dark eyes. She could see a sobriety there that had been missing before. He had done it. She was certain of it. He had put aside liquor, hopefully forever.

She smiled and touched his cheek. "I'm so glad you found me. I prayed you would come but thought it impossible."

"With God, all things are possible. You taught me that." Phillip grinned in the boyish way Ella had come to love.

"Why did you bring me here? Weren't you afraid Jefferson would be here?"

"We figured it was three against one, and you were in desperate need of warmth. It was the only place we could get you some immediate help. He was gone when we got back here with you. Abe and Robert and I took turns looking for him, but it was clear he saddled up and hightailed it out of here. We might have gone after him, but it was far too important to get you warmed up and tend to your feet."

"He figured I'd try to run, so he refused to let me have my boots or coat when I asked to go to the outhouse. I knew I couldn't let that stop me."

"I'm so glad you're safe." He pulled her up and embraced her for a moment, then gently eased her back against the pillows. "Sorry. I just had to hold you. I thought I'd lost you forever."

"I was worried you had too. Jefferson had grandiose plans for disappearing forever." She shook her head. "But what about you? How are you?"

"I'm fit as a fiddle and ready to dance a jig." His smile broadened. "That is, as soon as my best gal is well enough to dance it with me."

"I heard talking and figured you must be awake," her brother said, coming into the room. "How are you feeling?"

Ella could see that neither man had slept. They both looked haggard. "I think I feel better than either of you. You look exhausted."

"Yes, well, it's hard to sleep when you don't know if your baby sister is going to live or die," Robert said matter-of-factly. "Now that I know, I'll be happy to return home and rest."

She laughed. "I'm so grateful for what you both did. Abe too. I cannot thank you enough. When Jefferson took me, I feared I'd never see any of you again."

"We feared the same," Robert said. "I know what he's capable of . . . what he might do."

Phillip frowned, and Ella could see the concern in his expression. She gave his hand a pat. "He didn't hurt me. God protected me in every way."

A look of relief passed between Robert and

Phillip. "We prayed it would be so," Robert declared. "Mara and Mother were praying at home as well. We were so afraid of what Jefferson would do to you."

"I think he was far too consumed with his own well-being to give me any real attention. He knew the Pinkertons were after him and that you all would come searching for me. He had no rest, no peace of mind. I assure you of that."

"I sent a boy to wire the Pinkertons in Washington before we left the farm. No doubt they'll send a man," Robert said, fixing Ella with a serious expression. "Anything you can remember about where he intended to go or what he intended to do would help them greatly."

Ella nodded. "I understand. Jefferson didn't say a lot, but he did have plans. He intends to change his identity and disappear in the West. He has friends who will help him, and at least some money."

"You mentioned him going to California," Phillip said, stroking her hand with his thumb.

"Yes. He said he had a friend who would help him. I think he lives in the city of Riverside. Jefferson mentioned going there on the train. That's really all I know."

"That's more than we knew. It's hard to

say if Jefferson will change his plans now, but I have to believe he'll at least attempt to go through with what he set in place. Now that you're awake, we should start for home. I'll let Abe know." Robert headed for the door, then glanced back over his shoulder. "I feel confident that I'm leaving you in good hands."

Ella looked at Phillip and nodded. "The very best."

———◆◆◆———

Two days later, Ella sat in front of a Pinkerton man in the comfort of her childhood home. She felt completely restored, and even the cuts on her feet were healing well enough that she could walk on her own—although Mother insisted she use a cane just in case.

The detective had listened to her every word, making notes and asking questions as they went along. He now closed his little notebook and got to his feet.

"I believe that's all I need. It seems you have nothing new to add, so I will join the other agent back in town."

Robert stood as well. "You will let us know if you find him?"

The Pinkerton man smiled. "Oh, we will find him. We always get our man. But to answer your question, yes. We'll notify you when Spiby is in custody."

Robert walked him to the door while Ella and her mother remained seated. Ella reached for her mother's hand. "Hopefully Father's testimony will put him away for the rest of his life."

"I just hope your father doesn't have to face such a sentence. I know your brother feels confident he will be given leniency for his testimony, but I worry so."

"No matter what happens, you mustn't worry. Robert and Virginia will never abandon you. Robert has assured me you will always have a home with them."

Her mother nodded. "I have a feeling we're done for in this area."

"I had much the same thought," Robert said, returning to the front room with Phillip now in tow. "I doubt we'll ever be welcomed back into polite society around here. People who were forced to help our father and Jefferson Spiby's family will begrudge us for a great many years. Not to mention the authorities who willingly helped them for money. They have lost the extra benefits Father and Jefferson provided. There's bound to be hard feelings over that as well."

"The sheriff wouldn't even come out here after Jefferson took Ella." Mother's tone betrayed her anger. "Jefferson could have added her to his list of victims, and the sheriff wouldn't have lifted a finger to help us."

"Exactly. We will probably never again be able to count on his protection," Robert replied. "And even if he's replaced because of his part in all of this, I don't think people are going to be quick to forgive."

"Then what are we to do?" Mother asked.

Ella met Phillip's gaze and smiled. "There's plenty of land for sale in Montana."

⋄⊱═ TWENTY-FIVE ═⊰⋄

Y ou suppose Henry will hire us back on, since we're late getting back?" Phillip asked in a teasing tone.

Ella shrugged. "I honestly don't care one way or the other. I mean, I love performing, and I think another year or two of trick riding would suit me just fine. But I won't be bullied. I wanted to attend Abe and Mara's wedding and celebrate with them."

Phillip looked across the room to where the bride and groom were happily greeting their guests. "I think you managed that quite well."

She smiled. "I think 1903 will be a wonderful year for weddings. What about you?"

He looked down at her and laughed. "Are you proposing to me?"

"Well, what if I was?" she asked. "Seems one of us ought to."

Phillip hooked his arm through hers and pulled her along. They exited the back of Mara's church and walked a little while before Phillip spoke his mind.

"I didn't want to rush you. You went through a lot with Spiby, and you deserve to take as much time as you need."

"I've had as much time as I need. Jefferson plays no part in this, and I won't give him the satisfaction of delaying my happiness." Ella stopped and looked up at him. "I love you, Phillip. I love you, and I want to marry you."

He chuckled. "That sounds fine to me, because I want to marry you too. Maybe we should go back to the church and see if Mara's pastor can do the job here and now."

"Mother would never forgive me," Ella said, shaking her head. "Besides, Robert said Father will be home at the end of the week. That ought to be time enough."

Phillip looked around. The street was empty except for one old man loading a milk can onto the back of his wagon. Phillip pulled Ella close. "Care to seal it with a kiss?"

"Not until you ask me officially," she said with a smile. "I won't have it said that I forced the issue, but a gal likes to be asked."

"You want me down on one knee?"

"No. Just like this—with me in your arms."

"In the cold morning air with the taste of snow on the breeze?"

"Exactly." She giggled as he tightened his hold on her.

"Miss Ella Fleming—"

"Luella," she corrected. "The official name is Luella."

He nodded. "And we want this to be official."

"Indeed."

"Miss Luella Fleming, will you marry me? Will you love me forever and go where I go? Will you promise to always speak your mind and hear me out when I speak mine? Will you forgive me no matter how many mistakes or messes I make?" He bent down until his lips were just an inch away from hers. "Will you?"

"I will," she said, putting her arms around his neck. "Will you?"

"Most assuredly," he whispered. "What comes my way, comes your way too. We'll face it together, and with God's help we'll be just fine, you and me."

He kissed her then, leaving no doubt of his affection.

"Now, come on. It's freezing cold out here, and we're missing the cake." He pulled her back toward the church. "And you ought to know by now that Phillip DeShazer is never one to miss the cake. Although I would prefer we serve pie at our wedding. I'm partial to pie."

———◆◆◆———

On Friday, Ella wore her mother's wedding dress, marveling the entire time at the way Mara had been able to make it fashionable. Ella's parents had married in the early 1870s when the bustle was all the rage. Mara had managed to remove that feature and save the integrity of the gown. With a few snips here and there, she had maintained the front of the gown's original styling and yet given it a fresh new look. Ella was delighted, and so was Mother.

Phillip wore a store-bought suit that Mara had also altered. Robert had taken him shopping, and while her brother reported they were somewhat snubbed, their money, on the other hand, wasn't. The mercantile owner was happy to sell them what they needed, although he drew the line at alterations.

It was of no concern, however. Mara was happy to lend her expertise, and Ella even got into the act and hemmed the trousers. Together, Ella thought they made a very fetching couple.

The wedding was small but very satisfactory, as far as Ella was concerned. She had never wanted a large wedding with hundreds of people. So long as Phillip was at her side, the rest of the world could be a million miles away.

"I now pronounce you man and wife," the minister said with a smile. "Phillip, you may kiss your bride."

Ella smiled up at him as Phillip pushed her veil aside. He tenderly held her face and gave her a rather chaste kiss. Ella turned to see her parents smiling in approval while Robert clapped. Mara and Abe, who stood opposite Ella's family, did likewise.

"Well, now we'll have to do it all over again for Henry and the show," Phillip said as he straightened.

Ella laughed. "I don't mind as long as you're the one I'm marrying."

"I'd better be. You try this with anyone else, and I'm afraid I won't be very friendly about it."

"Congratulations, you two," Robert declared. "I don't mean to rush you, but you do have a train to catch, and I know Ella planned to change out of that gown before you made your way to town."

"I'll help you change," Mara offered.

"Oh, I wish you had allowed for more time, Ella," her mother said. "We can't even throw you a wedding breakfast."

"No one but us would come to it anyway," Ella said, smiling. "But even so, don't fret, Mother. This was the perfect wedding, as far as I'm concerned. I wish my sister could have been here, but even without her, it was lovely."

"Come on now," Mara encouraged. "The fellas will finish loadin' everything in the wagon, and we'll head to town as soon as we get you changed. We just have time if we hurry."

Ella hiked her skirts and dashed up the steps in an unladylike fashion.

The depot wasn't very busy when Robert stopped the wagon. They'd beat the train into town, and that was a great relief to Ella, who felt as if she'd been running the entire day.

Phillip jumped from the wagon and then turned to help her down. Instead of just assisting her, however, he pulled her into his arms and cradled her for a moment.

"Put me down. Someone will see us," she protested.

"And you would honestly care?" he asked, leaning down to silence her answer with his lips.

Ella sighed, put her arms around his neck, and returned the kiss.

"Enough, you two. The train is coming in," Robert said, chuckling as the whistle blasted.

Phillip lowered Ella to the ground. "Remind me later to pick up where we left off."

"Like you'll need to be reminded." Ella thought her heart might burst with love for him. How thankful she was for all God had done to bring them together. "Hand me my bag, please." She pointed back to the wagon, and Phillip retrieved her carpetbag.

"You'd better let me hang on to this. It weighs a ton," Phillip said, pretending to be overburdened.

Ella yanked it away from him. "It does not."

"What do you have in there?"

"Not much. A book, a few toiletries, a change of clothes."

Phillip laughed. "Not much at all."

The men managed the trunks while Mara made certain the tickets were in order. Ella, meanwhile, stood on the platform, contemplating the future. She turned back toward the main part of town, knowing she might never return. There was nothing to keep her here. Even Mother and Father were contemplating moving to Montana, and Robert had already agreed that he and Virginia liked the idea of relocating. Ella knew the Brookstones would be more than happy to assist them should they decide to settle in the Miles City area, and it gave her great peace of mind to think of them all being so close together.

"What's on your mind, little sister?" Robert asked, joining her on the platform.

"I was just saying good-bye to this place and to my childhood." She smiled. "I'm not sorry to leave it. There are a lot of bad memories here."

Robert shrugged. "Some good ones too."

"Yes, but I can't help thinking they were good only for my benefit, while others suffered to make them so. I can't look back on them without wondering what price was paid."

"I hadn't considered it that way, but you're right. I suppose now we must look to the future and put the past behind us."

"That's exactly what I intend to do." Ella put down her bag and hugged her brother. "I hope we shall all meet again very soon."

He leaned down and kissed her cheek. "I hope so too, little sister. I hope so too."

Phillip joined them and stuck his hand out to Robert. "Until next time."

Robert shook his hand. "In Montana."

"I think that would suit us all just fine," Phillip replied. "Ella and I figure this will be our last tour with the show, because we intend to have a whole passel of kids."

"Phillip!" Ella felt her cheeks warm. "Hush!"

"Why should I?" he asked, grinning. "It's true, and your brother understands. He's got a passel himself, what with that new baby boy."

"Mr. Fleming," a deep male voice called.

They turned to find the same Pinkerton agent Ella had talked to a few days earlier coming across the depot platform.

Robert went forward and met him. They spoke for a moment in hushed tones, then rejoined the group. The look on Robert's face was grave, and Ella felt a lump rise in her throat.

"This is Mr. Richardson, as you no doubt remember," Robert began. "He's come with news about Jefferson."

Ella reached for Phillip's hand and felt a sense of reassurance as his fingers closed over hers. "What has happened?"

"We were able to capture Mr. Spiby, ma'am," the agent declared.

"Thank the good Lord," Mara said, shaking her head.

Ella let out the breath she'd been holding. "Where is he now?"

Mr. Richardson exchanged a glance with Robert. "On his way back here."

"Here? But why? You aren't letting him go, are you?" Ella could hardly believe they would turn him loose.

"No, ma'am. You see, he refused to be taken alive."

"Jefferson is dead?" Ella said in disbelief. She looked to Phillip, and he put his arm around her for support.

"What happened?" Phillip asked.

"We caught up to him, and he wouldn't give up. He tried to run for it and shot at our men. They returned fire, and he was killed. I received a telegram just a short time ago and planned to ride out to your farm to let you know, but someone told me you were here."

"Yes," Phillip replied. "We're heading back to rejoin the wild west show."

Ella felt weak in the knees. It wasn't that she didn't feel relief knowing that Jefferson would never again be a problem to her, but the shock of it was more than she had anticipated.

"Thank you for letting us know, Mr. Richardson," she murmured. "I'm afraid I need to sit down."

"I'll get her on the train," Phillip said, moving her that direction.

"My bag!" she cried, suddenly remembering that she'd left it on the platform.

"I'll bring it, Miss Ella," Mara called after them. Then, like Phillip, she asked, "What in the world did you pack in here?"

Phillip chuckled. "I told you it was heavy."

He helped Ella up the steps and past the conductor. A porter stepped forward and directed them to their seats.

"All aboard." The conductor's muffled cry came through the closed window.

Mara and Abe brought the tickets and handed Phillip and Ella theirs. "We're set, all the way to Richmond. Abe and I will be in the black folks' car if you need us."

Ella looked at her lifelong friend. "I'll always need you, Mara. God gave us to be friends knowing we'd always need each other."

"I 'spect He did, at that."

The train jerked to life, and Ella reached for Phillip's hand with a sigh. "I'm so glad to be on our way. Glad too that Mother and Father plan to sell the farm and leave the state. I can't bear the idea of them being treated poorly."

Phillip stretched out his legs as far as he could. "I just want you happy. You deserve to be. You've put up with a great deal these last couple of years. Including my bad behavior."

"But you're changed now. I can tell. I could see it in your eyes the day you found me."

"A lot of folks who knew me before won't believe the change, but I guarantee you, I'm not going back to being the drunkard I was when you first met me. I promise you that."

Ella turned to better see his face. "I know God has totally transformed you. Now I need him to do the same for me."

He frowned. "What are you talking about? You're perfect."

"You wouldn't say that if you knew the thoughts in my head. Being with Jefferson made me realize I can be quite heartless. I hated him so much, Phillip. I honestly thought about finding a way to kill him. I'm not sorry he's dead."

"But that stands to reason. He was holding you against your will."

"Yes, but I didn't pray for his soul or that God would help him change. I just asked God to punish him—to hurt him as he'd hurt me. I wasn't kind, and I certainly didn't care that if he died, he'd go to hell. I just wanted him to die." She looked down at her lap. "I'm so ashamed of myself."

Phillip took his time replying. It made Ella nervous to think she might have changed his heart toward her. Finally, he touched her chin and raised her face to meet his gaze.

"You have to give it to God, Ella. Let go all your fears and regrets. Let go of the anger and hate. Like you told me about forgiving—God expects us to forgive in order to be forgiven."

Ella nodded. "That's true. I never gave much thought to forgiving Jefferson for what he did to me."

"Believe me, I wanted him to suffer too. I also thought about killing him, and I've never wanted to kill anyone. It scared me, I have to admit."

She nodded. "Me too. I didn't like thinking that I might be capable of such a thing."

"I don't think you would have been," Phillip said, touching her cheek. "Stop dwelling on it and give it to God. He'll help you to forgive Jefferson Spiby. I know this, because He's helping me forgive."

"I know you're right. But I don't think it will be easy. Despite what you think, I'm not perfect."

He grinned. "You're perfect for me, Ella DeShazer, and that's all that matters right this moment." He put his arm around her shoulders. "That's all that matters."

EPILOGUE

The new season was going as planned and seemed to be awakening an entirely new generation of children to the wonder of the wild west show and all it had to offer.

Ella watched from the sidelines as Mary and Chris finished their act and took their bows. She was glad they had decided to stay with the show and continue the act. Mary was such a dear friend, and Phillip and Chris were plotting out an idea for another book Chris might write about cowboys who roamed from ranch to ranch, looking for enough work to see them through another year.

Lizzy and Wes were no longer part of the troupe, of course, but the occasional letter came with news about the baby and the ranch in Montana. According to Lizzy, she had already taken Cora on several horseback rides, and the baby seemed to love it. No doubt

Lizzy would one day teach Cora every trick she knew.

Phillip had told Ella that he hoped they would one day end up back in Montana at the Brookstone ranch. Ella liked the idea as well. She liked being part of a large family. Maybe that was why she enjoyed the show so much.

As Mary and Chris exited and made their way toward Ella, the next act was announced, and Ella knew she had only a few minutes before she'd be called to perform.

"You two were, as always, amazing," she told them. "I find myself holding my breath every time you shoot at him, but especially when you turn your back and use the mirror."

"I do too," Chris admitted with a grin. "But I keep reminding Mary that if she kills me, she'll be a poor woman. I'm leaving all my worldly goods to charity."

Mary laughed. "He can leave his money to whomever he chooses, as long as I get him." She gave him a quick hug.

Ella watched as the other teams of Roman riders started their routine. She wouldn't be up for another few minutes. "Did you read my father's letter?" she asked Mary.

"I did. I'm glad there will be some help for those people who were wronged."

"I am too. Father said that since Jefferson had no family, the judge arranged the sale of all Jefferson's properties and for the money to be used to help relocate and settle those who were forced to indenture themselves to Father and Jefferson. I didn't tell you this, but Father decided to match the amount of Jefferson's monies. The judge said this showed Father's regret, and he weighed that heavily in showing mercy toward him."

"Money is poor consolation for the time and lives lost to their schemes," Mary replied.

"It's unusual that the judge or anyone would show concern for the victims, since they're black," Chris said with a shrug. "I, for one, am glad."

Ella nodded. "As am I."

Mary looked out across the arena. "It won't bring any of them back, but hopefully the families who've lost, as I did, will comfort themselves in knowing that decades of wrongdoing are over. I know August died trying to do what was right. I take comfort in that." She looked back at Ella. "Now, you need to get your focus on the show and your performance. I hear there's going to be a little something special tonight." She winked.

Ella smiled. "With Brookstone's Wild West Extravaganza, there's something special each and every night."

Ella stood atop her two-horse team and drove them around the arena, holding the reins in one hand while she waved to the crowd with the other. She focused on keeping her knees slightly bent and her suede-soled slippers firmly planted on the rough leather pads atop the animals.

"Isn't she amazing, ladies and gentlemen!" Henry Adler called through his megaphone.

The horses handled easily for her. They were used to the show and seemed to crave the attention they were given.

"Oh, ho," Henry called as Ella took hold of the lines with both hands and brought the horses back around. "Something is amiss."

The crowd's attention was turned to the rider approaching on the back of two matching blacks. Ella smiled at the sight of her cowboy husband standing Roman-style. Phillip had thought it would be great fun to propose to her on horseback, and for weeks they'd been practicing his trick. His agility and ability to master standing on the backs of moving horses had impressed everyone.

Phillip drove the team out to join Ella's matched white geldings. He lined up with her, and once the teams were even, Ella and Phillip brought them to a halt.

"Young man," Henry exclaimed, "this is

an all-female performance." The arena went absolutely silent. "I must ask you to leave."

"I won't go," Phillip declared. "Not until she says yes."

He handed Ella his reins as she planted her feet on the back of one white and one black horse. It wasn't easy to keep his balance, but as he knelt down, he grabbed a handful of the horse's mane to steady himself. Gasps could be heard all around the stadium.

Ella looked down at him with a smile as Phillip pulled a ring box from his pocket to the wild cheers of the crowd. "I think they approve," she said as the crowd broke into cheers. Phillip held the box up to Ella, and she nodded her acceptance.

"Will you look at that, ladies and gentlemen, boys and girls. We have a proposal and acceptance, Roman-style!" Henry called.

Phillip pretended to put a ring on her finger, then tucked the box back in his pocket and stood. He gave her a quick kiss. Everything was just as they had practiced, and the crowd was on their feet as Ella handed Phillip the reins and took her place back atop her own team. Once Phillip was in place atop his, they put the two teams in motion, running side by side. While they'd been stopped, the crew had brought out hurdles for them to jump. They went around the arena and made the jumps in unison. The audience applauded as Ella had known they would.

She looked at Phillip, who gave her a nod. Ella moved toward the center, and as she maneuvered to stand with her left foot on one of the white horses and her right on the black, Phillip did likewise and stood behind her while Ella took the reins of all four horses. Phillip took hold of Ella's tiny waist and steadied his stance as they moved around the arena one final time.

"Are you sure you know what you're doing?" he asked against her ear.

Ella laughed as they approached the hurdle one last time. The horses easily jumped in unison. She glanced over her shoulder. "I guess that answers your question."

Phillip laughed, and the cheers of the audience were deafening.

They circled one last time, waving to the crowd. Ella delighted at the wild elation of the people. She was happier than she'd ever been and knew that Phillip was too. Just a few years earlier, she had felt utterly hopeless about her future, and now it seemed the possibilities were endless and joy had replaced her despair. Lizzy had once told her that when God was at work, He could turn even the most desperate moment into something glorious and beautiful, and that was exactly what He had done for her.

One of the wranglers came to take hold of the horses as they exited the arena. Phillip jumped down from the back of the team and held out his arms for Ella. She jumped into his arms without a second thought.

"A superb job, Mr. DeShazer," she said, smiling as he lowered her to the ground. "You really should perform on a regular basis. I think you have a knack for it."

"As I recall, the Brookstone Wild West Extravaganza is an all-female show filled with women of extraordinary beauty and bravery. I think I'll just stick to wrangling horses and breaking broncs," Phillip said, putting his arm around Ella's shoulders. "Oh, and loving you."

She smiled up at him. "That suits me just fine."

Tracie Peterson is the bestselling, award-winning author of more than one hundred novels. Tracie also teaches writing workshops at a variety of conferences on subjects such as inspirational romance and historical research. She and her family live in Montana. Learn more at www.traciepeterson.com.

Sign Up for Tracie's Newsletter!

Keep up to date with Tracie's news on book releases and events by signing up for her email list at traciepeterson.com.

Also from Tracie Peterson!

From Montana to London, this series follows an all-women traveling Wild West show, with trick riders and sharpshooters who are on a mission to uncover a perplexing mystery and seek freedom in a world run by men. Will they all be able to overcome their pasts and trust God to guide their futures?

BROOKSTONE BRIDES: *When You Are Near, Wherever You Go, What Comes My Way*

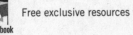**BETHANY**HOUSE

Stay up to date on your favorite books and authors with our free e-newsletters. Sign up today at bethanyhouse.com.

facebook.com/bethanyhousepublishers @bethanyhousefiction

Free exclusive resources for your book group! bethanyhouse.com/anopenbook

You May Also Like...

New to America, Nilda Carlson is encouraged by her wealthy mentor to better herself and her community. While her ideas to help other immigrants meet resistance, she finds delight in her piano lessons with a handsome schoolteacher. But with a detective digging into her past and a rich dandy vying for her hand, Nilda must decide what future she will choose.

A Song of Joy by Lauraine Snelling
UNDER NORTHERN SKIES #4, laurainesnelling.com

In this continuation of *The Tinderbox*, when young Amishwoman Sylvia Miller's world is upended by the arrival of Englisher Adeline Pelham—whose existence is a reminder of a painful family secret—Sylvia must learn to come to terms with the past while grappling with issues of her own. Is it possible that God can make something good out of the mistakes of the past?

The Timepiece by Beverly Lewis, beverlylewis.com

Mount Laurel Library
100 Walt Whitman Avenue
Mount Laurel, NJ 08054-9539
856-234-7319
www.mountlaurellibrary.org